Sugar Rush

JASMINE LUCK

Pencil & Page

Chapter One

Maddie

It's official. The universe has something against me.

In the last seventy-two hours, it had seen fit to shit on me repeatedly and from a great height. For example:

Relationship trashed (quite literally) by fiancé—tick.

Previously immaculate suitcase covered in mold—tick.

Drooled on by a sleeping man for (very delayed) flight duration—big, slimy tick.

I stood in the Louisville airport arrivals hall, limbs heavy with fatigue from the long journey, and considered the nearest row of plastic chairs. I'd read on a review that these chairs were the best place to sleep here—or the *least worst,* anyway. It was this or propping myself up at the altar of the 24-hour Starbucks several meters away until six a.m. at the earliest because every hotel within a twenty-minute taxi ride was full.

I parked my enormous suitcase by the nearest chair and

dropped down into it, weighing my options as I sat. *You know what? It's pretty comfortable. I could just nap here.*

Although that opened up the possibility of my possessions being removed as I slept.

I *could* call the man my cousin had arranged to collect me.

I held my phone, tapping my thumb on the screen as my thoughts tumbled over each other, flip flopping over whether to press the call button for one Rick Callahan, a man I'd never met.

It wasn't his fault that my flight had been so badly delayed. He probably wouldn't appreciate being called so early. Even if he'd been keeping tabs on the airline's website, he might have gone to bed.

All I knew about him was that he worked as a carpenter, and tended not to speak that much.

I imagined him, this grandpa-type man, sleepily rubbing his eyes at the shrill ring of the phone, then having to shake off the mantle of slumber.

No, Maddie. It's one in the bloody morning.

I'd wait until a reasonable hour.

Who crosses an entire ocean to avoid someone?

Me, apparently.

Welcome to Loserville, I thought miserably, not even smiling at my own crappy joke, and I always laughed at bad jokes. *Population: Me.*

I looked at my watch again. *Look on the bright side,* I told myself. *Only five hours to go until I can call Rick.*

The janitor, turning very slow circles in a ride-on floor polisher, gave me a long, sympathetic look. Or was it pity? Hard to tell under the harsh airport strip lighting.

I wiggled on the chair, but the plastic didn't give. Should I pillow my head on my hoodie, take off my shoes, try to get as comfy as the chairs would allow?

In the end, I lay down, draping my coat over myself, closed

my eyes, and mentally listed things I could do if sleep eluded me. I'd watched a video on the flight of fun ways to waste time at an airport, but I was pretty convinced that races on moving walkways were *much* less fun when I could only race myself.

Time passed. I let myself drift into a doze by the low rumble of the floor polisher and the white-noise quiet of the airport.

"Maddie Liu?"

Hearing my name jerked me awake.

I snapped my eyes open to see a man *so* gorgeous, I couldn't be sure I wasn't still dreaming.

He was big.

Tall, broad shoulders held my gaze for several seconds before I noticed his face. Sharp cheekbones. He'd broken his nose once, and the kink gave his face some character. His honey-coloured hair curled a little over his forehead, lending him a charming, rough-and-tumble look that belied the stern set of his mouth.

But it was his eyes that really held my attention. As the stranger stepped closer, I saw the quiet intensity in them. His irises were the deep brown of new acorns, shot through with just a touch of gold.

He wore dark jeans that hugged his hips, scarred boots, and a mustard Henley. The edges of a metal chain flirted with the open neck of his shirt.

"Sorry," I blurted automatically, British to the core. Perhaps he was some kind of weirdly hot, plainclothes security guard? "Am I not allowed to sleep here?"

He smiled slightly, and his handsomeness amplified. "Sure, but I thought you might prefer a bed. I'm Rick. Your cousin Jess's neighbor."

His voice was husky and deep, a good ol' Southern drawl that made my stomach flip over.

Oh. This is Rick?

I sat up, pushing hair out of my face. "How did you—"

"Jess told me the numbers of the flights you were on. Been followin' the carnage."

I smiled tiredly. "Carnage is a good word for it."

Hands tucked casually in his pockets, one hip slightly cocked, he looked like a walking advert for Southern men. They should put him on the airport billboard. "Didn't want you to be stranded. What kind of Kentucky welcome would that be?"

"I..." I swallowed the pang of lust *just looking at him* brought on. "Um. Did you have to walk around just saying my name at lots of sleeping women?"

Wow. My brain had *not* woken up enough yet to use a filter.

"Nah. You're pretty much the only one here aside from the security and janitors. Plus, Jess sent me a link to your YouTube channel, so I knew what you looked like."

He produced an ancient leather wallet, and flipped it open to reveal a driver's license with a grainy black and white photo of him.

"Oh." I vaguely remembered asking Jess if her neighbor could show me some ID before I got into a car alone with him. Better safe than sorry. "Thanks. Nice to meet you."

"Yeah. You, too. Welcome to Kentucky." Rick took the handle of my mammoth suitcase and slung my equally enormous tote over his shoulder as if it weighed nothing. His muscles bunched under his tee.

I blinked at him for a moment, trying to see through the haze of *oh my god he is so hot.*

This was my cousin's neighbor?

When Jess had described Rick as "a puppy with resting grump-face," I had imagined a sometimes-crotchety retired guy in a nut-brown pullover with five grandkids and a keen interest in sweater vests and period furniture restoration.

Not this *model*. This sharp-cornered Hollywood perfection with a honeyed bourbon voice.

Why had I imagined him as old? She had never mentioned his age.

I felt stupid.

"Thank you *so much*," I began as I stood and shrugged on my hoodie. "You've saved me from an awful night on those chairs."

Rick threw me a smile as I walked. "I hit the Starbucks first. I'm impressed that you even considered the chairs."

"I don't think I could afford enough coffee to keep me awake. I wasn't going to call you until at least six a.m."

"I was awake," he shrugged.

"Well, I really appreciate it." I snuck at a glance at his unbelievably hot profile as I walked. "I wasn't looking forward to several hours of vending machine roulette."

He laughed, flashing a slightly crooked grin. "You'd never get a Snickers. Damn things are rigged."

We waited for the elevator once Rick pressed the button, indicating for me to step inside first. Crappy generic sounds that could pass for music played us down the three floors to the parking lot. I stared tiredly at my reflection in the mirror. Even though I could only have slept for thirty minutes, I had bed-hair. *Compounded by plane-hair.*

Dark circles ringed my eyes, and those dark circles had their own circles. What a wreck.

The universe had started shitting on me from a great height earlier this week, and from the looks of it, it wasn't going to let up soon, even though I'd changed time zones and traveled several thousand miles.

"Here we go. Your chariot awaits." Rick led me to a dark blue pickup truck with the words *CALLAHAN CARPENTRY* emblazoned in pale gray on the side.

I stared at the door for a second when he pulled it open for me. Overtired, I hesitated for a moment, then thanked him before getting in. Rick climbed into the driver's seat after he loaded my luggage. I felt my eyelids droop as he started up the engine.

The combo of a long journey and lots of tears had started to take its toll. I felt myself begin to deflate like an old balloon.

"It's an hour's drive. Why don't you try to catch some sleep?" Rick suggested. His voice was so soothing.

I let my gaze linger on him; the line of his jaw under scruffy brown-gold stubble, the hazel eyes that seemed to see straight through me.

"What kind of person crosses an ocean to avoid some-one?" I mumbled, too tired to censor myself, not sure if I really wanted him to answer or not.

I fell asleep before he replied.

* * *

Rick

An hour later, Rick pulled up on the street outside Jess's house. Maddie was asleep next to him. She looked impossibly beautiful, her face relaxed in slumber. Soft lips, thick, dark lashes, raven's wing hair.

Who crosses an ocean to avoid someone?

He'd like to have several very stern words with that someone.

When Jess told him that her British cousin was coming from the UK to cover the family bakery for Jess' three-week honeymoon, Rick didn't know what to expect.

Of course, he'd watched Maddie's YouTube cooking videos, scrolled through her Instagram full of mouthwatering photos of apple-crumble bao and raspberry-filled angpao cookies.

But in those videos, she hadn't been like this. A tumble of bed-head raven hair, a crisp accent softened by tiredness. Wounded eyes. Jess warned Rick to look after Maddie, telling him she'd been through a lot lately. He'd figured that any friend or relation of Jess' wouldn't need too much looking after. His next-door neighbor was born independent.

Maddie Liu might not be bleeding, but she was absolutely walking wounded.

Rick stood by the passenger door for a moment. He needed to wake her up, get her settled next door.

In the quiet of the early May night, cicadas chirped.

Her chest rose and fell beneath the white t-shirt she wore under a soft pink hoodie. He sternly made himself not think about what might be under those clothes and opened the door. Gently, he nudged her shoulder. It was a safe area to touch.

She didn't stir once. Out cold.

He murmured her name. "Maddie. We're here."

At the lack of response, he tried again, slightly louder. She didn't budge. Not even an eyelid twitch.

For a few moments he chewed over the appropriateness of scooping up a woman without asking first. She needed the sleep, and he couldn't just start yelling at her in the street in the middle of the night.

He wasn't in the military anymore, after all.

Several options flickered through his mind, He could go through Maddie's stuff, find Jess' keys, or he could bring her into his house and settle her there. Might be easier. Would certainly be quicker.

First, he toted her stuff to his house, shouldered open the door, and shoved it inside.

When he got back to the truck, he found her still deeply

asleep, snoring softly. It was kind of adorable. Her lashes were thick, dark crescents against her cheekbones.

"Maddie," he said, louder, shaking her shoulder gently.

Her breath hitched, and she murmured something unintelligible, but slumbered on.

"Okay."

He unbuckled her seatbelt and lifted her into his arms. She shifted against him, pressing her face into his chest, cuddling in, and let out a long sigh. A happy sigh.

Rick would have laughed if he hadn't been so painfully turned on by the feel of her in his arms, warm, pliable, and soft.

He climbed the three steps to his house, trying to ignore the way she pressed her face into his neck, mumbling something in her sleep. The silk of her midnight-dark hair tickled slightly. Her heart beat lazily against his own. She moved a little, and her backside brushed his growing erection. He swore silently.

"Jess, you fuckin' owe me," he mumbled to himself.

Rick settled Maddie in his bed because his Ma had raised him too well to put a guest on his lumpy couch. He removed her shoes, placed a glass of water and a couple of acetaminophen tablets on the table, and tucked her in.

Unable to resist, and thinking of his sister Jenny's all too recent wrenching heartbreak, he leaned down to press a delicate kiss to her hair. "Sleep well, honey. You done crossed an ocean to forget him, so forget."

Her hair spread out like an obsidian halo on the white pillow. As he pulled the door closed, she turned, wrecking the fallen angel image of her hair, before pulling his pillow into her face as if breathing in his scent.

Her lips curved; her breathing evened out.

It nearly broke him to leave her there, warm and smiling,

and not just settle down behind her, wrap her in his arms, and keep her safe from whoever had turned her inside out.

Rick took off his boots and settled onto the couch before he dragged a throw over himself.

Sleep was a long time coming.

Chapter Two

Maddie

I startled awake in a strange bed. The last thing I remembered was getting into the car with Rick, then having his strong arms around me.

I slowly turned on my side, and looked at the rest of the bed, relieved I was alone. The last thing I needed was a throwaway one-night stand after crossing *an entire ocean* to avoid a confrontation with my ex-fiancé. Relief notwithstanding, I didn't think that anything about Rick Callahan seemed throwaway. Everything about his manner and kindness last night had relaxed me. He exuded peace and safety.

Being in this bed reminded me of how I'd felt last night, drifting into sleep whilst being supported by Rick's strong, sure arms, and I realised that this must be his bed.

Taking in my surroundings, I listened to the odd creaking here and there of an unfamiliar house. The birdsongs outside were so different from the horns and shouts of inner-city London.

The bedroom was minimalist, the beautiful wardrobes at the end of the bed the only real feature. The craftsmanship was stunning, the grain of the black oak visible all over the doors.

I sat up, ran a hand over my face, and saw the glass of water and the painkillers on the bedside table. Rick must've done that, thinking of what I might need or want, even at the late hour after the long drive

The sweetness of the painkillers and water gesture touched me. I took both, then left the bedroom, the wooden floor cool under my bare feet. The bathroom stood to my right, and I freshened up, washing my face and using the toilet. I stared at myself in the mirror for a moment.

Jet lag was a *bitch*.

I looked *tired*. Because I *was* tired. Exhausted, in fact.

I stared at myself in the mirror for another second, then willed the dragging fatigue away. "You're in another country now. Loosen up and forget him at least a few days. He's thousands of miles away."

I looked at my face, willing myself to accept what I was telling my reflection.

As I turned into the hall and padded down the stairs, the sounds of a baby gurgling caught my attention.

Rick has a family?

I followed the sound to the kitchen, where a mousy-haired woman sat facing a chattering toddler. Being fed was clearly a game to the little one, who clamped his tiny mouth shut just as the spoon was close. He laughed uproariously when the woman pulled away the spoon, and the whole thing repeated on a loop.

"Hi," I tentatively greeted her.

The woman looked up and smiled, unsurprised to find a

stranger in her house. "Oh, hi! Maddie, right? Rick said you were here."

I paused, wanting to just go back to bed and sleep. Was this Rick's family? And if they were his, why hadn't they been sleeping in the bed that clearly smelled of him with the ghost of a woodsy cologne partnered with sawdust and freshly cut grass?

But of *course* he had a wife and a baby. He looked as if he'd stepped off a movie theater screen, for God's sake.

"I'm his sister, Jenny. This little bundle of trouble is my son, Toby. We're living with him, temporarily. Bad break-up." Her tone was wry. "I hear that you're Jess' cousin from across the pond. Welcome to Redwing Falls."

"Thank you." I smiled woodenly, wondering what to do with myself.

"*Love* your concept, by the way! Asian-fusion is everywhere with dinner food but hardly anywhere in baking. I hope I'll get to try some of your stuff. I've been tempted to lick my screen when I look at your social media posts."

"Thanks so much!" The nervous knot in my stomach loosened a little because she was so lovely. "I'll do my best to make you something."

Jenny's lips curved, and she opened her mouth to say something else, but then Toby flailed and knocked the spoon from her hand.

She scolded him, telling me, "No one tells you this, you know? That the baby is awful cute and all, but I can't feed the thing *actual food* for love or money. He's a monster." She bent to retrieve the spoon, and wiped it clean on a muslin cloth.

Toby studied his pudgy little hands and giggled, then shot a killer grin at me.

"He *is* cute," I agreed, because it was true, and because I felt I needed to earn some conversation points with Jenny. I was an imposter in their house, after all.

"Coffee?" Jenny asked.

"I'll make it." I moved to the cupboards. "Just.... Um." I had not thought this through. "Just tell me where stuff is."

"Use the Keurig." Jenny used the baby spoon to gesture towards a sleek black coffee maker. "Rick allows us mere mortals touch it now. When I first moved in, I think he inspected it for fingerprints when he got home."

The words surprised a laugh out of me. Jenny was warm, immediately likable. "Really?"

"Maybe not *that* bad, but it was certainly his number one for a while. *Way* above me in the hierarchy. I mean, it's fair. He basically bought this house so Toby and I didn't have to be a burden on my parents."

I located mugs and set two on the counter. They were plain gray, the color of the sky after a storm. "How do you take it?"

"Cream with two sugars. I need all the energy I can get running after this one."

I turned to see Jenny moving a porridge-filled spoon towards her baby. This time she scored a direct hit, and the spoon went in, but Toby didn't seem happy about it.

The smell of the beans brewing made my senses twitch. I was waking up in increments.

"So, you've come to help your aunt cover for Jess while she and Connor take that big honeymoon trip, huh?" Jenny asked. "You guys must be close."

"We probably don't text as much as we could," I admitted, "And it's been four years since I actually saw her. Not on a screen, that is. I can't wait to work in a bakery in another country, though. It'll be a good experience for me. Plus, I get to test out my bakes on an American audience."

"I bet they're amazing," Jenny said. "You haven't tested them here before?"

"No. Jess and Aunt Laurie had only just bought the shop

when I visited last time. I helped them clear it out." I added a generous helping of cream and sugar to both mugs and carted them over to the table. *What the hell? I needed the energy, too.*

Toby sat proudly in his little chair, arms akimbo, face covered in porridge. It almost looked as if he was wearing a facemask. A huge grin lit up his face when I appeared.

"Is he always this happy?" I asked, unable to contain my delight. Babies' joy was so infectious. Instant serotonin.

Jenny laughed, taking the mug with a little grin. "Only when he beats the system and ends up with more porridge on the outside than on the inside. Scamp," she added, but with no real heat in the words.

She grabbed a wet wipe and cleaned his face.

I stared into my coffee, feeling like I was intruding on this family time, even though Jenny didn't seem at all bothered.

I slept in Rick's bed and now I'm hanging out with his sister...

Didn't I tell myself that these three weeks would be a total break from everything love-related? A chance to work out what on Earth to say to Seb when I saw him again, and a chance to lick my wounds out of sight of everyone I knew back in London.

Not so I could intrude on other families and definitely *not* so I could think about a tall, broad southern man with hazel eyes and a deep voice.

"Please sit," Jenny encouraged, nodding at the closest chair, and I did so as the big concertina door at the other end of the kitchen opened.

It was as if I had summoned Rick just by thinking about him.

He was framed by the doorway, hair rumpled, eyes soft and sleepy. The hem of his t-shirt was askew, riding up to reveal a sliver of his lower belly, lightly furred with an arrow of dark gold hair.

My mouth went dry.

"Mornin'," he half-muttered, half-grunted, running a hand through his already ruffled hair. His hazy stare found me, zeroed in. "You sleep okay?"

I tore my gaze away from his belly, looking into his sleep-softened eyes. My toes curled imagining waking up next to him looking like that, tousled and warm right out of bed.

"Yes. Thank you. I would've taken the sofa, honestly."

Rick chuckled, shook his head, and made a beeline for the Keurig. "And risk the wrath of my mother? No, thanks all the same. Guests don't sleep on the couch." He stopped by the coffee machine and stretched, giving me a tantalising glimpse at the tattoo just under his ribcage.

I swallowed back a surge of lust, wanting to get a closer look Who wouldn't have wanted to be up close with all that golden tan skin? He should have been a model. *He should have been illegal.*

Jenny nudged me. "You're staring," she whispered, amusement threading through her voice.

I jerked back so quickly that I nearly spilled my coffee, muttering. "*Shit.* Sorry. And God. Sorry for swearing in front of the baby!"

Toby seemed unbothered, sucking animatedly on one of his thumbs.

"You're fine," Jenny reassured me. "It's interesting. Rick doesn't really have women here, so I never get to observe. My brother's a known hottie, I get it. Doesn't make it any less gross for me, though."

I laughed into my mug. She was nice. In other circumstances, I'd really have liked to be friends. But I wasn't here for the long haul.

"You guys need more coffee?" Rick asked, yawning.

"No, thanks," we chorused, then chuckled at each other.

"Friends already, huh?" Rick muttered, clearly amused, as

the Keurig bubbled away in the background. "Listen, I'm sorry you woke up in my bed. I didn't wanna go through your stuff to find Jess' keys. I'm pretty sure she gave me a set once, but I couldn't think where they were."

Jenny scoffed. "You've gone soft since you left the military, Ricky."

Rick's scowl at the nickname made me laugh.

I could all too readily imagine settling into a life with these good people. It would be easy—in my head, anyway— to leave my old life behind.

For now, I would enjoy the holiday. Enjoy this break from the horrible mess my love life lay in, back home.

"I didn't mind," I said sincerely. "The bed's really comfy. Thank you. I'll get my stuff and settle into Jess' house this morning. Her bakery won't run itself, although I really hope that Aunt Laurie needs the help, and isn't just humoring me."

Toby fussed in his chair, and Jenny set her cup down. "Well, looks like breakfast is over for me, anyway. It was so nice to meet you." She scooped up her baby and made a face as she sniffed his butt. "Smells like someone's pooped!"

Toby wailed as Jenny carted him upstairs.

The room felt smaller with just me and Rick in it. He took his coffee to the table and sat, folding his long body into the chair.

I pushed the chair back, intending to stand.

"No rush on our account," he drawled. "It's Sunday, after all. I ain't gotta be anywhere for another hour, at least."

"Is it Sunday?" I blinked away the last of the jet lag sleepiness. "After I take a long flight, I never know where I am."

He sipped his coffee. Steam from the drink curled up into the air, hot and fragrant. "I used to fly a lot. In the military. Gets you all turned around, don't it?"

"That's an apt description of how I feel. Turned around." I finished my coffee. "I should go."

"You don't want breakfast? I make a mean omelet. At least, Jenny says so."

I went to say no, but my stomach grumbled loudly, giving me away. *Oh, God.* I felt heat creep up my cheeks. "Um. Yes, please?"

One corner of his mouth tipped up with his smile, and it was adorable. "Okay, then. You like spice in your eggs?" He unfolded his long frame from the chair, gulped the rest of his coffee, and crossed to the fridge, turning to look at me, the question sketched on his handsome face.

"No. I'm not that good at spicy stuff."

"Copy that." He bent into the fridge and took an armful of ingredients to the counter before he poked through some bottles, looking at their labels.

"My Asian father is *ashamed* of me for it. But then he serves himself eye-watering hot chili sauce with *everything*, so..."

I let my gaze linger on the broad line of his back as he cracked eggs and poured milk into a skillet, added butter and herbs, and stirred it around. A grinder sounded. The scent of black pepper and cooking eggs filled the space, and I breathed in hungrily.

"So, how long's it been since you were here?" Rick asked as he cooked.

"Almost four years. I bet things have changed."

He smiled at me over his shoulder. "It's small town America. Probably less has changed than you think. You missed anythin' in particular?" He pronounced it *anythang* and his accent was unbearably sexy.

"Well, one of the first things I need to do, apart from go and see my aunt, is say hi to the Han family. They run Lucky Star, the Chinese takeaway."

"The takeaw—oh, the delivery place. Yeah. I love their lo mein. Okay, this is done. Order up." He smoothly slid the omelet on to a plate and placed it before me with cutlery. "Bon Appetit."

"You're not eating?"

"Can't eat in the mornin'. Makes me queasy." He frowned, sitting opposite me. "Dig in. No need to wait."

I sliced the omelet open, the fragrant aroma bathing my face. The first bite melted on my tongue. "Oh, God. This is amazing."

Rick leaned back in his chair, a smile that almost seemed shy crossing his face. "It's one of the three things I cook well. If you're lucky, you might get to taste the other two before you fly back."

I'd like to taste anything you've got, I almost replied, but just about managed not to say it out loud. Instead, I ate the delicious omelet while Rick sipped his coffee, and it was all *so* domestic and *so* what I had wanted with Sebastian, who I was now avoiding by being on the other side of an ocean.

I pushed back the chair. "Thank you for breakfast. And the bed. It was really nice of you. But I have to go. Right now."

Rick stood. "Did I do—"

"Nope. Nothing. You're perfect. I mean..." I took a deep breath. "Please, don't get up." I scrabbled in my bag for the keys, and thankfully found them without having to upend up the entire thing because wouldn't *that* have been embarrassing? "Thanks again."

I shouldered the tote and tugged at the suitcase and then remembered I wasn't wearing shoes.

Rick slowly rounded the table, his expression serious, concern in his gorgeous tawny eyes. "If I said or did something wrong, you can tell me. No hard feelings."

My shoulders slumped. "I think I just want to be alone," I said slowly. "I'd planned to just help out my aunt, but now I'm having to be heartbroken in another country, and this is... it's just a bit too cozy. I'm sorry. I just need some processing time."

His gaze softened. "'Course. You need anything, you just call, okay? I know Jess gave you my number." His eyes lingered on my face for a moment, before he added, "I'll get your shoes."

I stood awkwardly while he headed up the stairs, long legs eating up the distance. I heard him have a muffled conversation with Jenny, and then he reappeared. "Here ya go."

"Thanks." My hands brushed his as I took my shoes, and awareness skittered up my arms. Lord, why did he have to be *so beautiful*? And so tall. "Say bye to Jenny for me."

Rick tossed off a lazy salute and picked up my suitcase. "Sure."

He followed me out of the door and stood patiently while I fiddled with the keys and let myself into Jess' house next door. The scent of citrus air freshener drifted from inside.

"I can take it from here," I bit off, too sharply, and then tried to soften it with a smile, but I knew it came out weak.

"Yes, ma'am," Rick murmured and crossed back to his own door. He slid his hands into his pockets. "Well, guess I'll be seein' you. Enjoy your trip."

I let myself drink him in for a moment. Morning-mussed antique-gold hair, sleepy-eyes, sharp jaw. Some lucky woman would wake up to this every day, but it couldn't be me.

"See you," I replied softly, hearing his door close after I closed mine.

Slumping between my suitcase and the wall, I cried for everything I'd wanted in my life back home, and for everything I was running away from.

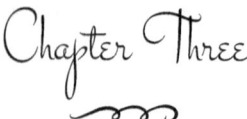

Chapter Three

Later, I microwaved a frozen meal (best before date: last week) and sent Jess a message telling her that Rick was a total gentleman and that I was safe, skipping the detail about sleeping at his house. I didn't want her to think I'd leapt on the first available man for rebound sex.

I texted my parents, too, adding a snap of me in Jess' kitchen to assure them I had arrived safely. They'd been very concerned as they saw me off at Heathrow. I'd been a mess of tears, half-wondering if I should put this trip off to try to fix things with Seb.

But finally, Mum had pointed out that I didn't break anything, so why was it up to me to fix it? As ever, she was right, and that made me get on the plane.

After eating lunch, I walked to the bakery and peered into the window. It was beautiful, the window frames and door painted in mint green, the awning the same color with white lettering spelling out the name *Cake Away,* with a little smiling cupcake as the logo. Jess loved to doodle cupcakes like that when we were teens. We had always loved food and creating, so it was no surprise that we chose it for our careers. She convinced her mother and now-husband to go into business with her, and on the foundation of working as a pastry chef in a hotel kitchen, I built an online following that expanded into custom cake orders.

A hanging basket of flowers protruding from the bakery wall provided a riot of color and a note of welcome.

The *closed* sign was on display, but my Aunt Laurie worked inside, rolling out dough. I knocked on the window and she glanced up at me. Her lined face broke into a big grin.

Her resemblance to my mum when she smiled warmed my heart.

She hurried to the door, apron flapping, and yanked it open, pulling me into a hug. She smelled of warm dough and chocolate, and fresh tears pricked at my eyes. She said my name softly into my hair as I melted into her embrace.

"Hi, Aunt Laurie."

"Hi, baby." She kissed my hair, then stepped back, floury hands cupping my face. "Let me look at you. You're *so* pretty. Your mom sends me pictures, but it isn't the same. I'm so sorry I didn't come get you at the airport."

"It's really okay."

She sighed. "It's not. I know I'm in danger of narrowing my world, but ever since Benny died, I don't like to drive too far, 'specially at night. It makes me anxious. Don't get old."

I squeezed her arm. "You're not *old*, Aunt Laurie."

She waved my compliment away. "Enough of that for now. Come. Let's bake stuff."

Her enthusiasm uncurled the nerves that had been budding in my stomach on the walk over. I let her take my hand and lead me to the big workbench in the back of the bakery-come-cafe. And when I took an apron from the hook - mint green, of course - and washed my hands with the lemony soap, it felt natural.

What I'd be doing right now, at home, if only...

I put those thoughts aside. This was a holiday, wasn't it? Not a pity party, at least, not right now. There'd be time for tears later. Now I wanted to enjoy my Aunt's company, and to settle into my happy place, which I always found when baking.

"Sweet tea or coffee?" Aunt Laurie asked.

"Tea would be great. We can get bottled sweet tea in the UK, but it isn't the same."

As she poured from a pitcher, I picked up where she'd left off, shaping beautifully layered puff pastry and rolling slim sticks of cold Belgian chocolate into them, ready for baking tomorrow morning.

"How was the flight?"

I patted the chocolate into the next pastry. "Fine. Uneventful. Watched that new action film, you know, the one with the electric dinosaurs."

Aunt Laurie smirked. "Worth a watch?"

"I was so tired that I fell asleep forty minutes in."

She laughed and set my tea down and smoothed her hand along my hair again. "I'll wait until it's streaming, then." She cleared her throat. "I just need to say this once. It's a crying shame you didn't bring that dirtbag down with you. There'd have been a long line to smash his face in."

I gasped at hearing my aunt speak like that. "Aunt Laurie—"

"A man hurts one of my family, and he's going to answer to me. Jess didn't tell me everything, but she told me enough. I was fit to be tied, Maddie. Still am. May his internet forever cut out at the most inopportune time."

I laughed in surprise. "That's a good modern curse."

"The best."

She moved to work next to me, and for a good long time, we baked together, mixing and shaping and glazing and proving. The scents of chocolate and cinnamon hung heavy in the room with us, new and familiar at the same time.

The sweet tea was delicious and tasted of my childhood. Aunt Laurie and Jess used to come over for holidays and make huge vats of the stuff, some of which my mum would freeze. I could never quite make it the same myself, and oh Lord, had I tried.

"So," my aunt ventured once I'd slid all the pain au chocolat into the fridge, "Rick picked you up from the airport?"

I eyed her. "Yes..."

She dusted her hands off on the apron. "He's a good man. He dotes on his nephew. Took the little boy and Jenny in when her ex turned out to be an asshole. Anyway, it's her story to tell."

I swallowed, feeling a pang of sorrow for a lovely woman I'd met briefly this morning. "There seems to be a lot of assholery going around. What's your point?"

Aunt Laurie smiled and folded her arms, leaning against the closed door of the giant fridge. "I used to be young once, too. I'm saying that he's not known for permanence, but if *I* wanted a little fun to forget my own asshole ex, you could do *much* worse than Rick Callahan."

I sputtered out a laugh, mildly scandalized. "I was *engaged* until a few days ago!"

She shrugged. "It doesn't mean you're not interested."

I laughed out loud. "I'm *not* interested."

"Honey, I could be *dead* and I'd still be interested. Have you *seen* him?"

I shook my head, still laughing. "Thanks, but you go ahead. I'm not here to sleep my way around town."

"Well, it's lucky then that you don't need to go around town. He's right next door."

I moved in for a hug. "You've really cheered me up."

She grinned cheekily. "Then, I've succeeded."

"Thank you. I'm looking forward to running this place with you. You're sure I won't be in the way?"

My concerns were legitimate. After all, I didn't have a huge amount of shop management experience. I'd worked in a couple of bakeries as a teen in college, and I had years of hotel kitchen experience, but every shop was different.

It looked like my dream of owning or co-owning a shop would have to be shelved a bit longer.

All my dreams had been very loudly interrupted when my fiancé betrayed me.

Betray seemed like such a small word for what he did, when he basically dumped our relationship in a bin and set fire to it.

I felt like I was in a sort of limbo, unsure how to move forward.

"Not at all," my aunt assured me. "I'll enjoy the company, and you could use a change. It's as good as rest, they say, but nothing's better than freshly baked cake for a broken heart." She squeezed me tight. "Now, you got dinner plans?"

I winced. "Well, there's another slightly out of date dinner in the freezer."

She tutted in a very my-mum way. "You're coming over. I've got some beef in the slow cooker and I always make too much. I don't take no for an answer."

Warmth bloomed inside me. "I'd love to."

* * *

Much later, when I got back to Jess', my stomach full of proper home comfort food, a little basket was sitting on the front step. The tempting scent of chocolate wafted out of it. A note was tucked under the dishcloth covering everything, and I slipped it out, unfolding it to read:

. . .

A welcome to Redwing Falls gift - cookies!

Because I know Jess only stocks freezer crap and let's be real, that stuff is not food.

Jenny x

A smile tipped up my lips, and I was grinning hugely before I knew it. I checked my watch. It was after eight o'clock.

Too late to ring the bell now and say thanks; Toby would probably be asleep or very close to it. But I'd go over tomorrow.

I could text Rick and convey thanks that way, but...

I wasn't going there. Rick Callahan was an inviting rabbit hole too dangerous to disappear down. Even *if* he was interested, and it was a very big if considering the impression I must have left this morning, a rebound fling was a bad idea.

It didn't mean I couldn't fantasize about it. I'd have to be blind not to moon over him, but that's where it had to end.

I let myself into Jess' house and dug into the basket.

The cookies were melt-in-my-mouth delightful, the chocolate still warm and a little gooey. As I boiled water for tea, I looked out of the window to see what looked like Rick's shadow in the opposite window. Broad chest, wide shoulders, moving around and maybe making dinner. One of his other two signature dishes? I imagined him frying and stirring, tasting, his tongue flicking out over his full lower lip, and my stomach flipped.

For a moment, I thought about going over, but in reality, he and I were just two strangers. He lived next door to my *cousin*, not me. In three weeks, we would be an ocean apart again.

Chapter Four

I was up early the next morning, and spent a half hour lounging in bed, replying to comments on a recent video. I'd have to upload something soon, and remind viewers and subscribers that orders were closed while I was away.

My phone pinged again with a message from Lara Han, daughter of the couple who owned Lucky Star, the one Chinese place in Redwing Falls. We messaged back and forth for a bit. She and her brother Marcus were around my age and we hung out when I was here four years ago.

The sound of vehicle doors being opened and closed stirred me into finally getting out of bed, and when I looked out of the bedroom window, I saw Rick loading his van with bags of tools. He bent over and I admired his ass in his worn, dark wash jeans.

My God, he should be a model. I wondered idly if agencies knew he existed. Someone should tell them.

On impulse, I cracked the window open. "Morning!"

He spun around before catching me in the window. The morning sunshine kissed the bridge of his nose. It picked out the gold in his yellow hair, the thick strands ruffled by the breeze, or his hands.

I'd certainly like to get *my* fingers in it.

"Mornin'," he called up, a smile kicking up one corner of his mouth.

"Tell Jenny thanks for the cookies."

His smile widened. It was devastating. "I will. Thank God you came. I couldn't keep eatin' 'em. I'd need new jeans once a month."

"Well, it's a shame for you that I'll be trying out lots of new recipes while I'm here, then."

Rick shook his head, chuckling. "Bigger jeans it is. I gotta get to work, building spindles on a staircase today. Customer wants 'em shaped like willow tree trunks."

"Rather you than me." I winced. "Baking is my thing."

"So I've heard. Can't wait to try some," he added, and grinned up at me.

I felt heat creep up my cheeks at his words. Flirting? Was he actually flirting? Surely, I was imagining it. My stomach flipped at the thought of feeding him a bite of cake, his lips brushing my fingertips as he ate. "Um.... Well, have a good day! Enjoy the staircase!"

I shut the window and pressed my hands to my face, hoping that I'd just die of embarrassment.

Enjoy the staircase.

Had I really just said that?

Grim.

After a few seconds, I heard the rumble of his truck's engine. I peeked over the lip of the windowsill, and he was gone.

I cannot get into anything with Rick Callahan, I told myself.

If he even likes me.

I cannot get into anything.

I was engaged until very recently.

I do not live in this country.

Shaking it off, I got ready and left to open *Cake Away*.

The old, clunky keys jingled in my pocket when I opened the door, pausing to consider how quiet Redwing Falls was this early in the morning.

Aunt Laurie wasn't coming in for a couple of hours, but that was okay. We had made the bulk of the bakery stock yesterday, and Jess had left explicit instructions, the kind that were completely idiot-proof, for the register.

When I let myself in, the welcoming scent of baked goods made my heart a bit lighter. This was familiar. This I could do.

I lined up the fresh cinnamon buns on the racks as people in work clothes passed by the big picture window. The scent of nutmeg and mixed spice filled the air, and I inhaled greedily before setting out the fridge section, filling it with the eclairs and other pastries my aunt and I had baked yesterday.

The racks and cake stands Jess had invested in were gorgeous. The small town, shabby chic vibe worked well for *Cake Away*. That was a great name for a bakery, but of course, I was biased.

As I breathed everything in, thinking how lucky Jess was to have Connor and her mum help her fund and run this place, the wholesale delivery truck arrived. My aunt had mentioned it and I signed off on the delivery of pre-packed sandwiches and the bakery's staples like flapjacks, carted them inside and set them out.

Jess, Aunt Laurie, and Connor made popular signature bakes like rainbow sprinkle cookies and chocolate muffins, but having the wholesaler bring sandwiches and treats helped with the baking load.

I flipped the sign from *closed* to *open* and, just as I stepped back, Rick Callahan opened the door, making the bell tinkle.

"Couldn't stay away?" I asked before I checked myself.

Oh, God. Stop it, Maddie.

He smiled, flashing a dimple. "This week's staircase build is across the street. Came for coffee."

"Oh." *Duh.* Coffee. Not because he wanted to see me. I needed to get my head on straight. "Of course. You want to try Jess' new blend? She says it's great."

He shrugged, stretching the white t-shirt that I liked because it showed off the bottom of what looked like a large shoulder tattoo. "Why not? Two cups, please." He flashed that grin again and my heart flipped.

I crossed behind the counter and pretended to rearrange some pastries, trying to resist checking out Rick's ass as he perused the pre-packed snacks and drinks in the fridge opposite the counter.

I failed. Man, those jeans did *obscene* things to his backside. Flat-assed Sebastian could eat his heart out.

What was my ex doing right now? Was he—

"You okay?"

I jerked from my reverie to look at Rick. "Yes. I'm fine. Why?"

He nodded at me. I glanced down at my knuckles, twisted so hard in my apron that they were white. "I'm fine. I'll get your coffee. Two cups, you said?"

"Sure," he said easily, but his hazel gaze was quietly assessing me. He could tell something was wrong, but I hoped he was too much of a good, polite southern boy to mention it. "Two cups. Got my apprentice on the job today. He might be over to get us some lunch later."

You won't come? I nearly asked, but thought better of it.

"Cream, sugar?"

"No sugar for me. I'm sweet enough, so my Ma tells me," he drawled, rolling his eyes for comedy, smiling at me.

God, he was self-deprecating and sexy and caring and *just so amazingly tall* and I could *not* allow this.

"Must not fall for Rick Callahan and his stupid sexy face," I chanted under my breath as the coffee machine puttered away. I glanced back at the man in question. He was texting someone on his phone and, for just a second, the little teeth of jealousy bit into me deeply.

But I had no right. I had not an ounce of claim on Rick. Not even a half ounce.

Sadly.

"Okay, order up." I placed the coffee on the counter.

"What's the damage?" Rick asked, his phone poised to tap on my reader.

I told him, entering the info into the register, and he paid with a robotic beep, my hands brushing his as I held up the card reader, and for a moment, awareness skated up my arm, and then he moved away and it was gone, and I missed it.

"Thank you, ma'am," he murmured, and his accent made my blood heat.

"Um, you don't have to call me that. Maddie's fine. Or something less formal."

That half-smile kicked up his mouth again. "What, like *darlin'?* It's mostly what people get called 'round here."

"Um. Sure. I guess that works." I tried desperately not to think about him whispering that over and over, telling me how good I felt around him as he ruined me up against the bakery wall, panting in my ear as he filled me in long, delicious thrusts.

No.

No bakery sex.

It's deeply unhygienic, for a start.

Even so, I could imagine myself wanting to do things with this man.

"Y'all have a good day now. See ya later," Rick called as he opened the door, disrupting my little my X-rated fantasy.

I sighed as the door closed. It was going to be a *long* few weeks.

* * *

Thankfully, a steady stream of customers to *Cake Away* had followed Rick, keeping my thoughts off him. Many of them had commented on my accent and said Jess had spoken about my arrival. I wasn't used to that. London, although my favorite place in the world, just wasn't that kind of small.

I loved the interaction. It was what I missed by having a mostly-online business.

That afternoon, I had a brief chat with Jess, who was fresh-faced and high from white river rafting (weren't honeymoons meant to be relaxing?), and then unpacked my enormous suitcase, which mostly contained video equipment.

My collection had grown with every how-to seminar I'd attended, and each video blogger I'd connected with. Each of them usually recommended equipment, which meant I'd started with a smartphone and a ring light, and now had more than a dozen different lights, a tripod, and various freestanding shades and lighting accessories.

I uploaded a video once a week, sometimes more if I had an email asking about a certain topic of baking, or if a London-based baking or food-related influencer offered to record a video with me.

Today I was making a Mississippi Mud sheet cake with matcha icing, in honor of being in the south. Jess permitted the use of her kitchen in the videos and I planned to give my viewers a mini tour, making sure I removed all the personalized knickknacks first so she wouldn't be identifiable.

I organized all the ingredients, measured them out in bowls. Even though I was recording rather than live streaming, if I messed up, I'd have to start over, so it was important to have everything ready.

I cracked eggs into a small, pretty blue bowl and as I did so, I was hit with a flashback of Seb accidentally gate-crashing one of my videos, leaning in to give me a forehead kiss and asking jokingly who I was talking to. It had been shared a *ton* of times.

I'd have to communicate the news that we'd broken up somehow, I supposed. Or, I could pretend it hadn't happened.

Maybe that was why I'd run away *across an ocean*.

To continue living in denial for another few weeks.

I preheated the oven, checked my make-up in the hallway mirror for the last time, checked the tripod height, and hit the record button. I could trim out the footage of me walking to the kitchen island later.

"Hi everyone! Thanks for joining me all the way from Kentucky today!" I enthused, settling back into my favourite thing of all: baking.

I chatted as I worked. Subscribers said one of their most-loved things about my videos were how cooking along with me was like cooking with a friend. I talked about stuff other than the ingredients. Today I rambled on a bit about the flight here, the airplane food, and the kind attendant who'd resembled a young, hot celebrity.

I made sure to say a few times, "Don't forget, the recipe will be posted in the comments, so don't feel the need to rush this. And you can pause me anytime! I don't mind at all!"

I always said this because some people, my own mother included, forgot about the pause function and tried to hurry along with the video.

By the time I was done, ending by showing off the finished cake, exhaustion dragged at my bones. I stopped recording and resolved to edit and post it later. I was too tired to do it justice now.

Besides, I still wasn't completely over the jetlag, and there was one more thing I had to do.

I sat down with a cup of tea, replied to messages from some friends in London while I waited for the cake to cool a little, then parcelled some up in baking foil and walked it over to the house next door. The grass was soft under my feet and, for a second, I thought about how different this small southern town was to my own concrete jungle.

I knocked. No response. Then, after a few seconds, the upstairs window opened.

"Oh, hey!" Jenny shouted down, smiling.

"Hey," I said, waving. "I have cake for you."

"Oh, my *God!* I'm *so* excited! Thanks! Leave it on the step, would you? I'm changing a diaper." The sound of wailing began and Jenny rolled her eyes, even though she was smiling. "That'll be my treat for having to deal with the third kiwi poop today. It stinks!"

I winced and set the cake down. "Enjoy!"

"Thanks so much!" I could hear Toby squealing from inside when she called back to me.

Once back inside, I made myself edit the video, watched it while I drank tea, and then uploaded it to my channels.

Then, I slept the sleep of the heartbroken and jet-lagged.

Chapter Five

Tuesday morning dawned bright, and I felt better. A lovely follower had sent me an Instagram DM saying she'd baked the matcha Mississippi cake and loved it and that it had pleasantly reminded her of the matcha tea her Japanese grandmother used to drink.

That message warmed my heart.

My second favourite thing after baking was connecting with people who also loved to create. Messages like the one I'd had just now made me fizzy with happiness inside. It made me want to have my own space, a real one, not just an online shop, even though it had become very successful and allowed me to quit my long-hours hotel job.

My mum had also emailed with some pictures of her and my dad doing *their* favourite thing: walking. They'd started walking holidays when I was a teen and they still regularly joined groups of other like-minded people in the wildernesses of the UK, if such a thing as "wilderness" could still be found in today's world.

Rather them than me. My mum liked to joke that I'd been

born on the wrong side of the family, seeing as all the bakers seemed to be over here in Kentucky.

I made coffee and replied to some of the order enquiries with a holding message, and then opened the kitchen patio doors to let some air in. The key turned easily; no rusty lock in a Victorian-era single glazed window here, thank you, America. I breathed in the morning.

In the distance, a dog barked. Someone mowed their lawn with a low, constant buzz.

It was small-town peaceful, but I'd be lying if I said I didn't miss the sirens and city bustle a little bit.

I messaged Aunt Laurie to see if she'd be up for selling the leftover matcha Mississippi cake and some brownies today. She replied with a thumbs-up.

It was my plan to test my Asian-fusion baking out on the audience of this town and I really needed to get a move on with that.

It would let me see people enjoy my baking firsthand, after all. When you dropped off a cake at a wedding or party, you rarely got to see the eating of it.

It was still early, so I rummaged through my ingredients and remembered with delight that I had brought with me two jars of white miso paste, in case I had a craving, as I often did, for miso brownies. I briefly considered washing my hair and showering so I could film this as a video, but thought, "fuck it". I did a video yesterday. I deserved a rest.

I made the brownies and slid them into the oven, set Jess' cat shaped kitchen timer, stretched, and after shoving my feet into my ancient Converse, made my way out onto the decking. The dark brown wood was edged with a handrail all the way around, bisected by three little steps down onto the lawn.

The view was gorgeous out here. Birds tweeted from the trees. Clouds drifted across a robin's egg blue sky.

Of course, I wasn't stupid enough to think it would be

this serene all the time, but I'd wanted a change of pace, and I'd got it.

I stepped further out onto the deck, admiring everything around me, thinking about taking some photos for my Instagram feed.

And I put my foot straight through the wood.

"Shit!"

My beloved Converse had protected my skin from the potential splinters. I grabbed the handrail and tried to tug my leg free. No dice.

Double shit.

With my free hand, I pulled my phone from my pocket and scrolled through my contacts. Aunt Laurie would already be at the bakery. I could call her anyway, but it'd take her some time to get here.

Or...

My gaze skittered across the lawn and over the fence toward Rick Callahan's house.

You need anything, you just call, okay?

The memory of his soothing, honey on grits voice came back to me.

Well, I was going to take him at his word, despite the fact that it was completely against the unspoken laws of all British people to ever impose on anyone for anything that wasn't inevitable death. Or, perhaps running out of teabags.

Even then it was preferable to die without, god forbid, having inconvenienced another human.

It rung once, twice, and, cringing, I was about to hang up, thinking that maybe he'd left for work already, when he answered.

"Maddie."

"Hi, Rick." I felt about sixteen. My face flamed.

"You okay?"

I'm fine, I started to say, automatically. Stupid. "Actually, I've put my leg through Jess' decking, and I can't get free."

He cursed. "Goddamn told her to get that fixed," he groused, his drawl stronger when he was annoyed. "Are you hurt? How bad is it?"

"I'm not cut. I can wiggle, but the wood has sort of closed around my leg."

"I'll be right over," he assured me. The rasp in his voice made me weak. God, this man made me feel like a lovestruck girl. Well, lust-struck anyway. "Stay where you are."

"Oh, that is *not* a problem."

He hung up. Before too long, I heard the slam of a door, and then I was treated to the sight of Rick Callahan walking across the land between the buildings. He rounded the side of Jess' house, the toolbox in his hand clunking when he set it down after climbing the small stack of stairs onto the deck.

"Well, shit."

I smiled. "That's one way to put it. Thanks for coming."

"Of course."

He looked good. Had he come right from the shower? He smelled like mint, crisp and fresh, the ends of his hair curled. The gray Henley he wore was rolled up to the elbows and hugged his broad shoulders.

I swallowed back a surge of lust. The fact that I was trapped in a plank of rotting wood did help to curb my libido, thankfully.

Did hot guys get some sort of a memo about shirts and sleeve rolling? How was it sent? Should I feel this way about another man so soon after my break-up with Seb?

Then again, the lizard brain wants what it wants, I reasoned.

And at any rate, I wasn't going to act on it, so it didn't matter.

I could enjoy my filthy thoughts about sliding my hands under his shirt in private.

Rick knelt by my stuck leg and opened his toolbox. I watched his hands work. Long fingers, wide palms, scars over a couple of his knuckles. A metal chain hung around his neck, and what looked like dog tags flirted with the open V-neck of his shirt.

"You were in the Army?"

"Yep." He took out a wicked-looking claw hammer. "Staff Sergeant when I got out."

"Wow."

"Yeah, I was in a long time. I liked it. Made some pals for life." He shifted onto his knees and then wrapped his free hand around my ankle. Even through the jersey of my PJ pants, his touch was warm, firm. "Stay still, y'hear?"

"I'm very good at following instructions. *And* I will do whatever you say as long as you get me out of this triffid."

Rick chuckled.

"Oh, you got that reference?"

"Sure did. Who doesn't love a yard full o' plants that might eat you?" He set to work with the hammer, using the claws to tease apart the wood trapping my leg. The rotten parts bent and broke quickly, and when Rick gave the word, I eased my leg free.

"Thank you! Thank you so much!"

"No problem. You might wanna tell Jess to get that looked at as soon as she gets back. I gave her an estimate, but I'll resend it to her email."

"Oh, I will absolutely tell her." I inspected my ankle. No signs of any splinters. "It seems weird to ask because you only live next door, but if you don't have to go to work right away, would you like tea? Coffee? I just made—Oh, shit!"

"What is it?"

I dashed inside the house, where the kitchen timer I'd set

was going off. I yanked open the oven, remembered at the last minute to get oven gloves, and pulled the brownies free. They were only burned at the edges, thankfully.

I silenced the vibrating alarm before it exploded. "Made some brownies before I put my stupid foot through the stupid decking."

He breathed in audibly. "They smell great. Chocolate?"

"Dark chocolate, yes. And miso paste. A deeply savoury Asian food. You want to try one?"

His brows rose. "Hell, yes."

I gestured to the stools by the kitchen counter. "Have a seat. Coffee, tea?"

"Coffee, if you're havin' one." He settled onto the stool. He was *so* tall and *so* broad and I was neck-deep in lust.

"Yep." I twirled the coffee pod carousel. "What're you in the mood for?" I asked, turning to look at him over my shoulder.

His gaze settled on mine for a long moment, before he finally replied, "Whatever you're havin' will be just fine."

I swear I hardly absorbed the name of the two coffee pods I plucked from the carousel. Every one of my nerves was alive with just having Rick so close. He looked amazing. He smelled amazing.

"How do you have it?"

"Black with one sugar."

I made the coffee as he worried one of the dog tags around his neck between his thumb and forefinger.

"Tell me about the Army?" I asked, setting a steaming mug and a plated brownie in front of him.

"God, this looks fan-fucking-tastic." He pulled the plate towards him. "What do you want to know?"

I sat opposite him, cupped my own mug between my palms. I loved the heavy, storm gray stoneware Jess had. "Why did you join?"

He smiled wryly. "I was seventeen. Couldn't bear the thought of takin' up my dad's carpentry business. Wanted to see the world. Leave this little town."

"But you have taken it up now?"

He nodded. "Funny how life works out." He took a bite of the brownie, and his eyebrows shot up. "Fuck! Sorry. That's really good. *Really* good. What do you put in here, solid happiness?"

I grinned, the coffee mug a breath from my lips. "If I told you that, I'd be giving away trade secrets. I'm glad you like it."

He shook his head, smiling. "It's... Don't tell Jess that I said these are better'n her brownies. I'll be strung up." He flashed a full grin again, and it made my stomach flop. He was beautiful.

He took another bite and the tip of his tongue peeked out to catch a crumb. I had to look away, pretending to pick at a bit of non-existent lint on my sleeve. *Hold it together, Liu! What are you, twelve?*

To distract myself, I took a bite of brownie. It was fudgy, sweet, and just salty enough for a sweet-salt tang. Perfect. These would sell well today.

"Your secret is safe with me," I reassured him.

"Good to know. You findin' your feet okay 'round here? Still feelin' jet-lagged?"

"It's not too bad, now. I'm getting used to it. Baking helps. Any kind of cooking, really. It orients me, if that isn't too weird."

Rick nodded thoughtfully. "It's how I feel about workin' with my hands, too. Nothin' like producing something at the end, ya know?"

"I do."

We contemplated this in companionable silence for a few moments, then Rick drained his coffee cup and stood. "I don't mean to be rude, but I've gotta get on. Staircases don't build themselves, and thank God, because if they did, I'd be out of a job." He flashed that smile again. It was deadly.

I stood up. "Take two of the brownies with you, for Jenny."

"She won't say no. 'Specially as she loved the other cake you dropped over yesterday. I didn't even get any. Thanks again."

"You're so welcome." I wrapped the still-warm brownies up, feeling his gaze on me. When I rounded the kitchen counter and offered him the foil-wrapped parcel, he lifted a hand to my face, close, but not touching my jaw. "You've got a little..."

"Oh..." I hesitated, but couldn't help myself from adding, "Can you get it?"

Gently, he stroked the pad of his thumb over my lower lip. Every sensory receptor in my body lit up; hormones sat up and begged.

Be still my beating heart.

I tried to tell my hormones that I should have been too heartbroken to feel lust, but they ignored me.

Perhaps this was what rebounds were made of. Pure gold dust lust.

I drank Rick in; his thick lashes lowered as he concentrated on the task at hand. His cheekbones would have been envied by any Hollywood star.

"Got it." He turned his thumb to show me the smear of chocolate, and then raised it to his mouth, licking the mixture off. "Hmmm. Fuckin' delicious."

I was going to die of unfulfilled desire. It was okay. Up until Seb's betrayal, I'd had a good life. I could die now.

"Thanks," I squeaked out, shoving the parcel at him. "I've got to, erm..." I stammered, covering my face with my hands. "Let's just agree that I'm still jet-lagged." I couldn't possibly admit I was all twisted up with desire. "Thanks again. For the assist."

He stepped back. "You're more'n welcome, Maddie. I'll see ya 'round."

I made myself refrain from watching him walk away. When the front door shut behind him, I could finally breathe easily again.

What the hell am I going to do?

At least I had a day of work at the bakery with Aunt Laurie to distract me.

Chapter Six

Both the brownies and the matcha cake sold out. I was delighted with this very early success. I tried not to read too much into it, but failed. People liked my cakes!

This was not a surprise, of course. I'd been baking to order for years, but, as most of the cakes I made were either mailed to people or delivered for an event, I rarely got to experience feedback firsthand, or quite so soon.

It was extremely gratifying.

Aunt Laurie sent me home at lunchtime when the college girls she kept on staff arrived for the afternoon shift. I was all too ready to fall into bed. The time zone shift was still doing a bit of a number on me.

I spent Wednesday sorting through my most beloved recipes to decide what to bake while Stateside. In the evening, I logged on to my tablet to check my emails, Instagram messages and video feedback, and to update my parents - the usual stuff. I had a quick exchange of messages with Jess and admired the pictures of her and Connor posing on a mountaintop, both grinning, Jess' nose covered in sunblock.

This morning before my shift at *Cake Away* I'd uploaded

another video, a short tutorial this time, for black sesame cook-ies, and it had more than fifty comments on it.

I scrolled through them.

Didn't Mr. Maddie come with you?

How long are you away for?

Have fun. Travel safe! You look tired.

Did something happen with your cute boyfriend?

I closed my eyes for a second, but I could still see the words swimming before my eyes. My loyal customers were concerned about me, but what did I tell them? The holding message of "this shop is taking a short break" obviously wasn't cutting it with those who knew me, or thought they knew me.

I'm sorry, I was sabotaged by the man I loved.

I'll be away for a while. My fiancé and I broke up.

I'm just helping my family out with their business for a few weeks.

I'm sorry, my fiancé thought that I should take a break from my lifelong dreams to bring up the children we had not yet discussed let alone brought into the world.

None of the potential answers felt right, although they were all true.

I had comments on another video, too. Questions about whether Seb had come with me to America. I hit reply and closed down the browser. It had never been the plan for him to come with me, but did I need to explain that? I was a chronic over-explainer because why use three words when you could use three hundred?

There would be time to decide what to say later.

I lay back on the bed in Jess' spare room, staring at the ceil-ing. A tiny spider made its way along a crack by the light fitting, and I envied it for a second. The little arachnid didn't have any of these cares, didn't have to navigate modern life, intrusive people, or broken hearts. Didn't have a mess waiting for it when it finally flew back home to face the truth.

My phone lit up on the bedside table, and I ignored it. It was probably Seb again. Apologizing. Thinking that *sorry* would be enough to make me forget that he'd figuratively and *literally* dumped my dreams in the trash.

I shut my eyes, but then curiosity got the better of me.

I reached for the phone and swiped the screen to unlock it. Four missed calls, all from Seb. I deleted those. There were also two messages from a number I didn't recognize until I read the message.

Hi! It's Jenny from next door. I always want to write Jenny from the block, but does anyone under 30 even get that reference? Jess gave me your number and said it's only for emergencies. But this is an emergency. My Mom offered to babysit Toby tonight and I have NO ONE to go out with. I know it's a school night, but please come out with me?

I smiled. Jenny was absolutely impossible not to like.

I saved her contact info into my phone and tapped out a reply.

Me: Sure. What's good 'round here on a school night?

She replied within seconds.

Jenny: Oh, thank God! I'm so excited! Pretty much the only place in Redwing Falls is Molly's. It's a bar, pool hall and diner all in one. It's nicer than it sounds. I'll knock for you around 7?

I shoved my hand through my hair. It really needed to be washed before I saw any other people. It was so oily, sometimes it felt like an animal on my head.

Me: Make it 7:15.

Jenny replied with three happy face emojis and two partying ones and I smiled again, surprised she didn't have a slew of girlfriends to call on. I guessed it was tough to keep up regular relationships with a small child to look after by herself.

I made myself shower thoroughly, and then I investigated

45

the clothes I'd brought with me to see what was suitable for drinks with a girlfriend.

I hadn't packed much aside from the basics, being too preoccupied with alternating between crying hysterically and fantasizing about ripping off Seb's balls.

I checked the time in the UK, and video-called my best friend Emma, a night owl who would still be awake.

True to form, she picked up on the second ring. "Hey!" Her sunshine-smile face, framed with chestnut brown hair, filled the screen, and I felt a pang at missing her, even though it hadn't been that long. "How's America? Are you drowning in sweet tea? How's the bakery? Did you find the Chris farm? Or any of the hot actor Chrises?"

"It's fine - it's pretty warm. Mad because I know it's practically Baltic there. I can currently still breathe, although I have been offered a *lot* of sweet tea. No hot Chrises yet, sorry. And the bakery's good, but it's shut now. It's five o'clock here."

"Only five! How's the past?" The screen shifted as Emma set her phone up on something, and then more of her appeared on the screen, her top half clad in a cute, thickly woven cardigan and an autumnal leaf-print blouse. Her free hand held a cup of tea.

"It's fine, but past me needs an outfit for drinks. I've been asked out by the woman next door. She apparently wants to be my friend."

Emma *tsked*. "And why wouldn't she want to be? Okay, what are the options? Do any of Jess' clothes fit you?"

"No, and even if they did, I'd feel kinda weird about raiding her wardrobe. At least without asking first. Here you go." I flipped the camera direction so she could see the clothes displayed on hangers hooked on the edge of the bedroom door. "Option one is this *deeply* unsexy blue dress with a huge snowflake across the boobs, which I somehow decided to pack even though it's Spring."

Emma winced. "You were heartbroken. It happens."

"Option two. This plain black top with maybe one of my two pairs of jeans? It's a bit boring but it doesn't have any flour stains, so for me, it's fancy. And it has a scoop neck."

"Uh huh."

"Option three is this stunning cheongsam which is also inexplicably here, but *way* too much for this one-bar-town. And option four is this t-shirt, which I really like because it has tiny sky-blue beads woven into the black, but it's also kind of dressy."

Emma *hmmm*ed. "But you left it 'til last which means you like it best."

Damn her, knowing my brain. She gave me some suggestions and we decided on the snowflake dress under the t-shirt. Our call ended when her takeaway arrived.

I squeezed in a return declaration of love before she disconnected, and the room felt big and lonely for a moment.

The bejeweled shirt made the hideous snowflake dress look like a plain blue miniskirt. Emma's suggestion was genius.

I twisted my hair up at the back of my neck, swiped on some eyeliner and blush, and finished a minute before Jenny rapped at the door.

"Hey, neighbo—*wow*. I did not get the dressing up memo!" She fanned herself. "You look amazing. The guys here won't know what's hit 'em."

"Doubtful, but thanks. It's the only dressy thing I have, aside from a *very* fancy cheongsam, and it's a bit much for a Wednesday, but.... Whatever."

"Yeah! YOLO! Isn't that what the kids say?" Jenny asked, voice shaking with laughter. She looked cute in red trainers, black jeans and a nautical print boat neck top. Red earrings dangled from her earlobes. "Take me to the bar now before I embarrass myself. I haven't even had a drink. How do people behave on nights out these days? I haven't seen anyone aside from my kid, my parents, and my brother for *so* long. What if we don't know what to do?"

I locked up the house and then took the arm she offered, feeling like a teen on a girls' night out, and it was *lovely*.

"You don't have to worry about anything," I assured her. "I know how to order drinks. We have bars in England."

"Oh, yeah." She patted my hand. "Woot! I'm out! I'm out! I might have to be up at six tomorrow, but I am *out!*"

"You'll have to show me the way."

"To town? It's basically one street," Jenny replied, amused. "You can't get lost. It's what's great and what's terrible about this place. I'll show you the way. Molly's is only around the corner and down from *Cake Away.*"

She led us down a few residential streets before making a turn that suddenly opened up into main street. I could see the bakery from here, realizing I'd been taking the long way this whole time.

She led us along the pavement and to an unassuming stone building with two big windows sheltered by a gray awning that read MOLLY'S.

The door was open and we could hear rock music from inside, punctuated by laughter and the click of pool balls. A neon sign in the left window read BAR IS OPEN, and below that COME ON IN.

So, we did.

I held the door for Jenny, performing a funny little bow for her. She giggled. I was in a much better mood than the one I'd started the evening in. I was starting to learn that Jenny had that effect on people. She was a bright light in any room.

I was envious of Jess, who got to live next door to her all the time. I didn't know half the people in my building in London.

The bar sat directly to our left as we walked in, and a woman in her mid-fifties with shoulder length curly hair, wearing a "100% THAT BITCH" tee nodded to us and smiled. "Hey, Jen," she called.

Jenny grabbed my hand. "Molly! This is Maddie Liu. She's Jess' cousin from across the pond."

"I'm helping my Aunt Laurie to run the bakery," I explained.

"Pleasure to meet you," Molly drawled. "Welcome to Redwing Falls. What can I get you? First one's on the house."

"Well, that's very kind, but—"

"We'll have shots!" Jenny exclaimed.

Molly raised her eyebrows. "Moms gone wild, huh?" she muttered at me.

I grinned. Similar to Jenny, Molly was impossible not to like. "Jenny's first night out in a while."

Molly poured the shots without measuring and nodded at a point over Jenny's shoulder. "Might not wanna go full wild just yet, Jen. Your brother's here."

Jenny paused with the shot glass halfway to her mouth. "Balls." She looked over. I followed her gaze across the wooden floor of the bar and *holy shit*.

Rick was bent over one of the three pool tables here. I recognised his ass in those jeans. No one had an ass that good, not that I made a habit of gawping at men's backsides in London, but sometimes it was nice to look.

The denim molded to him in a way that made me want to find out if it was painted on.

He took his shot, sinking a ball like he could do it blindfolded, and maybe he could, then he straightened up, leaning on his cue. The line of his back and shoulders was obscene in the gray Henley he wore, the sleeves rolled up to show off tanned forearms.

I swallowed, reliving my earlier fantasy of Rick railing me in the bakery, his gaze hot on mine, his hands cupped under my butt as he—

"Earth to Maddie?"

I jerked out of my reverie to find Jenny and Molly looking at me with *we know what you're thinking* expressions.

"Best ass in town," Molly said, like she was reading a fact from an encyclopedia.

"I wasn't looking," I blurted out, but my face felt very hot. *Great job, Maddie.*

Jenny linked her arm through mine. "Well, we might as well go say hi, then we can get on with letting our hair down." With her other hand, she tossed back the shot of alcohol. "C'mon, drink yours."

It was sharp, and it burned all the way down. I set it on the bar and thanked Molly.

"Another?" she asked, bottle poised.

"No. No, thanks."

"Suit yourself. Have fun, kids."

A guy with blue hair in a too-tight tee approached the bar, and she moved to serve him.

Jenny tugged me. "Let's go! Time's a wastin'! Let's go see my brother so he can tell me to behave, and I'll pretend like I'll listen, and then we can get down to business."

Hotel California was playing over the speakers under the chatter and laughter of the patrons as she led me to the pool table, where Rick was playing pool with a younger man, dark hair, full beard.

Rick looked up as we approached and met my gaze. A slow smile curved his lips, and I thought: *God, I am toast. I need to go.*

But I didn't make any move to leave.

"Evenin', ladies," Rick drawled, and I swore I could feel his voice in every part of my body. The Henley looked so good on him. The neck was open a few buttons, revealing a triangle of bare chest and a glimpse of his ever-present dog tags. "Didn't know you were comin' out."

"Ma offered to have Toby!" Jenny enthused. "I didn't know *you* were coming out, either." She beamed at him like she'd made a really good point.

Rick jerked his thumb at the younger man. "Eddie's my apprentice, and he did a good job today, so the beer was on me."

"Hey," Eddie said shyly, lifting a hand in greeting. Despite the beard, he looked no more than fifteen.

"I just came to say that I'm here to have fun," Jenny assured Rick. "So could you *not* glower at any man who so much as breathes within ten feet of me?"

Rick's brows lowered, and the corners of his mouth turned down, the beginnings of a bit of a snarl.

"Yes, that! Don't do *that*."

"No promises," he muttered.

She turned to me. "See? This is what I have to put up with." To Rick, she added, "I'll behave if *you* do."

He rolled his eyes. They really were the most gorgeous colour, deep brown, ringed with the faintest touches of gold. "That'll be the day. Go on then, enjoy your evenin'. Nice to see ya, Maddie."

"You, too," I replied once I forced my brain into gear. He was too handsome to be allowed, really.

Rick's gaze held mine as he asked, "Do you play?"

"Pool?" I swallowed, nerves butterflying in my stomach at his proximity.

"No, chess, darlin'." He grinned, that lazy tug of his lips that transformed his serious face into a boyishly handsome one. "Yeah, pool. Maybe we'll have a game while you're in town."

"Maybe. Can't promise to put up much of a challenge. I might need lessons."

That smile snuck onto his lips again. "That so? I've been told I'm a very good teacher."

I just bet he was. My mind raced with feverish, naughty thoughts, and I couldn't reply. Thankfully, Jenny pulled me away and guided us back to the bar.

Is he really just offering pool lessons? It felt like flirting? Maybe it's more?

Maybe I'm reading too much into this.

As we walked, I caught a glimpse of Rick, turning away to pick up his half-empty bottle of beer and tip his head back to drink, exposing the long line of his neck.

I felt seventeen again, trying to micro-analyse every little thing a cute boy did or not did not do, or did or did not imply.

Except Rick was all grown up, and oh my goodness, did I know it.

Chapter Seven

"Thanks so much for the cookies," I told Jenny sincerely as we sat down with our drinks.

We were tucked in the far corner of the back of Molly's, out of sight of the pool table, which meant, mercifully, that I could also not see Rick. "They melted on my tongue. They're all gone."

She clapped her hands together in delight. "Thanks! It's nice to have someone other than Toby, Rick and my parents to bake for. Ma's becoming critical now that I'm getting good." She rolled her eyes. "I remind her whenever she criticizes me that she taught me everything I know."

I laughed. "Parents. When I first started my business, my mum was deeply suspicious of all the social media involved."

Jenny sipped her mojito. "Do you want to talk about what happened? At home, with your fiancé. Jess only touched on it, but-" She closed her eyes briefly and shook her head. "No. You know what? We only just met. Please tell me to shut up and mind my own business."

I sighed, taking a swig of my delightfully crisp pear cider

while I thought it over. "Do you really want to hear about it? It's depressing."

Jenny leaned forward to take my hand. "If you wanna talk about it, I'm all ears."

"Okay. Well..." I chewed it over mentally for a second. As I let myself think about the week before I flew out here, the happy chatter around us and the dulcet tones of The Strangler's *Golden Brown* faded away. "Seb was so supportive when we met, or so I thought."

Jenny frowned. "Go on?"

"Given time, I wonder if I thought he was supportive because he organized our social life for me, planned all the stuff we did when we weren't working, but maybe I played into his hands by doing the things he wanted all the time, and not questioning it." I clenched and unclenched the fingers of my free hand, hurt and anger and sadness balling up in my stomach.

"I'd been working at a prestigious hotel in London, one of a team who made their cakes and desserts, while building my online following and making Asian fusion cakes at discounts for friends. I did the odd company cake delivery, too. It was slow, but steady. Long hours. By far, my favourite thing was meeting people at fairs and markets, seeing them enjoy my food firsthand, but I didn't have a car, and they clashed with weekend work at the hotel. I figured I would one day have my own space, if I did well enough.

"It took years, but the business grew, and I shortened my hotel hours. That was where Seb and I first met. He wanted to know who'd made this particular cake."

"He was obviously enthralled," Jenny interrupted.

I smiled. "Thank you for that ego boost. It was the hotel's most extravagant dessert, but he could afford it, he's a banker—"

"I know what that rhymes with," Jenny snorted.

Her words brought some light relief to the memory and I chuckled. . "Indeed. Anyway, by this point, I had twenty-five thousand subscribers to my platforms, two kitchen equipment companies sponsoring paid content, and I thought seriously about setting up shop somewhere. I would need a loan, or to co-occupy a space with another baker, but to see people enjoy my food right there? I'd started to think that was what I really wanted, long-term. To see the whole picture—make something, sell it to someone, see them eat and love it."

Jenny nodded, listening intently, stirring her mojito absently with the little cocktail umbrella that had come with her drink.

I looked over Jenny's shoulder, my eyes open but not seeing the bar scene around us, as I reminisced. "Seb had been constantly hinting that I should move in with him, so he could support me, but I wanted my independence - that's why I'd moved out of my parents' house.

"As my subscribers grew to thirty and then forty thousand, and orders piled up, I happily quit my hotel job. I could finally manage the rent on my flat without the extra job.

"Excited, I wrote to some shared shop spaces in the hip, foodie areas of the city. Seb suggested I use his address just for that, to circumvent my building's poor postal system. I didn't even think about anything going wrong. It made sense."

"On my birthday, he proposed. I was delighted. I temporarily forgot about a shop space, and started planning my wedding cake. I'd made countless bridal cakes. I couldn't wait to make my own. But I wanted to take my time planning the wedding. No need to rush. I'm glad that we didn't rush into getting hitched."

I swiped at my wet eyes, angry that just thinking about Seb could make tears spring up. I continued as Jenny listened, nodding sympathetically. "Time went on. I was happy. Anyway, last week, I happened to be at his place; I'd stayed over. He was in the shower. I went to the bin for something, glimpsed an envelope with my name on. Seb had received letters from the co-owned shop spaces, read them, binned them."

Jenny's mouth was hanging open. "What did you do?"

"I didn't wait for him to get out of the shower. I left the letters where he could see them on the dining table and I stormed out."

"Oh, Maddie," Jenny whispered.

I curled my hands into fists and felt my nails bite into the skin of my palms.

"And then what?" Jenny uttered.

"He called a bunch of times. I didn't answer. I rage-baked the last few cake orders I had to do before flying out here. I'm amazed they came out okay. He turned up at my tiny flat, and by then I'd cooled off enough that I decided to hear him out."

I inhaled slowly. Retelling it made me angry, rather than sad.

I imagined I would eventually get to the sad part, but anger still dogged my every waking moment, or at least every moment that Seb intruded on my thoughts.

"The turd," Jenny seethed. "What was his excuse?"

I gulped more cider. The sweet, sugary alcohol buzzed on its way down. I was beginning to feel a bit looser. "Apparently, he was doing it for my own good."

"Of course he was."

"I couldn't listen after that opener. I didn't even want to know what had gone through his mind. I demanded that he get out, and I started flinging things into my suitcase without really looking at them. He couldn't believe I'd still come here with that all between us, so I laughed in his face and told him there was no us, not anymore."

Jenny stared at me, her mouth agape.

Swallowing back the bad taste the retelling put in my

mouth, I added, "He begged me to stay, to hear him out properly, so we could fix it. So we could save what we had. But to me, he'd almost literally chucked everything I wanted for myself in the bin. I didn't see anything saving. I threatened to call the police if he didn't leave. He did, then I called my mum, and two days later I got on the plane here."

Jenny reached across the tiny table between us and squeezed my knee. "What an *absolute* ass hat."

"I still don't fully know his reasons."

"I'm sorry," she soothed.

"No, *I'm* sorry," I blurted. "We hardly know each other and you didn't ask for a full-on sob story."

"Do *not* apologise," Jenny commanded. Her eyes blazed brown fire. "Maddie, Rick was a Staff Sergeant in the US Army. He has *two* medals. He could make it look like an accident."

I laughed for what felt like the first time in an age, and I felt lighter inside. "I'll think about it."

Imagining Rick in combat mode was a hell of a distraction, and now I'd started imagining him in uniform, too. I tried to surreptitiously glance over my shoulder to catch a glimpse of him, and was rewarded when I saw him bent over the pool table, eyes narrowed in concentration, the low-hanging lights picking out the gold in his hair.

"Do that."

"Thank you so much for letting me vent." I drank the last of my cider and set the bottle down, then stood up. "This round is on me! What'll you have?"

"Another mojito. Why not? A hangover will be Tomorrow Jenny's problem."

"Coming up!" I strode to the bar, feeling warm inside, and a little freer now that I'd unloaded on Jenny. I hoped we'd be friends even after I crossed the ocean. Okay, long distance was tough, but that was what the internet was for, after all.

I leaned on the bar as Molly served another customer, but she gave me a little nod to let me know she'd seen me.

"How's your first night at Molly's treatin' ya?"

I jerked in surprise at Rick's words. His voice was really something, the sort that rumbled low inside you until all you could think about was how he'd groan your name during sex.

Or perhaps that was just all *I* could think about.

"It's good. Jenny's wonderful."

He held my gaze, and I got the strangest sense that he could see right into the heart of me. Finally, he said, "Yeah, she's the best. Has a huge heart. Can be a pain in the ass to live with, though."

"Really?"

"Yeah. She's the messiest person I have ever met. I don't love seeing my sister's bras lyin' all around the house." He grimaced. "There're some things a guy does *not* need to know."

I laughed. I really liked him. And that was becoming a problem.

He studied me for a long moment. On the overhead speakers, the music changed before Rick spoke again. "Did you live with him?"

"Who?"

"The guy on the other side of the ocean."

My stomach turned. "I told you about that?"

Rick smiled slightly, crossing his arms over his chest. He had excellent forearms, showed off to perfection in tonight's shirt. "You said, "who crosses an ocean to avoid someone?" Before you fell asleep in my truck."

I closed my eyes. "Oh, God."

"I ain't gonna tell anyone," Rick assured me in his measured drawl. "But whoever he is, I hope y'all won't give him the time of day once you're back across the pond."

"Oh, don't worry." I traced my finger around an old cup ring on the wood of the bar top. "I don't intend to."

"Good."

I looked up at him, letting myself get lost in the depth of his tawny eyes for a long moment, all the possibilities turning over in my mind. If he tried to kiss me now, would I let him? Would I have wanted him to?

Yes. I wanted him to.

Should I have wanted him to?

I was tired of these mental gymnastics.

"Sorry, folks. What can I get you?" Molly asked, and Rick's gaze cut from mine.

I swallowed, taking a deep breath. It was for the best. He was too attractive, too kind, and wasn't I here partially because of a break-up? It would be really stupid to indulge in any kind of relationship, even the very temporary kind.

Rick nudged my shoulder with his. "Ladies first."

"I was here first, anyway." I teased.

He just grinned. God, he was so handsome it hurt to look at him directly, just like looking right into the sun.

"I'll have a mojito and a Coke," I told Molly.

"Sure." She lifted the Coke tap and pointed it at Rick. "Watch this one. He could charm a bear out of hibernation."

"I can believe it," I said wryly.

Rick shook his head. "Teamin' up on me, ladies, I'm hurt. Hurt." He pressed a hand to his heart, and it only drew my attention to where the neck of his shirt opened, revealing his tanned skin and a very light furring of chest hair.

"He's all talk." Molly smiled as she set the drinks on the bar and told me the damage.

I paid. "Have a good night, Rick."

"You, too." He smiled, a slow smile that spread from one side of his mouth to the other, and I felt it all the way to my toes.

I carried the drinks back to Jenny. She was deep in conversation with a guy sporting a little goatee and wearing a beanie, and they were leaning toward each other.

She looked up when I approached, and she swiveled in her seat. I saw disappointment flash across the guy's face.

"Hey! Thanks! You were gone a while."

"Your brother was at the bar."

"Was he nice to you?" I watched her gaze dart back to beanie guy, who had taken his phone out but was also super-obviously keeping an eye on her.

"He was," I reassured her. I didn't make a move to sit, but I did lower my voice, passing her the mojito. "Do you want to carry on talking to him?"

Indecision paraded over her face. "Oh, no... I couldn't, because then you'll be by yourself."

Jenny had not enjoyed a night out in a long time. Who was I, someone she had known for almost literally five minutes, to get in the way of her meeting a handsome stranger?

"Well, your brother offered to teach me how to play pool, so..."

Jenny rolled her eyes. "He thinks he's the man. Don't let him mansplain the game to you."

"I won't. What I mean is, I could distract him from doing the glowering thing."

Her face lit up. "Really? Oh, I'd love you forever."

"Okay, then. Enjoy. He seems nice."

"He is," she whispered. "His name is Charlie."

I gave her a thumbs up and turned away to make for the pool table. When I glanced back, Charlie had already moved into my seat.

It was time to ask Rick Callahan to teach me how to play pool.

Chapter Eight

Eddie was leaning on the bar, laughing with Molly when I approached the pool table, which meant Rick was alone. He was coating the end of his cue in chalk, his gaze down, and I took a moment to appreciate his long lashes against his cheekbones. Why did men have such amazing lashes? It was deeply unfair. Meanwhile, I would probably be buying false lashes for another fifty years in an attempt to make my stubby ones even stand out on my face.

His gaze flicked up as I neared him, and he smirked. "Well, well. Back to test out your pool skills? Or come to distract me from that guy my sister's talkin' to?"

I laughed. "They're just talking."

"For now," he groused.

"How about you stand on the other side of the pool table, where you can face her, but where it isn't *completely* obvious that you're supervising?" I suggested, raising my brows cheekily at his big brother behaviour.

Holding his attention like this, being in his orbit, was intoxicating. I felt his nearness keenly.

"Fine." He shook his head, but his mouth curved. He

rounded the table, picked up a cue, and passed it to me. "How long since you played?"

"Years. Last time was university, about ten years ago." I hefted the cue in my hands and felt the weight. "This is a long one."

Rick raised his brows, mirth sketched across his face. "It's not the size, Maddie, it what'cha do with it. So I've been told, anyway."

"So you've been *told?* I'd have thought you'd know from personal experience," I teased.

He leaned over the table, practice-thrusting the cue through two braced fingers. "A gentleman *never* kisses'n tells, darlin'."

The endearment, although he'd mentioned everyone was called such here, still made a thrill race through me.

I mirrored him on the other side of the table, bending and positioning my cue just-so.

The scent of chalk floated up into the air.

"And are you a gentleman, Rick Callahan?"

"I'm offended that you even have to ask," Rick scoffed, but the twitch at the corner of his mouth gave his amusement away. "Aren't we in the South?"

"You can't tell me all Southern men are gentlemen," I countered.

He snorted, clearly entertained. "Oh, on that, I have to agree with you." He straightened, leaned on the cue thought-fully. "You wanna be stripes or solids?"

"Whichever one is rigged."

He laughed out loud. "I wouldn't do that to you. And more to the point, neither would Molly. She's as straight a shooter as you'll ever get."

He plucked a coin from the front pocket of his jeans and fed it to the machine. I heard clunk after clunk as the balls were released, and Rick set the triangle shaper on the forest-green table. I watched his hands as he settled the coloured spheres into place.

I could look at Rick Callahan forever. At the gleam of his golden-brown hair under the soft bar lights. At the broad line of his shoulders. At the one dimple that winked on the left side of his mouth when he smiled.

Even my bestselling miso-caramel brownies could learn temptation lessons from this guy and they took some beating.

It was a hell of a shame that I'd never find out if he tasted just as good as the fudgy treats. Or even better.

I'd bet on the latter.

"You need a rule refresher?" Rick asked as he gently eased the triangle shaper off the balls.

"You take turns to try to hit the balls into the pockets. Did I miss anything?" I asked, knowing I was being cheeky, but it was entertaining to poke the bear.

"All right, well, smartass, there's a *little* more to it than that." He pulled another coin from his pocket and offered it to me. "Flip for who goes first?"

The quarter was shiny and newly pressed, and warm in my palm from being near his body. I wanted to hug it to myself like a schoolgirl with a photo of her crush.

"Heads or tails?" I asked.

"Tails."

"Really?"

"Yup." He tugged down the left side of his shirt collar just enough to ease his shoulder out. His skin was that gorgeous golden tan all over, I learned, and then I saw the beautifully realised art of an eagle clutching a ribbon in its beak, its wings spread, the US flag billowing around it. "Always feels wrong to bet against the eagle."

"Wow. Did it take long?"

He let the shirt settle back in place, and I selfishly mourned the lack of ogling I could now do. Still, at least the image was burned into my brain. "Four hours, two sittings. Got it done the same time as some of my unit buddies."

"Do you— no, never mind."

"Do I what?"

I'd been about to ask whether he had any more tattoos, other than the one under his ribs and on his forearm, which I had yet to see in real detail.

But then I'd have to admit I'd been staring on Sunday. And *then* he'd know that I wanted to explore every inch of his skin with my fingers and then my mouth.

And I did. Fuck, I did.

I really did want to.

I might have very recently broken it off with my fiancé, but I had eyes. And those eyes, and the rest of me, were deep in lust. "Nothing."

The corner of his mouth turned up, and his eyes danced with mischief, but he shrugged. "All right, then. Keep your secrets."

"Oh, my God. Was that a *Lord of Rings* reference?" I laughed, even more drawn in by him. First John Wyndham and now Tolkien? He was a puzzle of a man, and the more I learned, the more I wanted to know.

"You know it was. Read the whole trilogy one tour," he confirmed. Was that a pink flush creeping up his neck? It was *adorable.* "C'mon. Put me out of my misery and flip that coin."

"This isn't over, Callahan," I muttered, but I flipped it.

The eagle looked up at me when the coin landed.

* * *

Rick

Rick's attention was slowly becoming centered wholly on the beautiful woman opposite him. He was trying to keep an eye on the beanie-wearing guy chatting up his little sister, but Maddie Liu was one hell of a distraction.

Her silky, raven hair framed a face created by angels. Her slight overbite made her rosy mouth more interesting, drawing attention to her top lip. It looked very soft. He'd have loved to find out just how soft.

He made himself think of Jess's reminder to look out for her cousin.

He didn't think sleeping with her would be included in that remit. Sadly.

"Looks like you're up first," she said, offering him the coin. The shiny metal glinted under the pool table lights. He took it, and her skin was warm and soft as his fingertips brushed her palm. Trying not to dwell on that, he shoved the quarter back into his front pocket. "Let's play."

It was tough to concentrate with her right there opposite him. The shirt she wore was covered in tiny beads that caught the light just so, casting an almost ethereal glow over her pale gold skin. The soft material hugged her in all the right places, reminding him of how she'd felt, cosied up against his chest when he'd carried her from the truck. Had that only been three days ago? He felt all turned about by her. A leaf in a storm, helpless to do anything but dance to the rhythm of the wind.

"Ready to get schooled?" he asked, trying to get his head back in the game.

"Big talk," she teased.

"For *you*, since you haven't played in years."

He bent over, positioning the cue and eyeing up the balls. The overhead pool lights glinted off their hard, shiny surfaces as he weighed his options, then set the cue ball down, and with a measured strike, broke the triangle of balls. His aim was a little off - one of the striped balls bounced off the corner, didn't go into the hole. "Rats."

Maddie just smiled serenely. "You were saying?"

"You're putting me off," he grumbled, wincing internally when he heard himself. "You're doing it deliberately."

"Uh huh. I'm just standing here, deliberately." She walked around the table and he exercised extreme restraint in not looking at the line of her ass in the blue miniskirt. With her free hand, she tapped her index finger on her cupid's bow and, like a moth to a flame, his gaze zeroed in there. How would she taste? Would her lips be plush and soft? "Okay, I think I see a shot."

Positioning herself, she bent over, slid the cue between the bridge she made with her fingers to get the feel of it. Rick made himself think unsexy thoughts. *Coffee-machine descaling. Eddie's Star Wars t-shirts.* Any-fucking-thing except how Maddie's delicate hands would look on pole-shaped parts of his own anatomy.

She made the shot and sunk a plain ball. "Big talk, huh?"

Rick rolled his eyes. "Beginner's luck."

Her second shot wasn't so good. It bounced off the side of a pocket, but she shrugged, nonplussed. "That's okay. I've lined it up for later."

From over Maddie's shoulder, Rick checked on Jenny. She was still talking to that guy. Just talking. Hands not touching. *Good.* He returned his attention to the beautiful Brit leaning on her pool cue, her free hand twirling over the chalked end. *Fuck.* The way her fingers danced made him think of other things she could touch just like that.

Rick shifted position, once again doggedly setting his mind to mundane everyday items. His mom's boiled cabbage. He hated cabbage. Good, that was good.

"We'll see about that," he tossed back.

He rounded the table, scanning the position of the striped

balls, picked one, lined up the shot and sunk it. He couldn't help checking Maddie's reaction. She stood with her index finger pressed to her bottom lip, thoughtful.

As she didn't say anything, he took another shot, but this one fell a little short, bumping the pocket but not going in.

Since he could feel her gaze on him, he pouted.

She laughed.

He could listen to that sound all day.

"My turn." She took her time looking over the balls. The shot Rick had just taken had knocked the ball she'd almost sunk last time off course, but there was another ripe for the picking. He spied it, and by the grin that flashed over her face, so had she.

Maddie bent over, showing off an *excellent* ass that certainly did not help his slippery grip on chivalry. Her ponytail slipped over her shoulder as she did so. The raven locks glinted under the pool table lights. She positioned the cue between her index and middle fingers, shot, and stabbed the tip into the grassy felt.

"Shit. Do I have to forfeit a turn now?"

"I'm feeling generous." He leant on the cue, smirking, unable to resist adding, "Want some help positioning?"

Her gaze flitted to him and then back to the cue ball. "Only if you're sure you won't mess it up."

He scoffed, chuckling, and abandoned his cue against the wall opposite. "I've been goin' too easy on you, champ. Okay, here we go." He stood behind her, caging her in, felt the brush of her ass against the front of his jeans, and made himself take a calming breath. "Bend over as if you're gonna take the shot."

She did so, and he went with her, positioning her arms and hands for the best possible shot. "This okay? Am I too close?"

"No, you're fine." But her breath hitched. Rick wondered if her pulse was pounding like his. His heart bumped hard in his chest at the proximity. He was dizzy from her perfume. It was cherries and something floral, something Rick would think about for some time to come.

"Okay, now feel the cue between your fingers. Is it steady? Don't move too fast. Breathe. There you go."

She slid the cue back and forth a couple of times, testing its weight. "Like this."

"Exactly. Too high and you'll hit the ball on the top, hardly moving it. Too low, and you hit the cloth instead of the ball. You ready?"

She wiggled to get comfortable and Rick's eyes nearly rolled back into his head with the sensation of her backside pressed tight against his crotch.

"The angle," she muttered to herself, "is everything."

Rick groaned internally. It fucking *was* everything. "Take it," he muttered against her ear. Her soft hair brushed against his cheek, and he inhaled a breath of Maddie, and *fuck*, it was too much.

It wasn't enough.

He wanted her so acutely he could feel it in every fiber of his being. He knew his balls would be blue by the end of the night.

She took the shot and sunk the ball.

"Yes!"

He straightened just in time to avoid being punched in the face by her pumping her fist in the air. She spun a little circle and hugged him, bubbling with excitement and jubilant. "Thanks!"

Rick put his arms around her automatically and wished he hadn't. She felt good. Too good. Soft and warm. The perfect height. The top of her head fit just under his chin. "You're welcome, darlin'."

The endearment just came out. Hell, he called near everyone in this town darlin', but with Maddie, it just hit different.

She drew back and smiled. The air between them had changed. He knew it, and it looked like she did, too. "I'll take the next shot on my own, now. Thanks, Rick."

He swallowed and nodded. It was probably best. He was at half-mast as it was. Getting a full-blown erection at Molly's, with his sister not twenty feet away, was *not* in his plans. "I'll, ah, be right back."

He marched himself to the men's room, shut himself in a cubicle, and willed his cock into submission. When he was confident he could look at Maddie again, he came back out.

She was gazing pensively at the table, her brow a little furrowed, lips pursed, and it was cute as hell.

He was *toast*.

"Can I get you a drink?" he asked as he reached her.

"Just a Coke. Thanks." She went to reach for her purse, but he cut her off with a gesture. "On me."

He threaded in and out of people to reach the bar, where Molly and Eddie were still yakking, Eddie's gaze on the game on the overhead TV. Rick glanced at it, but he didn't recognise the teams. There were always sports on at Molly's, just not necessarily the sports you wanted to watch or even knew the rules for.

Molly stopped slicing limes and looked up at him, her lips quirking. "You and English gonna get a room, or you gonna carry on making us all watch?"

Rick scowled. "It ain't like that."

"Bullshit it ain't." Molly pointed the paring knife she was using at him. "I can see the heatwaves from here. Just calling it as I see it."

Rick sighed. One of the downsides of living in a small town.

* * *

Jenny

"You want another drink?" Charlie asked.

Jenny shifted in her seat. Did she? Charlie was sweet, but she was starting to miss Maddie. She'd really needed a girls' night out, and instead, she'd just ended up talking to a guy. He was nice, yes, and she'd genuinely been excited not to be a mom for one night, to be seen just as Jenny, but the live band was setting up on the corner stage of Molly's, and she wanted to talk Maddie into a little dancing.

And she *didn't* really want to hear any more about Charlie's surfing adventures.

A girl could only listen to so much surfing terminology on a Wednesday night.

"No, thanks. I think I'm going to find my friend. I feel a little guilty about leaving her with my brother."

He lifted his near-empty beer glass in a toast. "If you change your mind, you know where to find me."

She made a quick trip to the ladies' room before bee-lining to the pool table. Maddie stood there, leaning on the pool cue, surveying the table with balls strewn across it.

"Hey, stranger."

Maddie's face lit up. "Hey. What happened to beanie guy? Are you okay?"

Maddie's concern touched Jenny. She'd forgotten quite how good it was to have female friends. "I'm fine. He was nice, really. And cute, which didn't hurt. Thanks for the distraction, but I realized as he was talking about how many killer waves he'd ridden on his latest surfing vacay, that I'd planned to spend the evening with *you.*"

Maddie grinned. "I'm knee deep in playing your brother at pool. Want to watch me kick his ass?"

Jenny laughed out loud. "So much. I'd even pay for it. Where is he— oh, getting drinks. I'll see if I can charm one out of him for myself."

"Good luck."

Making her way to the bar, Jenny leant her elbows on it. "Hey, Ricky."

He grunted at the nickname, and she grinned. "Got bored of that guy?"

She shrugged. "However exciting it was to talk to a boy *unchaperoned*," she wiggled her eyebrows, "I came here with Maddie and it wasn't fair to leave her with you."

"Don't worry. I'm takin' good care of her."

Jenny rolled her eyes. "I bet. Well, I'm back now. Buy me a drink? Please?"

"What do you want?"

"I'll be good and just have a soda. Changing diapers is no fun with a hangover. Thank you." She batted her lashes and laughed when he sighed.

Molly poured their drinks, and Rick paid with a folded bill.

"Great shirt, Mol."

"Thanks, Jen! My ex-husband gave it to me when we met to file for divorce. Asshole. I decided, fuck it, I'm gonna own this, and now I love it."

"Yeah. Fuck him!" Jenny lifted her glass in a toast and Molly clinked it with her bottle of water. She froze when she turned to find Maddie and Rick. The door of Molly's swung open and, for a moment, all the air seemed to leave the space around her.

Jenny didn't get out much beyond playdates and baby groups, and she almost never had cause to spend *any* time at the mechanic's on Salt Street. But once you'd seen him, Levi Russell was unforgettable.

It was impossible to miss his long-legged stride and riot of chocolate brown curls. Jenny had seen him slide out from under the hood of an old Corvette last week, hands and forearms covered in engine grease, white t-shirt sticking to him like a second skin, a sheen of sweat on his face. He'd been wearing old work boots, his pretty mouth scowling. Jenny thought about that for some time afterwards.

She jerked free from the reverie when he stopped a few feet from her, touching one finger to the brim of his faded old ballcap. "Evenin'," he murmured. The deep register of his voice was at odds with his big brown eyes, just as his soft mouth contrasted with his stubborn jawline.

If he'd been sitting on a stool here when she and Maddie had arrived, she'd never even have noticed Charlie.

"Um. Evening. Hi, Levi," Jenny uttered. "And bye."

She turned around and squeezed her eyes shut in shame, feeling Rick's gaze on her, then made a beeline for the pool table. When she chanced a glance back, Levi was leaning on the bar talking to Molly, his cap shoved in the back pocket of his jeans, thick curls gleaming under the overhead lights. A cigarette was tucked behind his right ear.

"Who was *that?*" Maddie asked.

Jenny jerked in surprise, almost spilling her drink. "Oh. He just works at the auto shop."

"Uh huh." Maddie sent her a look that said she wasn't buying it, but by then Rick had joined them and set up for the next shot, so she bent into position.

Jenny firmly put Levi out of her mind. He was younger than her, she had Toby to focus on, and not many men were interested in a woman who already had a kid. She cheered on her new friend, knowing there was nothing more fun than watching her brother get his ass handed to him.

Chapter Nine

Maddie

I beat Rick— *just.* By a hair. And I was sort of convinced that he let me, but I allowed it. I got in a few very good shots, if I do say so myself.

By the time the three of us headed home, I was merrily tipsy, my arm linked through Jenny's. I'd had a lovely time in this town. I liked the people. The live cover band, *Llamas in Limousines,* they were called, killed it on the stage at Molly's, and Jenny and I had danced and laughed until we were sweaty.

Rick had hung back, watching everyone boogie with an indulgent smile, shooting the shit with Eddie, Molly, and that guy who'd made Jenny hightail it away from the bar.

I was exhausted, and I'd enjoyed myself.

It was a shame I didn't live here, really. Maybe that was the alcohol talking, or the time I'd spent with Rick. Who wouldn't want to stick around with a ridiculously charming man like him on offer?

Except he wasn't on offer. He was Jess' neighbor, not mine.

I lived an ocean away, and I was fresh from a really quite bad breakup.

I needed to remind myself of that. On an hourly basis, it seemed. Especially when he walked me to my door.

"Well, I'm beat!" Jenny exclaimed from their porch, although she looked far from it. "Good night!" She let herself into the house, leaving Rick and I alone on my front step.

He was *so tall*. Why did he have to be so tall? That was one of my weaknesses.

Low light from the porch of a house opposite backlit him, picking out the gold in his hair, distracting me.

"Thanks," I murmured, searching his hazel gaze. He was way too beautiful. Men weren't this beautiful in real life. "For this evening."

"You're welcome." He slid his hands into his pockets, and I watched the movement, wishing he'd used them to touch me instead.

"You ever want the opportunity to get beat by me at pool again, let me know."

He chuckled. "Never heard that pride comes before a fall?"

"Heard it, lived it, but I'm still not above gloating at winning."

He let out an amused huff. "I had a really good time with you, Maddie. G'night." A muscle ticked in his jaw and I wondered if he was going to kiss me, and then he stepped back, the moonlight bathing his face in silver, and the moment passed.

What had I been thinking? Of course he didn't want to kiss me.

I was deep in lust and imagining things that weren't there.

He was being neighborly. I should have been grateful that he'd stepped back, really, and saved me from myself.

But I wasn't. At all.

* * *

I didn't have a hangover the next day, and I woke early, so the pint of water I'd downed before bed must have worked.

I made a big cup of coffee, and I tackled my work emails. I replied to requests for orders, telling customers when I'd be back. I answered questions about recipes on my blog, and I planned for the next video I'd upload.

I didn't answer any of the numerous questions about Seb. That could wait for a little while, but I was going to have to address it at *some* point. I regretted having him in some of the videos now, but his presence had given my online life another dimension, and, I reasoned, I'd planned a future with him.

How did I condense all that had happened into a few sentences? Could I? How did I do it without putting something I'd regret online?

I shelved that decision for now.

Nothing you gave to the internet ever really disappeared, not if you knew how to look for it, and I would bet some trolls did.

I was lucky not to have been victimized by any, but I had industry friends who'd had awful experiences.

My phone chirped, and I picked it up. A message from Jess, with lots of pictures of her and Connor looking loved up and sun-kissed, and a little "P.S. *please check the mail! Love you!*"

I shot out of my seat at the kitchen table. I wasn't used to an actual mailbox. In London, my mail was delivered into a little pigeonhole in the apartment block foyer.

I opened the door in my PJs and crossed to the end of the

lawn. The little red flag on the mailbox was down. What did that mean? New mail? No mail? I felt a flurry of excitement. God knew why. The mail wouldn't even be for me.

On bare feet, I padded across the grass, soft and warmed from the rays of the sun, and I opened the flap. There were about a dozen envelopes inside, and I flipped through them idly as I walked back to the house, then I stopped in my tracks.

I would recognise Seb's handwriting anywhere.

The *express mail* stamp told me he'd written it not long ago. Perhaps the same day we'd had the fight.

I started to crumple it up, but made myself uncurl my fist. I might want to read it later.

I might still want to burn it and dance around the flames, instead of reading it, but I'd decide that after another few cups of tea.

I stacked Jess and Connor's mail neatly on the kitchen counter. Nothing had red text or anything like URGENT on it, so I sent her a pic of the mail stack with a thumbs-up emoji. She replied with a heart.

I missed her. I was very glad she'd be back for a few days before I had to leave, so we could spend time together.

The envelope with Seb's handwriting dogged my thoughts as I messaged my aunt to ask about today's plan, and what time she wanted me. She replied almost instantly:

Aunt Laurie: It's after eight! Half the day's gone, girl. I've been up baking since 5!

She knew I'd been out with Jenny so I realised there was no heat in her words, but I'd been in the country for five days now, and I probably needed to start properly pulling my weight.

Me: I'll be there in thirty minutes!

She replied with a clock emoji and a whip. I laughed.

I jumped in the shower and, as I was drying off, I texted Jenny to see how she was feeling.

Jenny: Fresh as a daisy, but maybe a slightly crumpled one. Toby and I will stop by the bakery later for coffee!

I got dressed and locked up. Maybe I'd be able to find out from Jenny later who the guy in the baseball cap was. There'd been a proper *Casablanca* moment in the bar yesterday when they'd seen each other. He was definitely *not* just some guy who worked at the local auto mechanic.

Rick was loading planks of wood into his truck bed when I stepped outside. He wore a sleeveless grey shirt and his muscles bulged and pulled as he worked. I swear my temperature rose by a few notches just looking at him— hair tousled, tattoos on display, legs for days.

Eddie was with him, adjusting the stuff that was already loaded and reading off a clipboard.

"Morning!" I called.

Rick set an enormous tool bag in the truck and turned, a smile spreading across his handsome face. "Well, good mornin'."

"More spindles today?"

"Yup. Only twelve willow trees to go." He winced, pushing a hand through his hair. The sunshine picked out the gold strands within the dirty-blond. "Wanna get the job done, ya know? You off to work, too?"

"Yep. I'm late, actually. I better get a move on, or my aunt will relegate all the worst jobs to me." I gave him a jaunty little wave, then inwardly cringed. This man was turning me into a pile of jelly, which was not what I expected fresh from splitting up with Seb.

That reminded me of the letter. I promised myself I would read it after work. The more I procrastinated, the more I *would* procrastinate. I knew myself, after all.

When I arrived at the bakery, Aunt Laurie was serving a couple of older women cinnamon buns and coffee. I inhaled the scent greedily.

My aunt made a show of looking at her watch. "Well, look who's decided to turn up for work," she cackled.

"Sorry!"

She grinned. "I'm just teasing you. I hope Jenny had fun. That girl is welded to her little boy. Not that she shouldn't be, she's a brilliant mother, but children aren't the be all and end all of a woman's life."

I loved her so much.

"What can I do?"

"Get those cheese scones in the oven. People will be wanting their midmorning coffee and treat before you know it!"

I lost myself in the rhythm of baking for a few wonderful hours. To her credit, Aunt Laurie waited a whole thirty minutes before asking if I'd seen Rick on my outing yesterday evening.

I gave her the quick version. "And then he said goodnight."

I couldn't breathe, standing there so close to him, wondering if he'd kiss me. But I can't get into anything. Not that I want to.

I wasn't sure who I was trying to convince anymore. My aunt? Myself?

She just nodded, and wordlessly went back to basting scones.

Around one o'clock, the doorbell tinkled and Jenny walked in, Toby toddling ahead of her, wearing a little dinosaur backpack with reins that attached to a handle in Jenny's left hand.

"Hi!" I enthused, delighted to see my new friend.

"Hey there." She scooped Toby up. "Say hi to Aunt Maddie, baby boy!"

Toby gurgled, "Add!" and held out his chubby little arms. He really was gorgeous.

"Got any of the rainbow sprinkle sugar cookies left?" Jenny wanted to know.

I slid one out of the tray with tongs. "Kept this one back special, just for you."

He grinned, showing half a mouth of shiny white baby teeth.

"And a coffee, please," Jenny added. "And maybe a chat? About adult things? Literally any adult things. If you're allowed on break, that is."

I slid my gaze towards my aunt.

"Go on with you," she huffed, but I knew she was only pretending to be annoyed.

I snagged myself a bottle of water and a granola bar stuffed with cherries and almonds, and followed Jenny out into the sunshine. A few little tables were set up on the pavement for customers and we seated ourselves at one. On his mother's lap, Toby attacked the colourful cookie, sending a rainbow of sprinkles flying everywhere except into his mouth.

"I had fun with you yesterday," Jenny began. "I needed it."

Aunt Laurie arrived with Jenny's coffee, and she smiled up at my aunt.

"You're an angel."

"Oh, honey, I know I am," Aunt Laurie sassed, before disappearing back inside.

Jenny lifted the cup to her lips. "Thank God for caffeine."

"Same."

"Well, it's good to know that you Brits are as addicted as we are." She dug in her huge bag, stuffed into the basket of the stroller, and plucked out a little plastic puzzle thing, handing it to Toby, who squealed in delight. "Anyway, thanks for last night. Most of my pre-mom friends have moved away from Redwing Falls, and as we're still a small Southern town at heart, there were a few, shall we say, *ruffled feathers* when I returned as a single parent."

"In this day and age?" I asked.

"Prejudice is alive and well, my friend." Jenny took another sip of coffee. "Don't get me wrong, most folk were lovely, and, it's gotten much better recently. The gossips always move on to something else, eventually."

"We have that in common with the US, too. Although in London I'm kinda immune to that, thankfully. Big city and all that."

"Amen to anonymity," Jenny enthused. "But Jess and I are tight, and I'm so glad you came, too. I'm glad that we hit it off. I wish I could keep you."

I was about to say that I'd visit, but would that be true? The last time I'd come to see Jess was almost four years ago.

I settled for squeezing her hand instead, and then remembered an important part of last night. "Are you going to tell me about the guy who works at the garage?"

"Garage? *Oh....*" Her entire face went rosy red.

"Yes." I gestured to her blush. "That guy. What's his name?"

"Levi. But we're not going there."

"It certainly seemed like you *wanted* to go there."

She opened her mouth to reply, but Toby chose that moment to lunge off his mother's lap, and she moved at lightning speed to catch him. He started crying, and the moment was lost.

I left the bakery at two, when a college student arrived to take over. I had plans to make some of my favourite cookies, simple vegan shortbread-type biscuits layered with sweet red fondant to look like *ang pao* given out in Chinese communities on special occasions. They were typically filled with cash.

When I got home, cheese-scented and with aching arms from lifting baking sheets heavy with cakes, scones, and biscuits, the first thing I did was snag Seb's letter from the counter. I'd been thinking about it all day. Might as well get it over with.

I slid my finger under the seal of the envelope flap as my phone started to vibrate in my back pocket. I tugged it out to see my parents requesting to video call. I went into the living room where the light was better. It was late there, but we talked for over an hour about their trip away, Jenny, how Aunt Laurie was doing, and everything else under the sun. By the time the call had ended, I'd forgotten about the letter from Seb completely, and I moved on to making the cookies.

Chapter Ten

Mindful of pulling my weight with my aunt, I woke up at five o'clock the next day and used the last of my baking supplies to bake a batch of taro blondies, using taro powder I'd brought here with me. The smell of white chocolate filled the house, and I texted Jess a picture of me in front of the oven, with the caption: *wish I could send a smell!* I snapped some extra pictures for my online feed.

The *ang pao* cookie post already had over 17,000 shares.

The number didn't give me the most boost it normally did.

I think I'd been really set on having a space to display my bakes and sell them. The loss of that chance, for now anyway, coupled with Seb's awful behaviour, was depressing.

I was at the bakery by seven in the morning, arriving just as Aunt Laurie did.

She smirked. "Set your alarm for today, did you?"

"Yeah, yeah." But I was smiling.

I set down the stacked boxes and shook the feeling back into my fingers. Why did cake weigh so much? "I made taro blondies. These are one of my most viewed recipes on my blog.

At one point, I did three wedding orders for them back to back."

"Awesome." She leaned a little closer and inhaled. "Well, I feel like I've put on three pounds just by smellin' 'em."

"That's how you know they're good. I also made these cookies. Look!"

She looked. "I love those! They're *ang pao,* aren't they? Your dad always used to send them to Jess and Greg."

I shrugged off my jacket and bag. "Aunt Laurie, I meant to tell you. I got a letter from Seb."

She stopped with a tray in her hand. "And what did he have to say for himself? Or did you file it in the trash immediately?"

"I haven't decided what to do with it." I rattled around in one of the huge cupboards and found a pretty cake stand for the blondies, placing them in a pretty pattern to give my hands something to do. "I haven't read it yet. I'm torn between curiosity and just wanting to set it on fire."

Aunt Laurie started arranging perfectly round sugar cookies on to a clean square of slate. "You want me to read it for you and give you the summary, just say the word."

"Thank you." I fiddled needlessly with the presentation of the blondies. "I keep thinking, do I owe it to myself to at least find out what he wants? Or will I regret opening it and giving him even more headspace? Ugh. I don't know what to do."

"It'll keep another day."

"You're right. It will, it will keep."

I set the last blondie on the stack and carted them into the shop, laying them in the window next to the fat, flaky almond croissants. The combined scents of sugar, butter and taro wafted up into the air, filling me with happiness.

This was what had started to please me the most; baking things to make others sigh with delight, to feed people joy in solid form. It was how I'd built my business; making the recipes that made me happy, and sharing memories associated with them. Sharing the flavours of my culture with people through the medium of food made me feel bright inside, married the two worlds I felt I had a foot in.

The fusion of these in delicious bakes made me feel good and happy and *alive.*

I knew right then that I had to tell the people who'd helped me build up Maddie Liu Bakes about Seb and what had happened. If there was one thing I'd learned in my life, it was that telling the truth always made things easier going forward.

Lies were what made stuff complicated.

I'd had enough lies from my ex fiancé to last me the rest of my days. Who knew was else he'd lied about?

I resolved to make a blog post tonight about Seb. I'd keep it simple—no one except the two of us needed to know exactly what he'd done, but I really wanted to address the fact he wouldn't be showing up in my videos any time soon.

Or ever again.

Then, I'd read the letter.

Hours later, the bakery cleaned and shut, I sat down on Jess's couch with my computer, and opened a new window to start a blog post. I'd typed three sentences when a rap at the door interrupted me.

I looked through the peephole, then stepped back in surprise. Anticipation with a side of panic zinged through me for a moment.

Why is Rick here?

He stood on the porch, attractively rumpled, wearing a gray chambray button-down stretched over his biceps, tattered jeans slung low on his hips.

I'd heard men referred to as snacks often, but Rick Callahan was a *whole meal.* And dessert.

I tamped down on my libido as I opened the door. "Hey."

"Hey." He gestured with an envelope. "I brought over the estimate for the deck." He lifted his other hand, which held two beers, condensation dripping down the sides. "And somethin' to take the sting off the cost."

"Hey, it won't be me paying," I laughed.

"Yeah, I know, but if you're three sheets to the wind when you remind Jess how expensive it's gonna be, it'll be easier, right?" His cheeky grin was charming, and I was helpless to do anything but smile in return.

"Wanna come through? We can sit outside on the grass. I'm not putting my foot through that wood again."

"And at least if you *do,* you'll also have beer."

"I can't argue with that logic," I chuckled as he stepped into the house. *God,* he was so handsome and broad and a walking fantasy.

The combo made me weak.

Clearly fresh out of the shower, he smelled minty and addictive, his hair curling damply at the edges. I wanted him almost more than I wanted to breathe; I felt dizzy with it. I stepped back as he closed the door behind him, and I shut my eyes for a moment to calm my raging hormones.

"You okay?"

"Long day," I lied.

The frown that graced his lips told me he didn't buy the excuse, but instead of replying, Rick just gestured into the house, silently suggesting I should lead the way.

"You must know this house like your own."

"I don't come over *that* often."

I walked us through the house. The door to the yard already stood open, the weather sweet and mild. I grabbed a bottle opener from the top kitchen drawer and pocketed it before we walked out into the air together.

We sat on the edge of the deck, feet in the grass. Rick offered one bottle and the envelope.

I popped the tops for both of us, drank a little, and winced.

"Not a beer girl?" Rick asked, amused.

"Not often. I drink beer with a curry more than anything." I set the bottle down, the condensation running along the glass and pooling on the wood. "Now let's see what I'll have to deliver to Jess." I opened the back flap of the plain white stationery and unfolded it. "You have your own stationery. That's cute. I do, too."

"Stationery buddies."

God, I wanted to be so much more than buddies with this man.

I wasn't okay.

I scanned the text. "Wow."

"It's a big job. There're other weak points, not just the parts you put your foot through. The deckin's been here since before Jess and Connor moved in."

"I'll say. It looked old then. I should have known better than to come out on it. But you did say you'd been on to her to fix it for ages. Not that that'll take the sting out of it." I took another sip of beer. It went down easier the second time.

Rick drank, too. A bead of condensation escaped the bottle and ran on to his jaw, and I was helpless to do anything but follow its slow path down his neck.

Fuck, I'm toast.

I needed to get away. I should have made some excuse, but I just sat there, drinking beer with him in the sunshine.

"Any plans?" Rick probed. "First Friday night in the States, an' all."

I pulled my lower lip between my teeth thoughtfully. "Well, as you know, Jenny and I had our big night out earlier this week. I also have to go grocery shopping."

He laughed. "I'm honestly amazed you made it this long on the meagre supplies in Jess' place."

"Oh, she has a *ton* of supplies, but they're all baking related. I counted twelve bags of flour and sugar and seven bottles of vegetable oil."

Rick shook his head, smiling. "Connor does *all* the cooking. Jess might be a champion baker, but I can't say I'd accept a dinner invite."

I laughed out loud. "I've had *three* frozen dinners since I arrived. I can't eat anymore or I'll turn into a ready meal carton."

His gaze dropped down to my lips for a moment, so quickly I wondered if I imagined it, and then his eyes found mine again. "You'd be the prettiest damn TV dinner I've ever seen."

Heat crept up my neck, and I turned away, pretending to pick some lint off my jeans. I felt sixteen again, my stomach filled with the fluttery little butterflies of attraction.

"Thank you," I eventually murmured.

He took a drink. "God's honest truth."

I curled my toes into the grass. The sun was warm on my skin, and I wondered idly if I could stay in this moment forever. If I had to go back to what remained of my personal life in London.

"As you're here.... You wanna come to a baseball game?" Rick asked. "When in Rome, and that."

"Sure. When is it? I have the bakery to think of, but it's closed on Sunday."

"It's this Sunday afternoon. My cousin runs a little league. His kid's eight. Cute as hell. One of the parents usually does hot dogs. It's a whole thing."

"Baseball *and* hot dogs? I'll be killed if I go back to London without stories of those things. It's a date," I added automatically.

Rick's brow arched, a grin tugging at his *very* kissable lips. "It is?"

"I mean, yes, I'd like to go. Not that it's a *date* date. You know what I mean. God. I should really stop talking." I closed my eyes.

Rick nudged my shoulder with his own. "I'm lettin' you off the hook. I'll knock for you around one. Sound okay?"

"Great. That'll give me time to go grocery shopping. Where's good around here? To my shame, the last time I visited, my mum did the food shop."

"If you want a lot of stuff, the Sureway is only a ten-minute drive. But Otter Street has the little mom and pop grocery, and Molly's or the diner will do you a to-go box if you don't have time to cook. My cousin, the little league one, runs a butcher from behind his house. You don't gotta leave the Falls if you don't want to."

"I think I'll need some more unusual stuff for my bakes. But I'll definitely check out the grocer. And the diner. It'll be my first time in an *actual* diner. I don't think we went last time."

"Really? Well, you're in for a treat. Mrs. K's had it refurbed."

"Does it have a jukebox?"

"What self-respecting diner doesn't?" Rick countered.

"Truth." I lifted my bottle, and he clinked it with his own.

"So what's the story with Laurie being your aunt?" he asked, after taking a long drink from the bottle.

"My mum's American. Both she and my aunt grew up in Louisville. Their parents, my grandparents, owned a restaurant there. They had Aunt Laurie and my mum quite late in life, and decided to move into the suburbs to raise their kids."

Rick's gaze never left mine. He always seemed to be hanging on my every word; it was gratifying how he listened with his body turned to mine, fully engaged. "How did your parents meet?"

"My parents were pen pals." My whole heart warmed

saying it, and Rick's smile probably mirrored my own. "My Dad's family moved over to London from Hong Kong when he was five. He told her all about Chinatown in his letters."

"That's a cool story. What made your mom want a British pen pal?"

I grinned. "She wanted to meet someone who lived in the same country as the Royal Family."

We laughed together, and a knot I didn't know had been in my stomach unravelled.

A breeze fluttered my hair, and I pushed it out of my face with my free hand, only for it to catch on my nose again. I blew out a breath. "The trouble with flyaway Asian hair."

"Let me." Rick turned toward me. Awareness of his touch shivered through me as he gently freed the lock of hair and tucked it behind my ear. The tip of his index finger lingered just under my earlobe for a moment longer than was proper, and my gaze flew to his. A hundred unsaid words tumbled into the space between our bodies.

"Maddie," he murmured, that gorgeous drawl half an octave lower than normal.

"Yeah?"

He dropped his hand. His knuckles skimmed my bare arm. "Let me take you to the diner. First proper experience should be with an American, right? Well, Irish-American if you go back a little," he amended. "We're all immigrants here."

"Are you asking me on a *date* date?" I added before thinking, unable to help myself. Maybe I shouldn't have teased him, teased *us* like that, but I only had so much willpower. He was eroding it very quickly with his kindness and charm. Funny and cute and kind. The holy trifecta. I was powerless.

"If I was..." His hazel eyes warmed, going soft as he looked at me. "Would you say yes?"

My breath caught. It had only been days since I'd considered myself engaged.

"Sorry. I shouldn't have said *date* date. I need to tell you..." I let the words hang.

Rick lifted one shoulder in a half-shrug. "Don't gotta tell me anythin' you're not ready to."

He was too good to be real. "Can it just be new friends having dinner?" I asked, regretting my knee-jerk flirtation, not because of the flirting, but because I didn't want to hurt this man.

He was so handsome and sweet, but most of all *kind,* and that was my weakness more than anything.

"Of course it can," he said easily. "Happy to be your friend-date guide to small town Kentucky while you're here."

I wanted him to be so much more than that, but I had to remember that I lived an ocean away. And I was starting to think that Rick Callahan deserved much more than to be someone's rebound fling.

* * *

We agreed to go to the diner together on Saturday evening. The day before the baseball game. Should I have been spending a whole weekend with a guy I found *ridiculously* attractive, on the coattails of a bad break-up?

Probably not.

But was I going to enjoy myself and do it anyway?

Yes.

I'd tell him about the break-up while we were at the diner, I resolved to myself. He should know. He'd probably already realized that this wasn't going to go anywhere after I got back on the plane to London, but it sure wouldn't hurt to spell it out. For my sake, if no one else's, seeing as I seemed incapable of rational thought around Rick Callahan.

After waving him off, I took pictures of his estimate and

sent them to Jess, then sat down to try to compose the post about Seb.

It took a few hours, and *several* bags of crisps, but by the time bedtime rolled around, I had something I was happy with.

Hello from the other side of the Pond!

Many of you have commented on my recent videos or emailed me to ask about why Mr. Maddie, as I call him, isn't over here with me.

I'll be here in Kentucky for a few weeks, helping my aunt to run the bakery she and my cousin own, Cake Away. *I'll link to the website further down if you'd like a little peek!*

I've been keen to work in a bakery somewhere other than the UK for a while, and my cousin Jess has offered a few times now.

Just before I flew out here, I broke up with Mr. M.

Some things have happened between us that I can't get past, so he won't be making any more cameos.

In the wake of this, I needed to get away and clear my head.

I've responded to those of you who have order queries, but don't hesitate to hop into my DMs or email me via the website if you want to book in a future order. I've updated the website calendar for when I'll be back in the kitchen, and taking your orders. I look forward to them.

I've got a busy weekend coming up—my first Stateside food shop and then a baseball game—but I'll also be uploading another baking video as well, for my twist on a Lane cake, invented by Emma Rylander Lane in the 1880s, right here in the US.

Bye for now, and thank you for your support.

I added a few pictures I had taken while here, mostly of the bakery, one with my aunt smiling behind the counter, another early in the morning. The final one was of the view down Otter street. The sun had been shining prettily, catching on the bakery windows.

Chapter Eleven

Jenny

Jenny had managed to feed Toby four whole spoons of porridge, when Rick dragged himself into the kitchen, muttering "Mornin'."

"You've slept well, then?" she teased.

Her brother pushed a hand through his thick, tawny hair. "Feel like I've been hit by a damn train."

Jenny's heart softened. "Bad dreams?"

He jerked a shoulder as he stood by the coffee machine. "Some."

He probably hadn't fully dealt with his experiences in the US Army, Jenny knew. He'd had some therapy after deciding not to re-enlist, but she knew he'd lost more than a few friends under traumatic circumstances. Had he dealt with it? It was often hard to tell under the charming, rough–and-tumble, easy exterior he showed the world.

She was *very* happy that he attended a veterans' group every Sunday.

Not everyone in his unit did.

Some had been lost.

"Anything I can do?" Jenny asked.

He started to speak, then turned to face her, clearing the sleep from his throat. There was a big sleep-crease on his left cheek, and she was suddenly reminded of their childhood, when he used to build pillow forts for her, to keep out the monsters that she thought lived in the dark corners of the house.

He'd stay with her until she fell asleep, safe in the impenetrable bedsheet walls her big brother had constructed.

Rick had never stopped looking after her. He was doing it even now, in the best way he knew. He'd changed his life for her, and now he was making room for her and her son in his house, and in his heart, and she would forever be grateful.

"Actually, the truck's gotta have its oil changed this mornin'. Would you mind drivin' it down to Salt Street for me? I'll stay here with Toby."

At the sound of his name, Toby gurgled happily and offered his uncle a toothy grin.

"That's right, little man! You an' me can watch cartoons while Uncle Rick mainlines caffeine," he rumbled.

"Sure, I'll drive it over."

Only once she was in the truck with the engine going, did she remember that Levi worked at the auto shop. *Fuck.*

Well, she couldn't get out of it now.

Maybe he didn't work Saturdays, she thought as she made the drive.

Except that he did, and he was bent over the open hood of a grey Ford when she pulled up, his truly excellent ass on full view, clothed in worn, tight denim as music blared from speakers elsewhere in the workshop

"Morning," she ventured, trying not to drool.

He smoothly stood from the car, and she saw that his hands were dark with engine grease. The car's innards were shiny in the morning sunshine, wet with oil, all the metal parts akimbo.

It made her think of something her college friends had often muttered about boys. *I'd like him to rearrange my guts.*

She was thinking it about Levi now. He was pretty, with just an edge of rugged. The brim of his ball cap cast a shadow over his face.

His eyes were an utterly gorgeous shade of chocolate brown.

"Mornin', Jenny." He dug a rag from his front pocket and used it to wipe his hands. "What can I do you for?"

"Rick's truck needs—" she stopped when a smear of bright red appeared on the rag. "You're bleeding!"

He glanced down like this was news to him. "How 'bout that?"

Jenny crossed to his side without thinking about it, digging in her purse for wipes. "Good thing I always have these on me for Toby." She grabbed his injured hand, gently cleaning the shallow cut and the surrounding skin. "You're lucky it isn't deep. You should be careful."

"Yes, ma'am," he murmured, an amused smile tugging up one side of his mouth.

"I hope you aren't making fun of me, Levi Russell."

"Hell no. My mama would tan my hide for teasin' a beautiful woman, especially one tendin' to my stupid ass."

Jenny's face flushed, and she stopped scrubbing at his hand, offering him the small pack of wipes. "Well, I'm sure you can take it from here."

He bent his attention to his hand, and she watched his fingers work. How old was he? Twenty-eight, twenty-nine? Younger than her, for certain. He pursed his lips as he wiped away the oil on his skin, and she was struck again by a sudden urge to see if the skin there was as soft as it looked.

She had it *bad*.

"Um, I came to drop off Rick's truck. It needs an oil change."

"Right." Levi pushed the wipes and rag back into his pocket, and plucked a clipboard from a shelf built into the shop wall. "Oh yeah. He in a hurry to have it back?"

"He didn't say."

He scribbled something on the sheet of paper. His handwritten letters slanted to the left. "I'll drive it by before I close up. Sound all right?"

"Yes. Great. Thank you." He smelled of engine grease, lemon polish, and cut grass, and it was making her stomach clench with yearning. "See you later."

She'd turned away and had taken three steps before he called out to her.

"Jenny?"

This was it. He was going to tell her that she was too old for him. That he didn't need babying for a little cut. That he had a girlfriend.

"Yes?" she asked without turning back.

"You might wanna give me the keys."

Crap. She turned back to him with what she hoped was a casual smile. "That, erm, was a test, and you passed."

"Uh huh."

He held out his uninjured hand, and she dropped the keys into it. Their fingers brushed for the scantest moment, but Jenny felt the touch all the way up her arm. She took a step back. "Thanks again."

Levi nodded, his gaze bright on hers. His eyes were a captivating nut brown, the left one sporting a ring of green around the outside of the iris, an unusual and gorgeous heterochromia. "No problem."

She walked home thinking about the deep register of his voice, at odds with his doe-eyed gaze and that tempting mouth.

* * *

Maddie

On Saturday morning, I woke up thinking about Seb.

How we used to have coffee in bed on some weekend mornings—usually in his spacious Chelsea home, seeing as mine was the size of a cupboard— while the brittle light filtered in through the silky curtains. How he used to read out bits of the papers he found amusing to me, in different voices.

I missed the Seb I'd known before he tried to control my life.

I still didn't really know why the heck he'd done it.

I didn't want to be controlled by someone, ever.

Maybe I should have paid more attention. Made an effort to weigh into decisions he made about where we'd go on the weekends if I was free. Instead, I'd let myself be led, because I was flattered by his attention and too distracted by my business to voice my own preferences. Was I to blame, too?

Perhaps I was.

I lay in bed, playing with the ends of my hair, thinking about the letter.

Maybe I wouldn't open it. Maybe I'd burn it.

Did I owe it to him to read it?

Or did I owe it to myself?

He'd tried to call me another couple of times yesterday. I'd ignored both calls. I might continue to do so for as long as humanly possible.

Maybe I should have blocked his number, but I didn't quite have that in me, not yet. Every time my finger hovered over the BLOCK button, I felt a pang of sadness.

Birdsong reached me from the window, left ajar last night as I'd turned in. So different from the concrete jungle I called my home.

A change is as good as a rest.

Was it? What would be waiting for me when I got home?

I'd sent my dad— who had to be talked into refraining from cutting Seb down to size with his extensive collection of wood-working equipment—to collect the small amount of stuff I kept at Seb's fancy flat.

Dad hadn't said much about the encounter, but it was always hard to tell if he was just shielding me from bad news. I was an only child and my father had always babied me a bit. I didn't mind; I was a daddy's girl.

I eventually dragged myself out of bed by bribing my addicted body with coffee. I could afford a lie-in, seeing as Aunt Laurie and a couple of college girls were in charge of *Cake Away* today.

As the sleek little machine brewed, I searched a map on my phone for the Sureway that Rick had mentioned.

It only occurred to me after the first sip of coffee that I didn't have a car and that, although Jess' little Honda sat in the drive, I had no experience driving in the US, with the steering wheel on the other side and everything reversed to how it was in the United Kingdom.

Feeling sheepish, I texted Jenny. *How had I not thought this through?*

Me: Morning, neighbor! Fancy a trip to Sureway? I can promise you petrol money and cake for your trouble!

I drained my mug, and by the time I'd also polished off two pieces of toast slathered with peanut butter, she'd replied.

Jenny: Sure! Can Toby come with?

I replied in the affirmative, and she told me she'd be over in ten minutes.

Just enough time to make a list of what I needed and brush my hair. Not that it ever needed much attention. Straight was pretty much all it did, to my chagrin and to the envy of some of my friends.

I'd compiled a list on my shopping app by the time she knocked at the door.

"Hey, neighbor!" She greeted me perky as ever.

She looked cute; maple-brown hair scooped up into a ponytail, wearing a dark blue cotton shirt dress. "Toby's in the car. You ready for the mind-blowing experience that *is* grocery shopping in another country?"

"Yes, but I'm pretty sure it isn't going to live up to my expectations from recent films, like being hit on in the fruit aisle," I said, referencing a rom-com I'd seen a few weeks ago.

Jenny chuckled as she opened the driver's side door. "Probably not. I almost *never* see a hot guy when I'm grocery shopping. But then again, I think toting a kid along with me puts them off."

I got in beside her, waved to Toby in the back, and fastened my seatbelt. "Seriously, Jenny, anyone who's put off by you having a kid isn't worth your time. Someone worthwhile will take on Toby as his own."

She smiled, reached over, and squeezed my hand. "Thanks."

Toby shook a rattle and babbled to himself— I caught the words *duck* and *bread,* or at least those were the words I thought he said— as Jenny navigated us on to the highway and towards the store.

Anticipation raced through me. I loved grocery shopping anyway, but in a whole new *country?*

My imagination was in overdrive. The possibility of *more*

than two flavours of Pop Tarts had me clenching my hands in barely restrained glee

"What all do you need?" Jenny asked as we pulled up outside an enormous building.

"For once, I've got a list on my phone." I pulled up a shopping app. "You might have to tell me what stuff is. I know the usual things, like swede being rutabaga and aubergine being eggplant."

Jenny wiggled her brows. "Eggplant? Actually, I've never ever eaten eggplant, but I know all about that emoji."

She took me on a tour of the aisles. The place was cavernous. Huge didn't even cover it. I was torn between being overwhelmed and being in awe.

Toby munched happily on a carrot while we shopped.

"Everyone has so much in their trolleys!" I whispered to Jenny.

"Well, most people come to these huge stores for a big grocery run. Don't you do that in the UK?"

"Yeah, but I'm also much more likely to pop to the corner shop for something if I run out." We passed a man pushing *two* heavily laden trolleys. "This is on another level."

"Knock yourself out," she playfully directed as we reached the baking aisle.

Eighty-five dollars and six carrier bags later— and after help from packers, why didn't we have bag packers in the UK?! — we exited the shop. Toby was protesting out of boredom and Jenny promised him a trip to the park as a reward, along with an ice lolly. This placated him long enough to load him and the bags into the car.

"Thanks so much," I enthused as we got back on the road. "I owe you. Happy to babysit or bake for you any time. Well, until I leave," I added, a sour feeling settling heavily in my stomach,

"I just got used to you! You can't leave," Jenny joked. "Perhaps you could come over and sit with him while I take a bath? God, I miss baths."

"Now?" I jumped at the chance to spend more time with her. "I'd be happy to."

I unloaded the shopping into Jess' house, happy at making the fridge look inhabited at last, while Jenny tried to wrangle Toby out of his car seat. He was in a playful mood, grabbing on to the straps like an octopus as she tried to untangle him.

I locked up Jess' house and, when I strolled up to Jenny's door to knock on it in case Rick was home, he opened it before I could lift my hand.

Chapter Twelve

Rick

Had Maddie's hair always been so shiny? Rick wondered as she stood on his doorstep. The sunshine, dappled from the tree in the front yard behind her, casting leaf-shaped shadows on the lustrous black of the strands, flyaway and fine and soft. He knew how soft it was. He had to curl his hand into a fist to stop from reaching to touch it.

"Hi," he said, dumbly.

Way to go, his inner monologue sassed.

"Hey." If she thought he was dull, she didn't say it. "I didn't realise you were home. Jenny asked me to sit with Toby while she took a bath. We just went grocery shopping."

"Come on in. I always need a bath after I go grocery shopping."

She laughed at his joke, and it made him feel on top of the world. He stepped back to let her in, and caught a gasp of her scent as she passed. *Something sugary and cherryish.*

"Incoming!" Jenny announced as she barreled towards the door with Toby under her arm. He was howling like he'd been separated from a limb. "So much for my relaxing bath. I can smell something *heinous* coming from his cute little butt."

The sound of his wailing distorted as she carried him up the stairs, and then Rick heard her add, "Who's ready for the tickle monster?"

Squealing laughter ensued.

"I wasn't hanging out by the door," Rick added as Maddie toed off her shoes. "I was about to go check the mail."

"Of course." She furrowed her brow, smiling. "You don't have to justify yourself to me, Rick."

He'd wanted to, but didn't know how to say that, so instead, he asked, "You want coffee?"

"As you say in this country— or maybe you don't say it at all—does a bear shit in the woods?"

He snorted. "I have never personally said that, but my dad does all the time. Maybe it's generational."

He led her through the house to the kitchen. Sunshine streamed in, dappled on the wooden floors by the overhanging tree in the yard.

Maddie inhaled deeply as they reached the coffee machine. "You've already made a coffee, haven't you? I can smell it. Sweet, sweet caffeine."

Rick took the cup and offered it. "It was for me, but if you're about to keel over from lower than usual caffeine levels, please take it."

"I think I can last five minutes." She grinned.

It was easy, being with her. Exchanging silly banter. Making her coffee, the scent drifting through the air.

He wanted to make her coffee every day.

She dropped into one of the kitchen chairs. Upstairs, the sound of Toby squealing and Jenny saying, "Calm down! I'm just washing your hair! I even got the watermelon shampoo you like! This is meant to be *my* bath!" filtered down the stairs.

"I don't think I *ever* liked having my hair washed as a child," Maddie began as the coffee brewed.

"No kid does. Well, except maybe Kyle Brandon in my fourth-grade class. I swear he was part seal. Always in the water. I think he became a swim instructor." He rubbed his hand over his hair, threading his fingers through the strands. "I had a buzz cut for so long. Feels weird, long like this. Every time I go to shampoo it, I'm still a little surprised."

She tilted her head, appraising him. He felt the kiss of her attention as keenly as if she'd touched him.

And *fuck,* he wished she had.

"I like it."

"Oh, yeah?"

"Yeah. The colour is gorgeous. Sort of all tawny blond," she said admiringly. He loved her accent, the crispness of it.

The coffee machine beeped to signal the coffee's readiness. "Milk, sugar?"

"A little of each, please. I'm not sweet enough to forgo sugar yet."

Rick let his gaze linger on Maddie's face. "Really? I ain't sure about that."

He was gratified to see her cheeks flush a rosy pink. She ducked her head away from his scrutiny, but her face lit up when he settled the doctored coffee before her.

She breathed in deeply. "This is the *super* expensive stuff. I can tell."

"Ethiopian beans. They're the best, and I consider myself an expert in coffee. I drank shitty U.S Army brews for years."

"I love coffee, too. Every time a new place pops up in London, I make sure to try it. For a long while my best friend Emma and I had a spreadsheet running."

"Who doesn't love a spreadsheet?" Rick deadpanned.

"I know!" Her face brightened. "They're just so useful for logging stuff like recipe outcomes, storing info like ideal ratios for sauce thickeners—" She stopped, narrowing her eyes at him. "You're making fun of me."

"A little bit." He settled himself into the chair opposite her, enjoying her company immensely. "Sorry."

Their eyes met for a moment, and Rick wanted to lose himself in her warm honey-brown eyes, her entire countenance dancing with amusement. She was beautiful.

"Okay, you guys are up!" Jenny announced, carrying a squealing Toby into the kitchen. "He's bathed, and now *I* am finally going to have a long soak. Thanks so much, Maddie."

Maddie opened her arms to receive Toby. He squirmed and reached for Rick instead.

"That's my little guy!" Rick wrapped his arms around his nephew, giving himself one more minute to drink in the silky fall of Maddie's raven hair, and the sweet curve of her cheeks.

Then Toby stuck a little finger up Rick's nose and the moment was lost.

"Hey, little dude! Careful with the merchandise!"

"Nose!" Toby cried, going in again. Rick held him at arms' length, laughing, occasionally making his eyes really wide, which sent Toby into peals of adorable baby laughter. He settled the baby on his lap and faux pinched the little boy's nose.

"Now I got *your* nose."

Toby found this pant-wettingly hilarious.

They continued the game for another few minutes.

Rick loved this time with his nephew. If he'd stayed in the Army, he might never have experienced this, or, at least, Toby would never have grown so close to him. He'd be that uncle who worked away and came home on leave sometimes, a family member who was recognised but not well known or loved.

He'd never have wished such an awful break-up on his sister, sweet, caring Jenny, but he couldn't bring himself to be sorry, ever, that her pain had, in part, led to him knowing Toby so well.

Across the table, Maddie sipped her coffee, leaving a faint imprint of rosy lipstick on the cup. If he put his mouth right there later, Rick thought suddenly, it'd be like they had kissed.

He mentally rolled his eyes at himself. When did he become such a sap? The guys in his unit would rip the shit out of him for being so soft.

Toby interrupted his thoughts with a cry of "horsie!"

Rick winced. "Whoa, little dude. Maddie doesn't wanna see that."

Maddie crossed her legs, a devious little smile slowly curving her delicious mouth. "Maddie really, really does want to see that, cowboy."

The sultry tone of her voice went straight to Rick's cock, and he stifled a groan.

Hoisting Toby up, he told the kid, "Okay. She asked for it."

"Horsie, ick," Toby commanded.

"Okay, but you gotta hold on tight." Rick sat Toby down on the hardwood floor and his nephew clapped his chubby little hands with unbridled delight. He waited patiently for Rick to lie face down and then clambered on top of him, settling on his waist and grabbing handfuls of his t-shirt.

"You holding on?"

"Yes, ick!"

Maddie chuckled.

"All right, buddy, horse is ready." Rick slowly got to his hands and knees and lumbered along the floor at a glacial pace. Toby screamed joyfully with every inch of the floor covered.

Rick's heart warmed every time he got to do this with Toby. Sure, it was hell on his knees, but whatever. He'd take the ache a thousand times over for hearing his nephew's little squeals of happiness.

"Gidd-up!" Toby cried. "Gidd-up! Fasta!"

"Yeah, yeah, this horse is old. Last one left in the stable."

"Is that so? You look pretty decent for an old nag," Maddie commented.

Rick tried hard not to preen. "Know a lot about riding horses, do you?"

"At the moment, I'd quite like to."

Heat rushed through him at her words. They were absolutely flirting now.

The question was, did he want to stop at just flirting?

Did she?

Rick had to remind himself that Maddie lived on another continent and was taking this time to get over her break-up, which he was very curious about.

He was about to shoot something pithy and clever back when Jenny appeared in the doorway, looking rested and glowing. "I needed that bath. Could've stayed soaking in there forever." She scooped Toby off Rick's back. "Thanks, guys."

Maddie took another drink of her coffee and then set it down. "Thanks for the coffee, and the company, but I've got a socials video to shoot before dinner. I'd better get going."

Rick stood up. "I'll see you out."

"There's no need."

"Let him," Jenny said fondly. "Southern boys break out in hives if they don't exercise their good manners on a regular basis."

"Thanks, Jen," Rick snarked back.

"No problem, bro."

He walked Maddie to the door, where she slipped her shoes back on, and then he reached around her to open the door.

"See you for dinner? We still on for that?"

"It's a date." Her hand flew to her mouth. "I mean, you know. Sorry. I have to stop saying that. A *friend* date."

He tried to suppress a smile. "I thought we decided this was all theoretical anyway, didn't we? Theoretically, if it was a date..."

"...Which it isn't." Her gaze held his for a moment, and Rick wanted nothing more than to claim her lips in a soft kiss, taste the hint of coffee he knew would linger on her tongue.

But he just rested his hand on the open door and had to hope he wasn't making obvious heart eyes at her.

"Right. Good thing we've got that cleared up," he said instead.

She darted out of the open door. "I'd better, um, get baking. Thanks again for the excellent coffee. I'll see you later!"

* * *

Maddie

I made the Lane Cake with pandan powder. Usually pandan cakes were chiffon cakes flavoured with pandan root, but the powder was an easy fix. Plus, I wasn't entirely sure I would have been allowed to carry an actual plant through customs.

I talked to the camera as I baked, explaining the history of the cake. A sponge cake, Lane Cake lent itself well to pandan flavour and the end result of layers of the green colour with coconut frosting was a homage to the original as well as a delicious nod to my favourite cakes in Chinatown, London.

I edited the video, fixed the lighting, uploaded it, and then walked over to the Han family's restaurant. I knocked on the door marked "DELIVERIES" and Lara's voice streamed out with, "It's open! Come in!"

The tinkling of the bell, the hanging Chinese lanterns with silky red tassels, the ancient lion head on the order counter, the black lacquer with red Chinese calligraphy; it was the same as my last visit four years ago, and the same as when I'd come here as a little girl, when Lara and I had chased each other around the order counter, snapping open fortune cookies and reading them to each other.

I used to be so afraid of the lion head when I was very small. Now, it made me nostalgic and reminded me of running amok with Lara and Marcus.

She enveloped me in a huge hug. She was helping her parents prep for opening today, and she smelled of sesame oil and spring onions, and I breathed in greedily. We exchanged a flurry of greetings and exclaimed over each other's outfits before her parents, Pete and Sarah Han, emerged from the stripy plastic curtain separating the delivery area from the kitchen. Another round of hugs followed, and then they strong-armed me into helping them prep for an hour while we caught up.

It didn't take much effort. I loved food and being near it and making it, and while baking was my number one love, meals were a close second.

Peter offered me dinner, but I very reluctantly had to turn it down, explaining that I was meeting Rick at the diner.

"Uh huh," Lara said, giving me the side-eye.

"He has come home from the Army ready to have babies," Sarah said, using her huge cleaver to chop coriander at an alarming speed.

"Mom!" Lara gasped.

"Mark my words," she said, grinning at me.

Lara shook her head at me. "She said that to his face when he first came back. The perils of a small town."

I laughed, suppressing the urge to ask what Rick's response had been to the suggestion of babies. The image of little tow-headed kids with his irresistible grin flashed through my mind, followed by a pang that it wouldn't be my future. "Here. Let me take a picture for my mum and dad." I tugged out my phone and snapped a shot of us all working away diligently in the big prep area.

I was settling in. It was good to be here with people I loved.

Chapter Thirteen

Buoyed up by my time with the Han family, I practically skipped back to Jess' place to get ready to go to the diner with Rick. The pressure to find the right outfit was on, much more so than it had been for girls' night with Emma.

As much as I'd have liked the excuse to go shopping, I had no time, but what I did have was a best friend, so Emma and I messaged back and forth for a while until we settled on a cute, sunflower-print sundress topped with a cardigan.

I got dressed in record time, grabbed my purse and applied some lipstick just as Rick knocked on the door.

He looked tastier than ever. The tattoo of two koi carp snaked around his forearm, detailed and vibrant, and without thinking, eager to see it close up, I reached out to touch it.

A breath away, I withdrew my hand. "Sorry."

"Don't be." He extended his arm so I could inspect the work. "I like showing it off."

"It's stunning. Why koi carp?"

"My unit had these two soldiers. Brothers, Chinese-American. They each had a little tattoo of a koi on their wrists." His jaw clenched. "We lost 'em."

"I'm sorry," I murmured, unbelievably touched that he would honor his fallen brothers like this. "So now you wear them on your arm."

"Yep."

I looked up and met his gaze, and realized again that I barely knew him. He'd lived an entire life that I hadn't been part of, not for a moment, but I wanted to know everything, and that scared me more than a little.

Not least because I'd be flying home before too long. The days were ticking away.

"What happened? If you want to talk about it," I added. Maybe he didn't want to.

Rick swallowed visibly, his eyes closing for a second, before he took a steadying breath and told me about the explosive device in Afghanistan, and how the brothers' mom liked his tattoo tribute.

"She said they weren't really gone, so long as she remembered 'em." His voice broke on the last word, and he tugged on the brim of his cap, looking uncomfortable. It was the first little fissure I'd ever seen in his laissez-faire persona.

"It was really kind of you, Rick."

Every day so far, I uncovered something new about him; a gentler, vulnerable side to a multi-faceted man.

A man it would be hard to leave on the other side of an ocean.

Every minute we spent together made that clearer.

He made a little sound that could have been either agreement or *let's talk about something else.*

"So," he broke the silence, and just like that, the bared-raw part of him was smoothed over. "You ready for your first real American diner experience?"

I shut the door behind me and locked up. "I am."

"You look nice. You got a little..." He tucked a stray wisp

of hair behind my ear. His touch was gentle, but I felt it all the way to my underwear.

"Thanks. My hair does what it wants."

He started to walk and I fell into step behind him. "I am sometimes jealous of my mum's bouncy waves, though."

"You have gorgeous hair, Maddie," he replied softly.

We walked in companionable silence for a few heartbeats.

"I gotta warn ya," Rick began. "Don't judge a book by its cover with this place. It looks like it's one slammed door away from being condemned, but it does the best damn steak and eggs, and pancakes, I've ever had."

I looked up at him cheekily. "And do you make it your business to be an authority on such things?"

"Hell, yeah, I do. Any Southern boy who doesn't know a good steak or pancake stack should be stripped of the title," he grouched, then added, "In my opinion."

His smile was contagious. He was gorgeous. He was a walking invitation to fall deeply in lust.

But it was more than that now. I'd learned a little about his past, seen a few of the scars he carried, peeled back the layers.

It's getting to be more than lust. And therein lay the danger.

"I didn't ask," he suddenly said, stopping. "You wanna drive or walk?"

"I'm fine to walk."

Rick slid his hands into the pockets of his jeans as we strolled. Across the street, two kids of a similar age rode scooters up and down driveways. A small dog that looked to be part rat chased them enthusiastically.

"So, anything you really want to try at an American diner?"

I put my hands into the pocket of my sundress—I made it a habit these days to only buy dresses with pockets because fuck the patriarchy—to stop myself from sliding my arm through his. It seemed so natural and I could not give into my weak desires. Not after I had categorically denied that this was a date.

"What would you recommend?"

"Well.... If you want the full Kentucky experience? A hot brown. It's turkey, ham and bacon, on fried bread, covered in cheese sauce."

"I'm amazed it isn't called *a heart attack on a plate.*"

He snorted. "Honey, almost all diner food would have to be called that, so it'd never work."

My insides had gone all tingly at the sound of his delicious endearment. "Hot brown it is. And to drink?"

"Again, for the full experience, shitty diner coffee, although the coffee here isn't so bad. Alternatively, a chocolate malt milkshake."

I frowned. "I'm not entirely sure a hot brown *and* a milkshake will fit inside this dress."

"You'll make it work." He grinned down at me, his eyes dancing with good humour. "I believe in you."

"Well, as long as you, Mr. I-never-met-a-steak-I-couldn't-finish, believe in me, I can do anything."

He laughed. "I know you're being sarcastic, but I bet you *can* do anything. You've made your own business from the ground up, so Jess tells me. You had a bad break-up, but rather than stay and wallow, you flew half a world away to honour a commitment you made to family."

I shrugged. "I don't know. Crossing an ocean is just another kind of wallowing, isn't it? I ran away."

He tilted his head thoughtfully. "Maybe it's a matter of perspective."

I nudged him affectionately with my shoulder. "You should be available on prescription. I'd *definitely* listen to you narrate a seven-hour audiobook about perspective."

"I'll keep that in mind if work falls through," he chuckled.

This was so easy. Nice, warm, comforting.

Maybe I was only relaxed because I knew I was going home eventually, and so, that meant nothing could come of how I felt about Rick Callahan.

I wrangled my thoughts away from how good he looked and smelled and sounded.

Maybe I should rethink spending time with him.

And maybe I should stop overthinking and just fucking enjoy *a trip to the diner.*

Rick turned a corner and Otter Street, the main street of Redwing Falls, opened up. There wasn't much to it, but it was easy to navigate around.

A butcher, a grocer, a tiny lawyer's shopfront, an adorable looking giftshop and florist combined, a barber, two hair-dressers, and of course, *Cake Away.*

"There's a gym, too. Well, more of a one-stop fitness shop. It's got a boxing ring and a gym, and they do classes. It's a couple streets away," Rick explained. "In an old car parts warehouse."

"It's cute. The town, I mean. I doubt the gym would want to be described as cute."

He smiled. "I think *quaint* is the way a lot of out of towners describe it."

He glanced back and forth at the cars moving along the road, and my heart bumped when he grabbed my hand and made to cross.

I curled my fingers around his—he had calluses from all the woodwork and maybe from holding firearms, too— and he turned to look down at me.

"Sorry. I'm trying to remind myself to hold hands for when I walk Toby across the street. It won't be long."

I squeezed his hand. "It's nice. You're a great Uncle."

"Well, I hope Jenny thinks so."

His compassion was endearing and only made me like him

even more. I should have slipped my hand free from his grasp, but I couldn't.

Friends could hold hands, right?

"Here we go." Still holding my hand, Rick led us to the diner, an unassuming one-story white stucco building with a neon sign above the door that read *The Redwing Diner.*

"As you can see, the name is *very* creative," Rick uttered as I snorted. He opened the door. The bell rung to announce our presence, its cheery tinkle making me grin.

"Well, it's about time you showed your face 'round here!" a woman called from the counter at the back of the space.

She could have been anywhere between fifty and eighty. Her hair was coloured deep pink streaked with silver, and she wore a bright yellow polo shirt with the diner name embroidered across the left breast.

"Hey, Magda," Rick called to her.

A younger woman, who Rick introduced as Tori, appeared from a side door. She wore the same polo and a sunny yellow apron around her waist. She greeted Rick and he introduced them to me.

"Nice to meet you, Maddie! You've got fantastic hair. So shiny. I'm very jealous. Take a seat anywhere you want, and I'll bring y'all some coffee," Tori offered.

Rick led us to a table by the window and passed me a laminated menu as we sat down opposite each other.

I saw that the hot brown was listed as the special, but the diner also offered much of the stuff I'd expect to see at a greasy spoon, as we called them in the UK. Like my favourite greasy spoons, they also offered an enormous, heartburn inducing breakfast, all day.

"What're you getting?" Rick asked.

I noticed that his hand rested near the middle of the table. Should I take it? I wanted to, but I had a feeling that'd move us further from the friend zone and into the date zone.

"Still the hot brown. You? Will you be able to resist the lure of breakfast for dinner?"

He grinned, and it was irresistible; I was powerless to resist smiling back. "Everyone knows that dinner is the *best* time to eat breakfast." He grinned lazily. "But I think I'll have my usual, steak and eggs."

Tori appeared and set down two yellow porcelain mugs, pouring coffee into them. "Sugar, sweetener, and creamer are on the table. Rick, my grandma *loves* the spindles you made for her staircase. She says they look like they were always there. You made them just how she saw them in her head."

He beamed, his eyes crinkling at the corners. "I'm happy to hear that."

Tori turned to me. "How're you enjoying our little corner of Kentucky?"

"It's great! To be honest, I needed a break from home."

She gave me a knowing look. "Well, I sure hope Rick's takin' care of you."

I flushed. "Oh, it's not—"

"I still remember when he used to wear his underwear on the outside of his pants to play superheroes," Magda announced from the counter.

I bit my lip to stop from laughing, but the image of a little Rick, superhero-style attire in place, was very cute.

Rick closed his eyes briefly. To Magda he called, "Thanks, Mrs. Kriska. Appreciate the trip down memory lane."

"You're welcome," she called out.

When Tori had scribbled down our order and crossed back to the kitchen, Rick leaned back in his chair.

He was so *broad.*

It was hopeless not to be attracted to him. I could feel my strength waning.

I took my time doctoring my coffee to my liking. Rick did the same, and for a moment I observed him as he stirred, watching his arms move, admiring the planes and angles of his face.

"I'm gonna enjoy watching you try your first diner coffee."

I smiled. "You said the coffee here isn't bad!"

"It ain't. Which is why, before you go, I've gotta take you to the piece-of-shit diner off Route 65. That coffee's so strong you can stand a spoon up in it."

"I'll be sure to tell my fellow Brits that you like us to come to your country so you can torture us."

He chuckled.

Tori brought our drinks. The tall glass that held my milk-shake in was streamed with condensation, cream piled on top. "Enjoy the chocolate malt. It's my favorite."

We thanked her, and she left to take the order of three guys two tables over.

I pulled my shake over and took a sip through the paper straw. It was *ice* cold, as all milkshakes should be, deeply choco-latey, with a pleasant malty aftertaste.

I gave Rick a double thumbs up.

"Wait, wait." He palmed his phone from his back pocket. "Let me take a picture. A souvenir from your trip."

I posed with two thumbs up, sipping from the shake, and he snapped away.

I took a long sip, then shook my head at myself. "Brain freeze. I never learn."

"It's not a proper diner shake unless you give yourself brain freeze. Fact."

Tori reappeared through the swinging door to the diner kitchen with two enormous plates. She set the hot brown in front of me and the steak and eggs before Rick.

"Y'all enjoy now."

"Thanks," we chorused. I was slightly distracted by the heavenly scent of cheese and fried meat wafting up over my face.

Rick snapped another picture of me with my food, grinning ridiculously at the camera, as was the tourist way, and then we dug in.

"That steak is the size of your face," I observed.

"Told ya. Best in the county."

The hot brown was everything I wanted it to be. Hot and savoury, it hit the spot of beautifully greasy food. I was sad when it was done.

Rick grinned at me across the table. "And you said you couldn't fit a shake and food in that dress."

"I nearly couldn't. Thank *God* for elastic panels in the back. Never buying clothes without them in again. They should be standard issue."

He finished his beer. "You want a walk after eating all that? I could take you down by the lake."

I raised a brow. "The lake, huh? A popular make-out spot? Sounds like it."

I cringed. It was meant to *not* be a date.

Apparently, I couldn't help myself.

"A gentleman never tells, Maddie," he said softly.

I believed him, and in that moment, I wanted, more than anything, to throw caution to the wind and just take whatever he was offering, for however long he would offer it, from now until when I boarded the plane back to the UK.

After all, wasn't the best way to get over a man to get over another one?

That probably wasn't very good advice, even though it was so, so tempting.

"Let's go to the lake. I'd like to see it."

His grin was so pleased earnest and eager, and I felt like I'd got a glimpse into him as a younger man. "It's pretty. You'll like it."

Tori collected our plates. I dug my purse from my tote, but

Rick paid before I could. "Least I can do is give you your first proper diner meal in Kentucky."

"Thank you."

We waved to Magda and Tori, and the bell signaled our exit into the sunshine.

"It's about a ten-minute walk to the lake," Rick informed. When he took my hand this time, I decided not to resist at all, even though I was *pretty sure* it was no longer about Toby and road safety, and I laced our fingers.

Outside, it was busy, people milling around on an early Saturday evening, soaking up the sunshine. A few groups carried six-packs of beer back from the convenience store. Kids ate ice cream cones.

As we walked in companionable silence, the sounds of the main street drifted away. We passed the garage, closed for the day. I remembered the way Jenny had looked at that mechanic, and wondered what the story was there. He was good-looking in a boyish way, and I could see the appeal.

"Penny for them?" Rick asked.

Caught off guard, I said, "I was thinking about the guy who works in the auto shop."

"Wow. I *literally* just bought you dinner."

I laughed out loud. "No, silly. Not like that. I think Jenny likes him."

He frowned. "I don't want her to get her heart broken again. Ever. I mean, I know she can make her own choices, of course, but... Maddie, it was so bad, the last time. If that asshole ever shows his face in town, I'm gonna punch him into next week."

His face was like thunder, and I believed him.

"What happened? Not that you should tell me, if you don't want to."

He smiled slightly. "I'll let Jenny tell that story if she wants. It's a doozy."

It was on the tip of my tongue to tell him about the letter from Seb, to tell him about Seb at all, to just tell him everything, but I hesitated, and then we crossed the street into the most beautifully leafy park, and I forgot my train of thought.

In the distance, children played in a park with swings, a little splash pool and a climbing frame.

To my left, a row of trees had been cultivated into an arch and Rick led me under it. The sunshine was dappled under here. It felt private. We walked under the tangled branches and followed a path at the end down to a lake.

Several men sat on the grassy bank fishing, hats pulled down over their eyes.

The waterfall the town was named after sat about a half mile away.

Rick cast his gaze around, squinted in the still-strong sunshine. "Thank God my dad's not here. It'd really kill the mood."

"There's a mood?" I teased.

"Isn't there a mood? There's a lake, early evening sunshine. What more do you want? Are all Brits this romantic?" he snarked back, making me laugh.

We wandered to a big, sprawling oak tree whose branches overhung the lake. Rick sat at its roots and leant back against the trunk, spreading his legs and patting the space between them.

I hesitated.

His expression was open, soft. "You sit next to me if you prefer."

I did *not* prefer. I wanted to be close to him. So this was only my seventh day here, so what? I'd had a shitty time recently, and I just wanted.... To not have a shitty time anymore.

I sat down between his legs and wiggled backwards until

my back met his front. He was solid and warm, and butterflies ricocheted in my stomach when we touched.

Rick settled his chin on the top of my head. His scent surrounded me. The tang of the beer he'd drunk, the woodsy smell of sawdust, and under it, the fresh aroma of soap. It was a combination that made my hormones sit up and dance.

I tucked a stray wisp of hair behind my ear. It made my Hong Kong gold bracelet jingle, and that must have caught Rick's attention, because he touched a finger to one of the twelve animals dangling from the chain. "What're these?"

"That's the Chinese zodiac."

He held my wrist up a little, letting the sun catch the charms, studying them. "Tell me about it."

"Legend has it, long ago, the Jade Emperor wanted animals to be his guards, and said this would be decided by which of the twelve contestants got through the Heavenly Gates first. Competing that day were a rat, a pig, a dog, a rooster, a monkey, a goat, a horse, a snake, a dragon, a rabbit, a tiger, and an ox."

His skin brushed mine while he continued to examine the little gold animals in turn, listening to my story.

"The rat won the race by jumping on to the ox's snout at the last minute. So a rat represents quick wit and cunning. And so it goes."

"Huh." Rick reached the rat charm and stroked the tip of his index finger over its tail. "And what am I?"

I asked him what year he was born, and he told me.

"Ah, the ox. Auspicious."

"Even though I lose out to the rat?" He huffed.

I laughed. "No, the ox is great. You're persistent and diligent, but also not self-serving. That confirms everything I've learned about you so far."

"It does, hmm?" His chuckle rumbled against my back. "And what're you?"

"Well, I was born three years after you, so I'm a dragon. The most coveted of all zodiac signs. Ambitious and enthusiastic, and, depending on what translation you subscribe to, good-looking."

"Well, there you go. Must all be true," he said lowly.

"You're very kind." I smiled.

We sat together, contentedly not speaking, for a little while. I gazed out across the lake. Sitting here, I was reminded of being in Regent's Park on a sunny afternoon. I wondered if I'd ever get to take Rick there.

"I know we hardly know each other. I know it's been all of about five minutes. But I like you, Maddie," he murmured.

I half turned in his embrace, my side pressed to his chest. He cupped a hand over my knee, his thumb tracing gentle circles there, making awareness dance up and down my leg. "I like you, too."

"I wanna see where this goes. But I know you're just coming out of a break-up, and you don't live here..." he trailed off, holding my gaze with those intense hazel eyes. He looked sincere and my heart warmed.

"I want to see where it goes, too," I admitted.

He lowered his head a little.

I waited for him to kiss me, every fiber inside me buzzing, but instead, he just rested his forehead against mine, and we breathed each other in. Everything went quiet inside me. I let my eyes drift closed, anchoring myself in the moment by curling my fingers into the open neck of his soft, well washed shirt. The material was warm against my skin. I wanted to burrow inside it and never leave.

Somehow, this moment was more intimate without a kiss. He just wanted to be here, with me, with no expectations, and that made me want him so, so much more.

He murmured my name, and the syllables in his honeyed voice were the best thing I'd heard in an age.

My phone rang aggressively, startling me slightly out of his hold.

"Ignore it," Rick whispered.

I did, snuggling back into him. Every iota of me was on fire for this man. I wanted him desperately. In sexy physical ways, but also in small ways. I just wanted to stay in his orbit, absorb the relaxed, safe feeling I got around him.

But who was I kidding? I also wanted to touch him and be touched by him.

Learn what made him sigh and what made him groan with pleasure.

The thought made my inner muscles clench with thick, hot *want*.

The phone kept ringing. "Sorry. I'll just answer it real quick." With regret, I shuffled away from him, and plucked my phone from my purse. The display showed a number I didn't recognise. "Hello?"

"Is this Madeleine Liu?"

Beeping could be heard in the background.

"Yes."

"Is Laurie Heywood your aunt?"

The greasy snake of dread coiled up inside me. "Yes."

"I'm calling from the University of Louisville Hospital ER. Your aunt has been admitted."

Chapter Fourteen

"For Heaven's sake. It's just a broken arm! You'd think I'd been near death!" Aunt Laurie complained when Rick and I were finally let into her hospital room.

She looked a little pale, her right arm immobile in a cast, but otherwise she seemed like herself. The hospital gown hung off of her, and for the first time since I had known my aunt, I thought she looked old.

"Does Jess know?"

"No." Aunt Laurie glared at me. "And you're under *strict* instruction not to ruin her vacation by telling her."

I sighed internally. I was going to be in big trouble for this. I knew it.

"She'll only cut it short and come home," my aunt added. "And she and Connor have saved up for this holiday for so long."

I chewed over that for a second. She was right.

Beside me, Rick squeezed my hand, and I was very grateful for his solid presence. I squeezed back.

"Are you in any pain?" I asked instead. "Do you need anything? Books, magazines, food?"

Aunt Laurie sighed. "Just a little company would be nice. And I probably need to do a brain dump about the cake commitments I have comin' up. The most important being the wedding at the ranch next Saturday."

I let go of Rick's hand and sat on the edge of the bed, and took out my phone to make notes. "I'm all ears."

Rick cleared his throat. "I'll leave you to it. Maddie, you'll text when you need a ride home?"

"Oh, you don't need to worry about that. I can get a cab."

His gaze lingered on me for a second, and he settled his hand on my shoulder. "I don't mind stayin' in the waiting area."

The thought of him just waiting for no other purpose than to be there for *me,* just in case I should need him, made me melt inside. But I didn't want to rely on him. My stomach twisted with how complications things were becoming.

"You should go home," I said instead.

He inclined his head, but didn't agree verbally. Instead, he kissed the top of my head. "You'll call?"

"I'll call," I confirmed, my heart warming.

Rick nodded at my aunt, and quietly exited.

"Well, that one's a keeper if ever I saw one," Aunt Laurie observed. "Thought it ever since he quit his career in the Army and moved back home to take care of his family."

"Would you *stop?* This is not a romcom movie. "

She looked at me with innocent, wide eyes. "I'm only saying."

"Well, don't. I live far away from here."

She pouted dramatically. "Can't you indulge me? I'm sick!"

I laughed. "But you're also not five. Sorry." When she gave me a look, I rolled my eyes, then patted her leg. "Give me the information dump."

Accepting the subject change, Aunt Laurie frowned

pensively. "Most pressing one is the wedding in seven days' time. I'm set to do a three-tier cake. The specifications are on my computer at home." She huffed. "I don't know how long it'll take me to bake like this."

I gaped at her. "You can't be serious. *You* can't bake at all. *I* will bake."

"*And* manage the bakery? You can't leave the college kids on their own. They're not ready yet."

"I'll figure something out," I said with a confidence I didn't feel. My mind was already racing with what I would do and how I'd get help. I wondered if Jenny would be interested. She'd said several times she was keen to get some variety in her days. Would her mum babysit Toby?

Aunt Laurie looked unconvinced. "If you're sure. We can always drop the hours, so it's less time to fill."

I opened my mouth to ask how hard it could be, but I stopped short. Those words had never served anyone well.

Instead I asked, "What other cakes do you need made? Besides the ones the bakery sells."

She rattled them off, and I typed as quickly as I could.

"Oh, and *Lord*, someone needs to feed the cat! Poor thing, he'll be rattling around the house by himself. I feel a bit lonely there, even with him," she mused. "I could text my neighbor, I guess. Then there's the seventieth birthday cake for Eric at the retirement home. He's got special dietary needs, so it's a little complicated."

I smiled, typing on my phone. "No worries there. I'm from London. I've seen every dietary need and preference going, don't worry about that. Wheat free, dairy free, no soy, no nuts—I'll cover it."

"You're an angel, Maddie."

I preened, making her laugh.

"Oh, nearly forgot. Pass me my purse." Once I'd handed it over, she snapped it open and palmed her purse. "Take the bank card for *Cake Away,* so you're not spending your own money on ingredients for this wedding cake."

"Thanks." I carefully slid it into a slot in my own purse. "I'll keep all the receipts. Are you *sure* I can't bring you anything?"

She considered this. "The TV up there's stuck to CBS. Maybe you could bring me some magazines? Or better, books."

"No problem."

We chatted for a little longer, and I stayed while a petite nurse came to take observations.

"You *are* an angel," Aunt Laurie said after I re-read everything she'd told me. "You should go. I think Rick's waited for you."

"I doubt it. I asked him not to. It's been two hours!"

She smiled slightly. "Even so."

I gave her a hug and told her to behave herself around the attractive doctors. She made no promises, and I left her to relax. She had her eyes closed when I gently shut the door behind me.

I pulled my phone out to contact Rick, but, when I turned the corner, I saw him folded into one of the very unforgiving plastic visitor chairs in the corridor. He was reading an extremely dog-eared copy of *Elevator World* magazine.

He'd stayed.

For no other reason than to be here when I came out.

If I hadn't been completely gone for this man before, I was now. There was no use fighting it.

Could you start falling for someone after seven days?

I swallowed back the surge of emotion and managed to collect myself by the time he noticed me. A smile spread slowly over his face, his ridiculous handsomeness amplified by the expression.

"A gripping read?" I asked.

"Huh? Oh." He looked down at the magazine and chuckled. "I guess it's an important read if you wanna know how often to update your copy of the *Vertical Transportation Handbook.* They're on edition four, ya know."

"Wow. I did *not* know that."

"Well, I know what to order for your birthday." He closed the magazine and dropped it onto the table wedged between the two uninviting chairs. "How is she?"

"Surprisingly well. Mostly grumpy at the fact she can't change the TV channel."

Rick started for the exit and I fell into step beside him. He caught my hand in his, and I tangled our fingers.

"Thank you for staying."

"'Course. Anyone would."

"No, you're wrong about that. Not everyone would." I squeezed his hand. "I'm grateful."

He pressed the button for the lift and it whirred as the cables worked behind the shiny gray doors.

"You're welcome," he said softly.

We walked out of the hospital and to the long stay parking lot in silence, still holding hands.

Rick was a steady, warm presence beside me and, for a long moment, I allowed myself to fantasize that this was my life and that I got to curl up beside him after a long day.

Pathetic. I'd known him what, five minutes?

I needed to get a serious grip on myself, but Aunt Laurie's injury had been such a shock that I didn't have the energy to tell myself off right now.

Rick unlocked his truck with the key fob and opened the passenger door for me.

"You don't have to do that."

"Once a Southern boy, always a Southern boy."

I dropped into the comfy seat with a big sigh.

He started the engine. The evening sun slanted through the window and bathed his koi carp tattoo in rays of gold.

"I'm so glad your aunt is okay. How'd she do it?"

"Trying to reach something on the top shelf of the bakery. She slipped off the footstool. Thank goodness the window cleaner was passing, or she'd have been alone there for God knows how long!" I scrubbed my hands over my face. "It's just a reminder that she's getting older. You know? When I was young, Aunt Laurie was this superwoman. Invincible. In that bed, she seemed small."

Rick navigated us out of the parking lot and onto the highway. "It's a hell of a thing, ain't it? When your elders suddenly become human? They're not meant to have weaknesses."

"Exactly! They're meant to always be there."

He reached across the space between us and took my hand, intertwining our fingers. "My dad had a stroke 'round about the time Jenny got left high an' dry by her ex. Those two things led me to drop out of the Army. My family needed me. It was a tough time."

Sympathy for him made my chest tight. "I'm sorry."

He lifted one shoulder in a half shrug. "I don't regret it."

"Were you career Army? Jenny said you were a Staff Sergeant."

"Yeah, I guess I was in it for the long haul." He took a deep breath, and I watched his chest move as he did so. "I'm not anymore. I did it to travel, expand my horizons. Get outta bumfuck, Kentucky, you know? Made some friends I'll have for life, but on the whole, it's good to be back here. I was ready. I wanted to look after my folks when they need it. I was worried that Jenny's douchebag ex might come after her, an' Toby. I wanted to be here. For them."

It was more words than he'd spoken in a row since we'd

met and I listened greedily. I wanted to learn everything there was to learn.

"You're a great brother. And son."

He smiled. He didn't bother to deny it, but he also didn't say anything faux-modest, like *I try*. He just accepted the compliment. It was refreshing.

"This way, I get to see Toby grow. It wouldn't be the same, only hangin' out with him on leave, seeing him every couple'a years."

"What about your dad's business? Did that happen organically?"

He rolled his shoulders as he took the exit. "At first, yeah. Someone had to take over, at least temporarily, and I knew some carpentry, because Dad had taught me the ropes when I was younger. Every damn summer break from when I was twelve, I worked with him. Back before I got a wild hair 'bout escaping Redwing Falls an' seein' the world," he chuckled. "And the damn thing about it was, I *hated* helpin' him out over summers as kid, but then, during downtimes on deployments, what did I do besides read? Carve stuff. Funny how that works out."

He shook his head, smiling, before he continued.

"It was a steep learnin' curve, though. But I found that I liked it, much more'n I expected. Much to my dad's amusement. I like making things with my hands, producing somethin' that makes someone happy."

"You and me both. You're clearly extremely good at it, according to Tori in the diner, anyway."

He ducked his head, but I saw his mouth tip up.

He was adorable.

"You want a ride tomorrow? If you're plannin' on deliverin' your aunt some books and such."

Realization dawned. "Oh, God. Will you have time? How will you fit it in with work?"

"I do have some estimates to work up with my dad tomorrow, but if you need me, I can make it happen."

I chewed this over, my heart warmed by his offer. "I have to run the bakery full time with Aunt Laurie out of commission. I was going to chat to Jenny first thing, to see if she wants some hours. She can bake like a dream and she seems like a fast learner. Would your parents have Toby, do you think?"

"I'm sure they would, in the short term. They'd be pooped." He smiled as he made the turn into his street. "But I think they would. Especially as it'd help the community out. Also, they adore Toby, so it wouldn't be a hardship that way."

The sun had almost fully set by now, and the houses looked pretty in the twilight. Rick shut off the engine and walked around to open the truck side door for me.

"I'll walk you to the door."

"I am staying *literally* next door."

"Even so."

I told myself not to get used to this as he walked me across the front lawns and to the door of Jess' house. When I got to the porch, I looked up, and our eyes met. He cupped my cheek with one big hand.

I leaned into his palm.

I desperately wanted to ask him to come in, to throw all caution to the wind, with my arms around his neck and kiss him until I forgot my own name, forgot that my time here with him had an expiry date.

His gaze flicked to mine, a question in his eyes. I threaded my fingers into the soft hair at the nape of his neck and tugged his face closer, answering him without words.

It was time. I was ready to kiss him, and I wanted it *so* badly.

A shiver rippled through me at the first touch of his lips on mine. His kiss was gentle, exploring, soft. After a few moments, I opened for him and heard his sharp intake of breath. Our tongues tangled. He kissed like a dream. Not too wet, not too possessive; gentle with a fiery lick of need.

I stepped back, my shoulders coming into contact with the door, and Rick slowly pushed forward, crowding me in. I welcomed the press of his big body, sliding my hand under his shirt to meet warm, smooth skin. Tilting my chin up gently to get a better angle, he groaned softly into my mouth. The sound made a beeline to my lower body, pulling everything tight. His other hand settled at the small of my back, settling me closer to him.

As if I wasn't already in thrall to this wonderful man.

Almost unconsciously, I moved against him, feeling the hard ridge of him almost right where I needed it.

I sighed his name, and he muttered a quiet *"fuck."*

"Bit soon for that," I joked, softly, with a touch of regret.

He huffed out a soft laugh. "I'm not after that, Maddie. Well, not now, but it's sure hard to say good night when you're near me like this. All soft'n warm and kissable."

I groaned. "You're not making it easy for me to go inside alone."

He smiled, pressed a soft kiss to the corner of my mouth. "I'll see you tomorrow. At the game. All right?"

"All right."

He stepped back, let out a long breath. "Lettin' you go now is probably one of the harder things I've done."

"Rick, please. My control is perilously thin right now. Good night."

"G'night, honey."

He waited until I turned my key in the door to step back off the porch. The light caught on the gold in his hair and picked out the barely-there shades of green in his brown eyes. He was *gorgeous*. I bit my lip and let myself have one final look at him before I shut the door behind me, slid down it and suppressed a squeal of utter joy at the feeling of wanting and being wanted in return.

I felt alive; butterflies swarmed in my stomach. I felt I could do anything.

Chapter Fifteen

After I recovered from Rick's kiss, and allowed myself a full half hour to relive every detail, I messaged Jenny.

Me: Jen, are you still up?

Jenny: Yeah. Unfortunately.

Me: Are you ok?

Jenny: Toby's teething. He's gone back to sleep now, but I'm wide awake. I just heard Rick get in. How's Laurie?

Me: News travels fast.

Jenny: Welcome to small town, USA.

We texted for a while. I updated Jenny on the past few hours—my aunt was okay, but would undoubtedly be a bear with a sore head once her meds wore off. As I hoped, Jenny bit my hand off when I asked her to assist in the bakery. She thought she'd be able to ask her parents to watch Toby, considering the sky-high cost of daycare.

When she asked about Rick, I pressed my lips together, remembering the *epic* doorstep kiss. I was *very* eager for him to rock my world again.

Jenny: Did you have fun with Rick? Up until the hospital, that is.

Me: We had a nice time, yes. I had a hot brown at the diner.

Jenny: Is that what they're calling it these days??

Jenny: Jk.

Jenny: Unless....

Me : Good night.

Jenny: Party pooper.

* * *

I rummaged in the top drawer of Jess' coffee table for what felt like an *age* before I found the tiny envelope with the key to my aunt's house. No wonder Jess affectionately called it her "hell drawer." It was stuffed with random chargers, loose change, unused plasters, single earrings, and the assorted detritus of modern life.

I had the morning free before I went to the baseball game with Rick - if I was going. I needed to prepare for opening the bakery tomorrow, with Aunt Laurie out of action.

My phone beeped, and I snatched it up eagerly to see a text from Jenny letting me know she was available.

Jenny: I'm all yours, all day if you need me!

Me: Fantastic. If I give you the bakery key, would you find the order sheet and message me a picture of it?

Jenny: No problem.

Me: Thanks so much. I'll give you the key before I go to Aunt Laurie's. I need to mine her computer for information.

I gulped down a mug of the tea I had packed with me— I had to hope a pack of two hundred and forty would be enough to tide me over— and shoved my feet into my Converse. In addition to my other tasks, I needed to do the washing today, or I'd very shortly run out of clothes, and I couldn't really justify the time to go and buy stuff.

And I needed to read and respond to the comments on my latest video.

I'd better be careful or everything was going to start snow-balling. I already had a hell of a balancing act to do, and Rick was fast becoming a big distraction.

Aunt Laurie had reminded me of the walking directions to her house, and I dropped the bakery key off to a sleepy but excited Jenny before I left.

Rick was nowhere to be seen, and I was half disappointed but also half relieved; I'd never have made a quick exit if he'd turned up all rumpled from rolling out of bed.

Just the idea made my stomach clench with yearning.

I made the ten-minute walk in a little less time, aware that I was *very* on the clock if I wanted to get everything done *and* make the game with Rick later. That could be my treat for bossing it with my tasks.

My aunt lived in a cute little two bed, single-story red brick house on a quiet street. I knew it well from my visit here a few years back. It hadn't changed.

Birds in an overhanging tree tweeted busily as I let myself in, almost getting knocked over by an enormous, short haired tabby cat. I didn't remember him, he must have been an addition since I'd last come here.

"Oh, hey baby!"

The cat meowed plaintively. I bent to stroke his fuzzy head and he glared at me.

"Right, sorry. Food, you want food."

The cat led me to the kitchen and jumped on the counter, butting his head against the plastic box of kitty food, meowing constantly, as if to say *finally, stupid human.*

I couldn't blame him.

I rinsed his bowl out and filled it, making sure to provide him some fresh water, too.

The cat's purring went stratospheric when he started to munch.

I headed through the house to the spare bedroom, where Aunt Laurie said she kept her computer. I glanced around as I booted it up. Her home was warm, cosy and full of personality. Books were *everywhere,* on shelving and in little piles on the floor, and I loved that. I didn't trust people who didn't have books. What did they *do* in their free time?

I scanned a few of the titles, but didn't get very far before the login screen appeared. I fished out my phone and copied over the details. I got the blue wheel of death for a moment, which told me Laurie's computer was *pretty* old, and then her desktop background appeared, a picture of her, Jess and Jess' brother Greg, who had moved to Washington to work for the US Government, in front of a gorgeous waterfall.

I felt a pang of guilt not telling my cousin about her mum's injury. I was stuck between a rock and a hard place.

I had to hope that the Redwing Falls gossip mill got to her soon enough so that she wouldn't be mad with me.

Putting it aside, I looked at my notes and opened her file explorer. It didn't take long to find the word document and email it to myself. As I was turning the computer off, I texted my aunt to let her know I'd fed the cat. She replied saying that her neighbor had agreed to do it until she got home from the hospital, and that he pooped outside so I didn't need to worry about a litter tray.

Can't say I wasn't relieved about that.

As I locked everything up, my phone pinged with a photo message of the order list from Jenny. Everything was going according to plan. So far, anyway.

I power-walked back to Jenny and Rick's house, already

sweating under the warm sunshine. Jenny opened the door as I approached.

"I just got back, and I'm child free!" She started jumping.

"Maybe shout a little louder? Not sure the people on the far side of town heard you."

Unembarrassed, she did a little dance on the doorstep. I was pretty sure I was in love with her - I'd certainly be very sad to leave this woman. "I don't care! I have two free hands! Count 'em!" She wiggled them in the air and whooped. "What do we have to do?"

"First, we need to go to Sureway and get all the ingredients for the two cakes Aunt Laurie needs me to make, plus the baking I want to do for my channel. I'll carry on selling that stuff in *Cake Away*." I continued listing off our plans to Jenny. "There's a wedding cake and a seventieth birthday cake, but the wedding cake is the priority."

"Roger that."

"Then, we'll go to the bakery and I need you to start on the stuff we need to get baked and ready for the usual hours tomorrow."

"Coffee on the way?" she asked hopefully.

"Yes. Coffee on the way. I also need coffee."

"Is that Maddie?" Rick's voice floated out from inside, and then a second later he appeared, with Toby on his hip. The image of him, all sleep-rumpled, with Toby clinging to him, jam smeared over the toddler's mouth, sent my hormones into overdrive.

"Hey," he greeted me. His slow, warm smile would be my undoing. His eyes were soft from slumber and there was a sleep crease on his left cheek.

"Hey." I wanted to pull him back to his bed and get in there with him. I was pretty sure he'd be amenable.

However...

My resolve not to have a hot-as-the-surface-of-the-sun fling with him was weakening by the second.

I *had* to tell him about what happened with Seb. He deserved to know, and if I was going to be intimate with this man, he deserved honesty.

But first, I had a *lot* to do. And my primary reason for being here was to cover my cousin's bakery, not have sex with her hot neighbor.

Sadly.

"Mom's busy for the first couple of hours this morning," Jenny informed me. "So, Rick's watching Toby."

"Thank you for your sacrifice," I said, mock-gravely when Toby yanked his uncle's hair.

"Hmm," Rick replied. "Well, it's a great— ow!—opportunity to spend time with— *ow, quit it!*—him. I'm taking' him to the park and over to see Dad, so we can work up some estimates." He held the toddler at arm's length.

Toby swung his arms, delighted at the new game.

His joy was contagious and I found myself chuckling. "Ready to go to Sureway?" I asked Jenny.

"Am I ever." She ducked back into the porch to get a handful of reusable bags and then practically bounded down the steps. "Bye, Rick! Thanks for watching Toby!"

Toby chose that moment to stick a finger up his uncle's nose without even a second of warning.

Rick's face promised retribution, and I suppressed another giggle as we headed to the car.

"He's a good brother."

Jenny grinned. "The *best*. I never expected him to come home from the Army, you know? At least, not right away. But he did. He saw that we needed help, Dad and Mom and me, and he came, and he never made out that we owed him or anything."

My heart squeezed.

"Rick bought the house next to Jess," Jenny continued.

"He moved all his stuff out of that tiny apartment he kept in Louisville. I had no idea. I was staying my Mom and Dad, and he just turned up, and said he'd bought a two bed so I'd have more space for Toby." She swiped at her eyes with one hand. "He didn't have to do any of that, Maddie. He had a great career going."

"Did he like it? The Army, I mean."

"I think so? He doesn't talk about it a lot." Jenny drummed her fingers on the steering wheel. "Sometimes when he's had a few drinks on a weekend night, he'll open up a little. He has that one tattoo for friends he lost, and I know he's told Dad more than me." She rolled her shoulders pensively. "Men don't talk, you know? They should. Stupid society. Making men think they can only fight or fuck." She slapped a hand over her mouth and then laughed. "I swore! I thought for a moment that Toby would hear and then I'd be *that* mom, you know."

"You're safe here. Swear away."

She laughed. "Rick goes to a veteran's group though. It's more than some people do, so I have to be content with that." She sighed, pushed a hand through her hair. "You want to get coffee on the way?"

"*Yes.*" She drove a little further until a sign for a coffee shop came into view. As she flicked on her indicator and took the exit, I thought about all there was to do today, and without preamble, an image of the unopened letter from Seb flashed in my mind.

I needed to deal with it... Later.

We pulled up at the drive-through and Jenny leaned out of the window, glancing back at me. "Want anything?"

"Iced mocha."

She ordered it, plus an extra-large cappuccino for herself, and I took them from her and set them in the cup holders. She paid and thanked the server and we drove away towards the supermarket, where a frantic thirty minutes of shopping ensued. Jenny seemed to have boundless energy, or maybe that was the coffee. We finished in record time.

As she drove back, I called in the order of pastries, blueberry muffins, and bread rolls to the wholesaler, who promised to deliver it tomorrow. We might be a little late opening the bakery, but better late than never.

I slid my phone back into my bag and put my head back, closing my eyes.

"You okay?" Jenny asked.

"I'm just thinking about all the stuff I need to do."

"Delegate. What needs to be done?"

I opened one eye to look at her. "You're the hero I need, Jenny, even if I don't deserve you. I said I'd bring some magazines and other stuff to my aunt, conveniently forgetting that I don't have a car."

Jenny pursed her lips thoughtfully. "We can outsource that. Lemme make some calls when we're back home. You're in our town now, and we look after our own, okay?"

Everything seemed a little more manageable. "Okay. Thanks."

She reached over and squeezed my leg. "Anytime."

I was *really* going to miss her.

* * *

Jenny was as good as her word. Within the hour, someone had been sent up to the hospital with a raft of books and magazines, and a phone charger, leaving Jenny and I to prepare for tomorrow's opening hours at the bakery.

The house was quiet.

Rick had taken Toby out for a couple of hours, so we spread everything out on the solid oak dining table Rick's father had made. It was gorgeous, and had been well loved through the years, but the knocks and scrapes gave it more charm. My own flat in London was filled with old furniture I had picked up dirt cheap at car boot sales.

We mixed and shaped and stirred, setting everything out in big plastic trays that we'd take over to the bakery and cook in the morning. We could probably have cooked some of it here, but the whole process would be faster in commercial ovens, and fresher was better for customers, anyway.

Jenny was a dream sous chef. She followed instructions to the letter, and she was a fast learner. I had no doubt that she'd easily find a job once Toby started school.

While she laid out everything in trays and labeled them, I looked through the photos Aunt Laurie had of the wedding cake ideas she'd been sent by the bride. The wedding was next week on the Two Rivers ranch, three miles outside Redwing Falls.

Thankfully, *Cake Away* had only been commissioned for the wedding cake and not a groom's cake or any extra cupcakes or edible favors.

I'd made wedding cakes before. This one required some fiddly fondant work, but nothing I read sent me into a panic spiral. Phew.

I toggled over to my Instagram page to scroll through comments and see if any needed to be replied to or deleted. Sometimes I got a troll, or someone with a mystery vendetta against me.

Most of the comments were sweet, like *my grandma used to make this cake* or *I'm definitely going to try this soon*, but there were some darker ones about my split with Seb.

He was too good for you, one wrote, and another, *you were always punching way above your weight with him, he can get someone prettier now.*

Thanks, internet. You had to love the general public.

Or not.

I replied to the sweet ones and the genuine question ones, and I left the mean ones hanging. They said more about the mentality of the writers than anything about me. I'd learned that after several years of putting myself out in the public domain.

Sometimes it still hurt, though.

The general response from the internet was one of the reasons I loved posting and had done for years, but also one of the reasons I was keen to explore a shop space.

All real people. No internet trolls.

As I was about to log out when a new comment popped up from Seb's account.

Seb: Please call me.

I wasn't going to.

He could take a long walk off a short cliff.

But I *did* need to read the letter. It nagged away at my consciousness.

I should have read it already, probably could have made myself. I was just busy, I reasoned, and of course Rick was the most delicious distraction that had ever walked the earth.

But did it mean anything that I didn't miss Seb, that he only crossed my mind because of some unopened correspondence?

I put that away to think about later.

While Jenny worked away, I spent twenty minutes searching the cake supply cupboards at Jess' house. Thankfully, I found all the icing nozzles, shaping tools and decorative bits and bobs I would need to make this cake a showstopper. That was a hell of a relief.

I sketched the cake out on some spare craft paper with the dimensions needed and found the relevant cake tins, and then my phone alarm went off.

It was time to shower and get ready to go to my first Stateside baseball game.

Chapter Sixteen

Rick drove us a little way out of town to the big field where once a month, all the little league games were held. He introduced me to his cousin Ralph, a mountain of a man with a fierce-looking face but a soft, kind voice. I told him how excited I was to be making his wedding cake, and I apologized for the change. He enfolded my hand between his two giant ones and said that he was sure I'd do a fantastic job. I hoped that his future wife would be as calm about it.

Aunt Laurie had said the bride had panicked a bit, but who wouldn't with a last-minute change like this? I could relate.

The kids were running about while the adults prepped for the game. Our section of the field had a small row of bleachers. Some adults sat on them, eating sandwiches or enjoying cans of light beer. Others stood around the portable barbecue, offering advice on grilling the hot dogs. It was a scene I was well familiar with, just not in conjunction with baseball.

A small table was full of sauces, as well as two kinds of relish, grated cheese, and a steaming pot of sliced, recently fried onions, the edges of the slivers caramelized a golden brown.

It smelled divine. My stomach sat up and begged, despite yesterday's huge deposit of hot brown and milkshake.

Rick led me to the bleachers and patted a spot beside him. When I sat, he tugged a baseball cap from his pocket and offered it. "I got this for you."

It had *Redwing Falls Little League* embroidered on it, with a bird wearing a cap. Warmth filled me at his thoughtfulness as I smoothed my thumb over the bird's little face, perfectly captured in thread. "Thank you!"

He took it and slipped it on my head. "Perfect. Now you fit right in. You just need a hotdog."

"They smell amazing."

"My uncle Jay is an ace at barbecue. Today it's just hot dogs, but they've had cookouts where wild game has been on the menu," he praised, just as the man in question shouted, "Grub's up, come and get it!"

Rick stood. "What do you want on your hot dog?"

"You don't have to serve me. I'll do it."

He snagged my hand, and led me to the barbecue. I loved feeling our fingers wrap around each other. There was already a queue of kids with paper plates ready, discussing what they were going to put on their dogs.

"Mustard is the best."

"Ew! Mayo only."

"Everything else aside from the onions is crap, dude."

I had to agree with the third kid. I only wanted onions. I told Rick as much as he raised a brow, mocking me.

"Do you wanna do this properly, or not?"

I sighed. "Okay, *dad*. I'll have whatever you tell me to have."

He smiled. "Can't go back to the UK saying you had a hot dog with *only onions* on it."

"I guess there is that," I conceded.

He snagged two paper plates. We made a beeline to Rick's uncle, an older man with crinkly, laugh-lined eyes, who beamed at us. "Rick! Is this Maddie? Boy hasn't shut up about you," he told me.

"Yeah, thanks Uncle Jay," Rick deadpanned.

Jay leaned toward me. "By that I mean he mentioned you once, and since he hardly speaks, I inferred you to be of great importance."

I laughed.

Jay grinned widely. "It's nice to have gossip. A small town runs on it. Two dogs?"

"I've been told I have to have *everything* on mine," I said gamely.

Jay nodded, half-moon glasses slipping a little down his nose as he did so. "Yeppers. If it's your first time, sure." He dropped the dogs into ready-cut buns that looked cloud-soft, and set them on our plates. "Load the girl up, Rick."

"Yessir." Rick tossed Jay a lazy salute and went to *work*. Ketchup, mustard, relish, and onions.

"I'm not sure I'll be able to actually fit that in my mouth," I told him.

"Well, that's the fun of it. C'mon, they're gonna start soon."

I carefully carried the loaded plate back to my seat. I was pretty sure it was at least half a day's calories, but when in Rome.

Rick's cousin Ralph started to divide up the players into batting order, and I watched the proceedings with interest.

Rick pointed out the adults. "You know Eddie. That's Keith, the umpire. And that little guy in left field right now is my cousin's kid, A.J. It's Andy James, but he hates being called that."

"A.J. is way cooler," I agreed. "They look cute in their uniforms, don't they?"

"Sure do. Eat your hotdog before it goes cold," he added. "You don't get the full experience otherwise."

"All right, all right." I lifted the loaded bun with two hands and bit in.

I had to admit it was perfect. The tangy, sweet onions, the spicy relish, the mild mustard, the fluffy bun and the warm, greasy hot dog.

"This is amazing," I said, managing to wait until I'd swallowed before speaking.

His grin lit up his entire face. It only magnified his handsomeness, if such a thing was *even* possible. It shouldn't have been. "Told ya."

"Yeah, yeah. Has no one ever told you it isn't nice to gloat?"

He just smiled bigger and tucked into his own hotdog.

The game began. Rick explained various bits to me as I, a complete newbie, watched and tried to take it all in.

He was a fantastic cheerleader for A.J, standing up to enthuse when the kid hit the ball with a satisfying *thwack*.

At one point, things looked as if they might be a little ugly between one mum and the umpire, but Eddie managed to intervene in time.

"Is that normal?" I asked.

"Over-involved parents? *Yeah.* You can't tell me you don't have those in England."

"Fair point well made." I leaned into him. He was solid and warm, and magnetic, and I wanted him *so* badly. Couldn't I just stay here forever?

He tipped up my chin with a gentle hand. "You know what else is well made? Your mouth." And he kissed me, soft and gentle.

I smiled against his lips. "That is the worst pickup line in the actual world, Callahan."

He kissed me again. "It seems to be working, though, doesn't it?"

"You're making a lot of good points today. Can't argue with 'em."

He chuckled, and he kissed me again. I was dizzy with need for this man. He set every nerve inside me alight. What was I going to do when I was half a world away from him?

Was I on the rebound? I must have been, right? I couldn't possibly feel *this* intense about someone I'd only known for a short while.

It felt like longer.

I should have had whiplash from the speed of all this. But he made it so easy. He was easy to be with, like slipping on a comfy t-shirt.

Only the t-shirt filled me with unspeakable yearning.

All this from a single kiss. If we got any further, I'd combust.

I settled against him as we watched the remainder of the game. Afterwards, the kids played tag and then split into little groups to mainline snacks and watch videos, or whatever kids were into these days, on their phones. The adults cracked open a few beers. Rick got me a Coke from a nearby ice bucket.

"You ever make out under the bleachers, or whatever your UK equivalent is?"

"Snogging behind the bike sheds. Nowhere near as cool." I looked up at him from my position, with my head on his shoulder. "I can't very well go back to England without making out under some bleachers. It would mean that my favorite singer has taught me nothing."

He chuckled, stood, and tugged me gently by the hand. "Far be it from me not to enrich your visit to the United States of America."

"A crime," I agreed. "I never did, by the way."

Rick paused mid-step to glance back at me. "Never did what?"

"Snog anyone behind the bike sheds."

He raised a brow. "Because all the boys in your school were blind?"

I felt warmth creep up my neck at the compliment. "I had a lazy eye, so I had to wear correctional glasses for a couple of years. That sort of thing doesn't exactly score you a fleet of boyfriends."

Rick sent me a sympathetic look. "I had braces. But didn't we both get glow ups?"

I had to laugh at his self-confidence. It was warranted, though. He was gorgeous as hell.

"I had an eye patch, briefly, too," I added. "Because the glasses didn't work."

He smiled. "Well, now I *know* the boys in your school were idiots. Pirate girl? Hot."

"I can't tell you how good you are for my pride."

"Honey, I could be good for lots of things."

I laughed as he led me behind the bleachers, the wood charmingly sun-weathered. It was cooler here, the sound of the kids playing and the music a little muted. It reminded me of the willow tree in my grandma's garden that I used to retreat to if I wanted to be alone. Its leaves saved me from mortal embarrassment should I have been discovered writing about boys on the lined pages of my discount store faux fur diary, complete with shitty plastic padlock.

"Take a lot of girls here, do you?"

"Not for a long time, actually." The surprise must have shown on my face because he added, "When I was in the Army, it would have sucked to make someone wait for me back home."

"Still. You must have been beating them off with a stick."

He smiled slightly, his eyes warm. "A *gentleman* never kisses and tells. Anyway." He settled his hands on my hips and tugged me close, shadows from the hard lines of the bleachers casting grays and yellows over his handsome face. "Less telling. More kissing."

I wholeheartedly agreed with him there.

I lifted my face up to his, and he kissed me. Teasingly and softly at first, as if testing the waters, then deeper, more firmly, our tongues dancing. He tasted of the tang of ketchup and the sweetness of lemonade, and I knew I'd never forget today for as long as I lived.

Why did he have to be here, an ocean and several time zones away?

I let myself enjoy the moment; tried to push the worries to the back of my mind. Rick and I knew the score. We were consenting adults, and we both wanted to see where this would take us. If it ended when I got on the plane, so be it. I'd already had my heart stomped all over. I couldn't feel any worse, could I?

Besides, Rick's warmth, humor, and apparent desire for me was nothing but a balm on my soul.

He was one of the good ones.

"Man, you have no idea how much I wanna ask to be invited home with you," he murmured. "I'd invite *you* back, but a toddler eavesdropper is not the best setup for long, slow making out on the couch."

I dropped one last kiss on his gorgeous lips. "I wish I could, but I have a million things to do. This evening, I've got to call your cousin's fiancée and talk through the cake. She, quite understandably, wasn't happy when Aunt Laurie called and said I'd be the one making it, not the best baker in town, so I think I have some ruffled feathers to smooth out."

He squeezed my hip comfortingly. "Cathy can be intense,

but she's a good person. Fair. She'll deal, even if the curveball set her off balance."

"I hope so. I do, I *really* do, get how important weddings are." I'd been in the middle of planning my own, after all.

He gave me a sympathetic smile, but said nothing. I liked that about Rick. No meaningless platitudes from this guy.

"Then, I've got to visit the Two Rivers ranch and scope out the layout of the wedding to work out if there'll be any issues getting the cake in situ—"

"Be my date."

I stopped mid flow to stare at him in surprise. "What?"

He threaded a gentle hand through my hair. "Be my date for the wedding. I've got a plus one, even though I RSVP'd without one. Ralph, the cousin you met just now, keeps trying to set me up, but so far I've resisted."

"Do you need to check with him?"

"I will, but I'm sure it'll be fine."

My stomach clenched. "I don't have anything to wear. Honestly, I arrived here in kind of a state. I'm sure it was very obvious when you picked me up at the airport."

"You mostly slept."

"You're just being kind."

He pressed a gentle kiss to my forehead. "If you don't want to come, I understand. But I'd love for you to be there. I bet Jenny has something you can wear. Or, I could take you shopping."

"Um." My brain had short circuited.

"No pressure," he added. "I don't want to freak you out."

Sweet man. "Honestly, I'm not freaking out. Not about being your date, I mean. My brain is just glazed over, imagining you in a suit."

"A tux, actually. It's black tie."

"Oh, my *God.*"

He tipped my chin up, pressed a lingering kiss to my lips. "So... You'll think about it?"

"I doubt I'll be thinking about anything else. A tux. My God, it's like you're *actively* trying to kill off my brain cells."

He grinned, and his smile, as always, was deadly. "I mean, think about the invite." He let me go, and I immediately wanted to burrow back into him, snuggle into his broad warmth and never have to leave. "Shall I drive you back?"

"Please." I gave in and slid my hands up his chest, tugging him back for one more kiss. It lingered until a group of kids passed and wolf-whistled in our direction, and I broke the kiss reluctantly, red-faced.

I steadfastly looked out of the window on the short drive, determined not to be distracted by how *fucking* sexy he was.

When he opened the passenger side door for me, and walked me up to the house after a long, heated kiss, it was really all I could do not to drag him inside and peel off his clothes item by item.

"Rick."

He gazed down at me with eyes darkened with want, and I looked away to stay on track. "I'd like some time with you. Soon. I want to be upfront with you about my ex, and about why I broke it off with him."

"Okay," he agreed, kissing the corner of my mouth. "When you're ready to talk, Maddie, I'm here to listen."

After he drove away, saying something about an extra errand, I flopped down on the bed to try to cool off, but ended up with my hand between my legs, his name on my lips as I climaxed.

Chapter Seventeen

Rick

Rick should have gone inside his house after dropping Maddie off, but he didn't.

Instead, he drove out of town, kept right at the fork in the road, driving away from Two Rivers Ranch and towards the lake. He drove past the popular spots, near where he and Maddie had sat together— had that only been *yesterday?*—and further up the rough logger road, the gravel surrounded by trees.

He parked his truck in a layby and shut the engine off, then smacked the back of his head against the seat.

What was he doing?

She hadn't made any insinuation about living here. Fuck, he was crazy about her.

Hell of a thing that the first woman to make him feel like this was fresh out of what seemed like a horrible break-up, and a resident of a country an entire ocean and a handful of time zones away.

She'd been on his mind constantly since they'd met. She haunted dreams that made him wake up with hard-ons. Just thinking about her now tented his jeans. He eyed his dick, sighing.

If she'd invited him into Jess' house, he wouldn't have been able to keep his hands off of her.

He'd been half-hard leading her to the bleachers to make out, and damned if that little session hadn't made every nerve in his body stand to attention. Thinking about taking her shopping for a formal dress to wear *as his date* didn't help him calm down.

The sun was setting. Pinks and reds bathed the rear window of the cab of his truck. Maddie would look sensational in this light, the colors kissing her pale gold skin and catching on the tiny flecks of lion's mane gold in her brown eyes.

Opportunities to meet women since he'd moved back here a year ago had been few and far between, what with taking on his dad's business, emotionally supporting his mother, and moving his sister into this house and worrying about her.

Maddie was the first person he'd met, for a long time, who made every fiber of his being sit up and beg.

He wanted her in every way.

Letting his eyes close, he pictured Maddie as she'd been in their make-out session, rosy-cheeked with excitement, her breath coming out staccato. She'd been just as affected as he was. What would her mouth feel like on other parts of his body?

Giving in, Rick unsnapped his jeans and tugged out his cock. "You're gonna get me in a lot of trouble, you know?"

And then he sighed and wrapped his hand around himself, picturing Maddie's small, slim digits. The look on her face as she'd work him over. The press of her breasts against his chest. She'd taste of whatever sweet creation she'd been baking, and he'd take his time finding out how she tasted everywhere else, too. Her nipples. What would they be like? Rosy or dark? Large or small? Both options would please him. And what sound would she make when she came? Would her back bow? Would she groan his name?

With a groan of his own, Rick thrust up into his hand, wishing Maddie was here with him, wishing it was her lips or tongue wrapped around his dick. Longing to feel the silky fall of her hair skim along his bare stomach, lower, lower.

Would she look up at him as her clever mouth worked? Trail her hands over him, greedily, or kneel at his feet with her eyes closed, lashes thick and dark against her cheeks?

He wanted either. Both.

Settling into the rhythm he liked and had perfected —a man got *really* good at jacking off in the Army with close to no women around—he felt the first tingle of an orgasm build low in his belly.

He just wanted *Maddie,* period. Whatever way he could have her.

Man, he was toast. Falling for someone who lived half a world away.

* * *

Jenny

Very early on Monday morning, Jenny parked Rick's truck outside the back entrance to the bakery and contemplated how to unload all the trays in the back by herself. She'd needed to borrow the big vehicle to fit everything inside.

Maddie would be here soon to help, but dammit, Jenny wanted to impress her new friend.

You don't gotta do it all yourself, Rick always said to her. But she often found herself having to. Toby was a case in point. After Jenny's ex tried to convince her to either have an abortion or adopt Toby away, neither of which were ever in her plan, she'd decided to take some other advice he'd had a habit of giving her and lose some weight. Just over two-hundred pounds of useless ex-boyfriend, to be exact.

Man, had it felt good. Ever since, she'd done it alone. With the much-needed support of her family, but essentially, the buck stopped with her.

If she could birth a child and raise him, do the night wakings and all that other stuff, she could fucking well carry six big trays of sweet treats into the back of the bakery.

She stared at them, wondering if they had been quite so wide last night.

She bent over and grabbed the top two trays. Could she take a third?

"Mornin'."

At the low drawl of a greeting, Jenny stood up so fast that she almost took the trays with her. Like a shot, Levi was behind her, steadying the load, his body warm against her back.

"You gave me a fright."

"Sorry." He let go, took a step back, and then she could breathe again. He looked contrite with those big brown eyes, shadowed by the battered denim cap he always wore, soft chestnut curls peeking out from beneath it, kissing the nape of his neck. His habitual cigarette was tucked behind one ear. "Gettin' ready to open?"

"Yep. I'm hired on while Laurie's arm heals."

"Can I give you a hand?"

"I wouldn't say no."

He easily carried three of the loaded trays at once. Jenny took two, trying not to look at Levi's ass in those jeans.

"Why're you up and about so early?"

He glanced over his shoulder at her. "Headin' to the butcher's shop a few doors down to get some scraps. There's this cat that comes around the auto shop and always looks hungry."

Jenny's heart softened. Of *course* Levi took in waifs and strays. He couldn't just be a regular asshole that she could tell herself to avoid. "A stray?"

"Ain't got a collar. Not sure 'bout a chip. Thin fella. Where d'ya want these?"

"On the counter there, the wide one. Thanks."

He moved past her and again she caught a hint of his scent, freshly cut grass, and some woodsy cologne. She tried not to draw too greedy a breath. "I'll get the last one."

She liked that he didn't assume she needed help with the two she carried, or say something patronizing. He just helped.

"There you go. That all right?" Levi asked, setting down the final tray, heavy with raspberry-studded blondies.

"Perfect. Thanks."

"You need anything else?" His gaze held hers and she saw a muscle in his jaw move, like he was chewing over something to say.

"Um. No. I don't think so." He made some small move, a precursor to leaving, and of its own volition she heard her own voice add, "Want a coffee? I was going to make one for myself, so...."

"Sure. Thank you." He took his cap off, ran a hand through his tumble of curls and shoved the hat back on again. "What can I do while you brew it? Ain't used to bein' waited on."

Jenny jerked her chin towards the big commercial oven

across the space from them. "Can you preheat that oven? Three-fifty should do it."

"You got it." He bent to the task and Jenny exercised superhuman restraint in not gazing dreamily at him like a horny teenager. Like the horny teenager she apparently still was inside.

"How'd you take your coffee?"

"One sugar," he replied as he moved the dial. "What else?"

The coffee machine sputtered into life as Jenny took out sky-blue mugs from the cupboard above the counter. "Um, could you switch on the fridges out front? Then they'll be ready to put the sandwich fillings right in. The switches are at about knee level on each fridge."

"Yes, ma'am." He crossed into the shop space, and Jenny took a deep breath.

She hadn't felt this way about a man since Dustin, and look how that had turned out.

She sternly reminded herself that she did not need a man in her life right now, that Toby was the only male for whom she had time.

If only her libido also believed that.

"All done," Levi announced as he appeared back in the doorway. "That coffee smells like ambrosia."

"It's ready." Jenny offered a cup. "Here you go."

"Thank you." A grin tugged at the corner of his mouth. "You run on coffee, too?"

"Along with most of America."

He toasted her with the mug. "Amen to that." He leaned back against the counter, his expression hard to read under the ballcap.

"Tell me about this cat. Have you named him?"

"It'd be stupid to do that. He's only been comin' around a week or so."

Jenny hid her smile behind her mug. "You have, though."

"Might have," he muttered.

He was adorable. Why did he have to be adorable?

She opened the fridge. "Does this cat, that you may or may not have named, like milk? I can give you a little bottle."

Levi's face softened. He was even more handsome like this; relaxed. "That's kind. Thank you. Reckon he'd appreciate it."

She located a little plastic bottle from the odds and ends piled up in a box by the window and filled it with milk. "It's not free. The price is one picture of this cute kitty."

Levi grinned. "Mangy is a more accurate word, but sure." He dug in his pocket and held out his smartphone. "Put your number in. I'll text the photo to you."

Jenny hesitated.

"No pressure if you don't want to," he added softly, and that made the decision for her. She took his phone and typed her number, and her name.

"There you go."

Their hands brushed when she returned the phone and she felt the touch all the way down to her toes.

I have it real bad. What am I, twelve?

Levi set his empty mug down on the counter. "I better get goin'. I hope your kid's doin' well. Toby, right?"

It touched her that he remembered. Even if he only knew because of the gossip mill that had dogged her when she'd returned to town, like being a single parent now was akin to having plague in the 1600s.

"He's fine. Thanks."

He touched one finger to the brim of his cap. "Be seein' you."

The door banged behind him and Jenny sagged back against the preheated oven, her heart pounding ten to the dozen.

* * *

Maddie

I ran around the house, getting ready to open the bakery.

Jenny, God love her, had phoned already to say she was there. She'd sounded a bit breathless, but insisted she was okay. Just in case, I hurried myself along. Thank goodness I didn't have much to carry as I had no car. I hadn't really thought this through.

I arrived at the back door of the bakery to the scent of baking - the raspberry blondies and the pastries smelled like they were well on their way.

"Hi!"

"Hi!" Jenny greeted me with her usual happy grin. "Everything seems to be going well." She dusted her palms off on her jeans.

"And you're okay?" I searched her face. "You sounded a bit winded on the phone."

"No, I'm..." She chewed her lip, then turned to busy herself at the coffeemaker. "Levi was here."

"Le—*Oh.* The mechanic." Interesting. "What did he want?"

"He was in the area buying butcher's scraps for a stray cat."

"Aww."

"Right? Ugh." She made coffee for us both and set the filled cups on the counter. "He can't just be a regular asshole, can he?"

I thought about a suitable answer. "There's still time, I guess?"

That surprised a laugh out of her and she giggled until she wheezed. "Thanks. I really needed that."

It was on the tip of my tongue to ask who had hurt her,

and how she'd like me to kill them, but I wasn't sure she'd want to tell me, and even if she did, we didn't have time for a proper talk right now.

"Anyway," she added. "Everything is pretty much ready, but I haven't got the sandwich fillings and such out of the big fridge yet."

"I can do that." I strapped on one of the branded aprons. "How's Toby?"

"Excited for a day with his Grandma. I expect he'll come back full of sugar and having had no discipline, but, them's the breaks with free babysitting." She didn't seem cut up about it. "And once again, I have two free hands! Count 'em, one, two!"

Her enthusiasm was contagious, and I was already a morning person. Between us, we got the bakery ready in no time, and when the wholesale delivery arrived twenty minutes before opening, we were prepared to take it in.

Jenny was a *damn* good employee.

And an even better friend.

Maybe I could take her back to the UK with me in my pocket.

I mean, I *wished* I could. Toby might have something to say about that, though. I doubted there would be room for them both in my tiny flat.

Customers arrived almost as soon as we flipped the sign. I recognised some of them by now, but Jenny was a *pro*. She chatted the chat and convinced people to try our new pastries without them even knowing they were being sold to.

She would be a fantastic asset to whoever hired her on.

Not for the first time, I wondered what her story was.

Once or twice, she saw someone coming towards the window and murmured to me if I could serve them. Perhaps these were the vapid people whose feathers had been ruffled when she'd dared to come back to her own hometown with a child.

I wanted very badly to tell them to go get served elsewhere, but since Jenny hadn't given me any information, I couldn't do anything but behave as normal.

Everything else went great. As I met people and served them—some of whom asked after my mum and dad, which was sweet.

Laurie video-called me at around eleven a.m.

"I can go home today! Thank the *Lord*. There's a woman next to me who snores to beat the band. I was genuinely considering smothering her with one of her own sweaters."

Jenny snorted from behind me.

"I'm glad! I bet you've missed your own bed. I always do."

"Oh my, I really have. And, I can come back to work—"

"Oh, no you don't," I warned her. "Your arm is *literally* broken."

"Fractured, technically. I can still work the cash register."

"Not if you know what's good for you."

She scowled. "Sassin' me, girl? You should respect your elders."

I bit down on a smile. "Not if *they* don't respect their own health."

I had her there. I could feel her bristling *through* the screen. "Perhaps I'll see how I feel tomorrow," she finally said, a bit of fight still firm in her tone.

I wouldn't have expected anything less.

"You do that. You want me to come over this evening? Do you still love the Han's food when you have takeaway? Shrimp lo mein, extra dipping sauce?"

She sighed. "You remember my vices. Yes, I'd love the company."

"Good. You can also look over my sketches for this bridal

cake. If you behave yourself, I might let you make some of the fondant decorations later in the week."

"Watch it," she said fondly. "See you this evening."

I hung up to see Jenny watching me, amused.

"She pissed?"

"Oh, yeah."

Jenny chuckled. "She's a do-er, not a watcher or a waiter, like me. And, like me, she hates to be sidelined." She turned back to the counter to serve an absolutely adorable pair of teenage girls in matching pink dungarees. As I watched, she served them bottled Coke and then *upsold* them a warm, salty pretzel each.

She was too good to be real.

As if she'd read my mind, she turned to me, grinning, hands on hips. "I'm doing good, right?"

"You're doing amazing." I took advantage of the lull in customers to say, "Your brother asked me to be his date for the wedding."

Jenny's eyes went gratifyingly big. "*The* wedding? Oh, my *God*. What're you gonna say?"

"Um, I was thinking about saying yes."

"YEAH!" She threw her hands up in the air and danced around, joy in every muscle.

"I mean, that's great," she added sheepishly. "I was hoping he was going to ask you. Do you need something to wear? You have free reign over my wardrobe. I don't wear my fancy stuff hardly *ever* anymore. People tend to give you the side eye if you show up to baby massage groups in cocktail dresses."

I loved her, I really loved her.

"Thank you so much. I do need something to wear. What are you wearing?"

"Something nice, but not too fancy. Toby still vomits sometimes after I feed him, so... But still, this is going to be so fun! Girls bedroom fashion show! Can I do your hair? Not that it needs doing. It's beautiful as it is, not frizz central like mine."

The bell chimed with another customer and I didn't want to share Jenny, at least, not for this moment.

"Can we still be friends when I move back to the UK?" I blurted out, suddenly terrified of losing our friendship.

I seemed to be incapable of resisting anyone in her family. Must have been something in the Callahan genes.

Her face softened, and she pulled me in for a big, squeezy hug. "I'd be so mad if we didn't keep in touch," she said into my hair. She smelled of sugar and fresh bread, and, not for the first time, it struck me how lucky Toby was to have her for a mother.

I considered what was here, and what waited for me back home, and I promised myself that I'd read Seb's letter when we closed up the bakery for the day.

Chapter Eighteen

We'd made a good amount of money for the day. Laurie was going to be *very* pleased.

Jenny swept the floor while I finished cashing up. As I reconciled the day's takings on card and cash, and locked the notes and coins in the safe, she snapped lids on containers of cookies and muffins.

"I couldn't have done it without you."

She grinned. "You could. Just maybe much slower."

"No, I genuinely couldn't. Drinks when things quiet down?"

"Absolutely." Her smile was tired, but happy. "I've enjoyed today. Feeling like a functional member of society again."

I folded up my own apron, hung it on the peg by the back door. "I'm sorry that society ever made you feel you weren't. Even if you never get another job, Jenny, you still belong in society. You're raising one of its future residents, after all."

She huffed. "I wish you'd been here when I came back to town a year ago. You'd have put all those gossipy bitches in their place. I *know* you would have."

I squeezed her arm. "I'd have been delighted to. No one

puts a gossipy bitch in their place like a British person."

We shared a smile for a second, and then Jenny's phone chirped. "Rick's here to pick me up. And you, if you want. I drove his truck here earlier, but he needed it today to cart around some oak for a hardwood floor he's doing a couple towns over."

Every iota of my being ran hot and cold with excitement, but I managed to say, "Oh, cool."

Jenny snorted. "Never go into acting, okay? C'mon, we've slaved away all day."

She opened the door, and I busied myself making sure I had all the right keys and switching the lights off. My heart pounded at lightning speed. I hadn't seen Rick since yesterday's addictive make-out session.

"Hey!" Jenny called out to her brother.

I locked up and finally turned to look at him. He wore a short-sleeved gray tee, tattoos on full display on his arms, and just the sight of all that tanned, inked skin combined with his unruly golden hair and hazelnut brown eyes made me weak at the knees. It might've been a cliché, but that didn't stop it from being true.

"Ladies," he said, leaning slightly out of the truck, one arm folded on the open window. "How'd it go?"

"Your sister is a dream in human form, and she belongs to me now," I stated simply, hooking my arm around Jenny's shoulders.

"What she said," Jenny agreed.

"Well, I sure am gonna see a reduction in my utility bills." He grinned, and his dimple flashed. I needed to stop being so goofy over him.

Although, now we'd made out... And now that I was *probably* attending a wedding with him. Was there any point in dialing it back? Should I just put both feet in and swim with the current?

I wanted to.

"Nah, you'd miss Toby and me too much," Jenny sassed, as she opened the back door of the truck and hopped in.

Rick jerked his thumb to indicate the passenger seat upfront. "Maddie, you want to ride shotgun?"

"Sure."

He smelled of sawdust and coffee. It was addictive, the combo of how he looked and how he smelled, especially now that I *knew* how good his arms felt around me.

I slid onto the seat, closed the door, and buckled in, feeling Rick's gaze on me. When I turned to meet his eyes, his gaze lowered to my lips, and I felt like he was asking me a silent question. Could he kiss me in front of Jenny?

I leaned in, answering him without words, and let my eyes close as his lips brushed mine. I felt safe with Rick. How many times had that happened with men in my life?

Rick was the first. He'd stormed into my heart, and he could have trampled all over it, but instead, he handled it gently. Handled *me* gently.

All too soon, although perhaps for the best since we had an audience, he broke the kiss and I had to clench my hands on my lap to keep from reaching out for more. I wanted to grab him and never let him go.

"I'd better get us all home," Rick said at length, but I felt the heat of his eyes on me.

I pressed my thighs together, trying not to think about all the things he could do to me if we were alone here in his truck, closeted around the back of a row of now-empty shop buildings.

Jenny chattered happily about nothing in particular on the drive home, and thank God, because I couldn't concentrate on anything except the line of Rick's thighs in his worn, dark-wash jeans, and the way his throat looked when he swallowed.

I hardly heard a word Jenny said. I was a terrible friend.

We pulled up outside Rick's house, and I had the door open almost before he stopped, because I was worried about what I'd do if I didn't get out right then.

I wanted him almost more than I wanted my next breath.

"Thanks so much for the lift. And Jenny, I couldn't have done it without you."

Rick caught my hand as I unbuckled my seatbelt, and squeezed it for a moment. His was calloused, and I *really fucking wanted* to feel his touch on my bare skin. On every inch of my skin. I wanted him to do everything, anything he wanted.

"See you later?" he asked. "Tomorrow, maybe?"

"Yeah." I slid my hand up to his wrist, and held his gaze for a moment. His eyes had rings of green around them, and he was beautiful in the early evening light, motes of sunshine dancing around the truck's cab and giving his hair a tawny, sun-soaked cornfield hue. "I'll text you?"

"Okay."

Jenny rolled her eyes good-naturedly at me as I scurried off like some sort of wimp.

Scratch that, I *was* some sort of wimp.

And thinking about my cowardly status reminded me *again* of the letter. Fuck, I needed to deal with it.

Before any-fucking-thing *else* interrupted me, I locked the door, grabbed Seb's letter from the kitchen counter, and tore it open before I could change my mind.

He addressed me as Madeline. He only ever used my full name when he thought I was in the wrong, or after we had a fight. His letter began by him saying he was sorry that *I* was upset by his actions.

"Fucker," I muttered. Classic non-apology apology.

I had to write, as you have declined to answer my calls.

Had he always been like this? Surely not, I reasoned. It was like reading a letter from the King of England, not the man I knew and had been planning to marry.

I believe I did what was best. We wouldn't have been able to make a real go of our lives together with you struggling to make a shop space work.

I rolled my eyes so hard that I almost caught a glimpse of my own brain. How did he know I'd struggle?

It would have been long hours, and no guaranteed income. You wouldn't have been able to concentrate on our family, something we'd talked about a lot. You wouldn't want to have missed seeing our children grow up.

My eyebrows shot into my hairline. We'd briefly talked about children, but I was thirty-two. It wasn't even as if I was already pregnant!

Reading this, I suspected Seb would have been a double standard kind of guy, in that it wouldn't have been right for *me* to miss any family time.

But obviously it would have been okay for *him* to miss key moments like changing nappies and night-time feeds because of work.

Sexism was alive and well and living in the veins of my ex-fiancé.

Of *course* he was worried about *me* working too much. He hadn't been concerned when I'd worked twelve-hour days in hotel kitchens, though. Apparently, his concern had limits. Of course it had limits.

I made myself continue reading.

I love your passion for making and creating, and I never meant for you to lose that. I only wanted you to take some time for us, and then later, I'd have funded that shop for you.

I scoffed. Now that I had some distance, I realized that he'd always thrown his money around like this, showing off with fancy dinners out and such, and I'd been too busy with my work to notice.

Had I loved him? Or had he just been *there*, and I'd been flattered because he was good looking and charming and he made time around my hectic schedule?

I was starting to think I'd loved the *idea* of him.

Especially since meeting Rick.

Being with Rick was easy, and more, I *wanted* to be with him.

If I couldn't see Seb due to work commitments, it hadn't been a big deal. But you know what, it should have been. I should have missed him.

He'd been wrong for me, and it took an event like this for me to see it.

Come home, please, and we can talk about this.

Your mother returned the engagement ring to me. A little presumptuous, don't you think? We had one fight.

One fight that *he* had very much instigated.

Your parents seem upset.

Of course they seemed upset, because they *were* upset. They'd found out that their daughter was engaged to a Class A douchebag.

My parents were pleased I was taking some time out for myself to figure out what to do next.

I picked up the letter and started to tear it, but my phone buzzed in my pocket. I fished it out to see Seb's number and pressed END before even thinking about it. Imagining his frustration across the pond should have made me smile, but actually, I felt...

Nothing.

I still didn't want to speak to him, though, so I immediately switched off my phone.

* * *

An hour later, my feet still achy from the long shift at *Cake Away*, I walked over to Aunt Laurie's house. The evening air hung with the promise of summer. It had taken almost all my mental effort not to knock on the door of Rick's house and throw myself at him.

My aunt answered the door wearing a plaster cast and a smile. The cat wound itself around her legs as she stood on the porch.

I enveloped her in a gentle hug. "How are you feeling?"

"Ugh. Looking forward to my own bed. When you get to my age, even one night away from your orthopedic memory foam mattress takes years off your life."

I snorted. "As if you're old. My mum says hi. You hungry?"

"Hungry for anything that doesn't involve mashed potato. Is hospital food *meant* to make you feel worse?"

I followed her through the house and into the kitchen, where the mess made it apparent that she'd been trying to make things too complex for people with the use of only one arm. "I've only been hospitalized once and I have to say, I did feel that the catering staff were actively trying to kill me off."

She laughed heartily. "Oh, my darling girl, you've cheered me up. Thanks for coming. How's Jenny doing?"

"She is a Godsend. She is everything I could want in both a colleague and a friend."

Aunt Laurie grinned as she opened the fridge. "Glad to hear it. That was a good idea you had. Wine?"

"Yes, a thousand times, yes."

I caught her up on news from my parents, and she told me about the colorful cast of characters she'd met whilst in hospital. She was an excellent narrator, and I laughed my way through two glasses of a chardonnay.

By the time we came to order food, we were both more than a little squiffy. Laurie took charge of the order process, laughing with the Hans on the phone, and thirty minutes later, Lara gave us our order, carried in an insulated bag on her electric bike.

The food was salty and strong-flavored, and perfect.

As we ate, I filled Aunt Laurie in on Seb's letter. Her face darkened.

"That rat *bastard*."

"I didn't know anyone actually said that outside of films."

"Well, I'm bringing it into circulation, especially for your shitty ex."

"You swore!" I gasped, because it was so entertaining to hear someone who had once been an authority figure when I was a kid swearing.

"You should have heard me when I broke my arm," she chuckled. "I turned the air blue."

I dug into the steaming plate of shrimp lo mein. It was the perfect umami flavor, and the fat curls of shrimp were juicy enough to burst between my teeth. "He's that and more. But the worst thing is that I really thought I knew him. I guess, better now than when we were already married." I shuddered, just imagining it.

"That's the truth."

After we ate, I showed her my sketches for the wedding cake. Aunt Laurie pored over the designs, nodding, adding a few tweaks here and there with a pencil.

"It looks fantastic," she said decisively. "And I *will* be back to run the cash register for a day, or longer, so you can make this sucker."

"Only if you feel up to it," I insisted. "I can use the evenings if I need to. How's Jess' honeymoon going?"

"She keeps sending me pictures taken from snorkeling boats or from the tops of exotic mountains." Aunt Laurie smiled. "I'm happy for her. I hope they come back with some extra luggage, if you know what I mean." She circled a hand over her stomach and I laughed. "Are you coming to this fancy wedding? Other than as a supplier, I mean?"

I pushed my empty plate aside and took another sip of wine, as Aunt Laurie snapped a shrimp cracker in half. "Well, Rick's invited me. And I think I'm going to say yes."

"Good for you. He's a catch." my aunt grinned, sipping more wine, and then topping up both our glasses.

"Oh, I know. And you've been plenty vocal about it if I hadn't been sure."

She laughed.

I was going to be hungover tomorrow. Reading my mind, Aunt Laurie said, "You can stay here, if you like. Plenty of room. Spare bed is always made up, because I always judge other people on whether their spare rooms are ready, and if I'm gonna do that, I have to ensure my own house is in order first."

I almost choked on my wine, sputtering out a laugh. I loved her. She was so similar to my mum, and I felt a pang of homesickness.

Before I could drink too much wine to type, I texted Jenny.

Me: Going to say yes to the wedding.

Jenny: OMG! We need a makeover montage.

And then I texted Rick.

Me: Yes. I'd love to be your date at the wedding. X

He replied as I was pouring Aunt Laurie and I our third glass of wine, which I was absolutely going to regret tomorrow morning when I was at work early.

Rick: Great to hear. I'll come by the bakery and see you tomorrow.

Chapter Nineteen

I wasn't at my best the next day. Only the knowledge that Rick would be coming by made me wash my face with extra care. Luckily, my hair needed close to zero fiddling with, and Aunt Laurie had some tinted moisturizer that made me look much less zombie-like.

Downing a cup of coffee before leaving also helped.

To her credit, Jenny didn't laugh when I showed up at the bakery early in the morning, less than perfect. She'd been about to sip her cup of coffee, but she wordlessly handed it to me instead.

"Wow. Is it that bad?"

"How many glasses of wine?"

I winced. "Can you speak quieter? And at least three."

Jenny bit back a smile. "Sit. I'll do most of the prep."

I gingerly set myself down on one of the stools in the back area of the bakery. "Will you marry me?"

She mixed something in a bowl that smelled of cinnamon and vanilla. A recipe in my aunt's handwriting was laid out on the counter. "For a British passport? Of course!"

I sipped the coffee. It was pure ambrosia. "I'm not sure it

works that way anymore." I let my gaze take in the kitchen. "You already made the chocolate cookies?" She'd laid them out on a sheet and they looked fabulous, chocolate chips thick and glossy.

"Yep. Got a head start."

"Jenny Callahan, is there nothing you can't do? You should come on prescription."

She flushed. "Stop."

"Seriously. Any company would be lucky to have you if you decide to start job hunting when Toby's a little older."

Like a pro, she started scooping the batter from the bowl into laid out cupcake cases. "I sure can't live with Rick forever, great as he is." She sighed. "And I can't go live with my parents, either. They've done their time with us, and I can see my Dad getting older by the day. Since the stroke, he's seemed to age a decade."

"Oh, Jenny." I set my coffee aside and caught her in a big hug. She pressed her face, eyes wet, against my neck. "Do you want to talk about it?"

"Nah, or not right now. I'm hormonal, is all. I promise, I'm happy. And it's *so* nice to be needed. Like when I got your text last night. I'm so looking forward to the makeover montage, I've even got a playlist for while you try on clothes."

I laughed. "Excellent."

"I think I just haven't been this happy since I moved back, you know? I mean, I seem happy all the time, because I'm naturally an optimist, but sometimes, I feel really fucking lonely."

Hugging her tighter, I kissed her hair. "If the other women in this town don't see what a fantastic friend and person you are, more fool them. And more Jenny for me."

She squeezed me back, and I knew that whatever happened, I wanted to be friends with her always.

We got back to work, Jenny in a lighter mood, and me

filled with nervous, giddy anticipation at seeing Rick. I had to stop myself from jerking my head up hopefully every time someone approached the front of the bakery.

* * *

Rick texted later that morning. Seeing his name flash up on my phone gave me a stomach full of butterflies.

Rick: I'm working near a dumpling place. Want me to bring you some? I'm almost finished up here.

My mouth watered just reading his text. Redwing Falls was many lovely things, but culturally diverse was not one of them. Even though it had been four years since my last visit, the only non-Western takeout was still Han's.

Me: PLEASE. Do they have xiaolongbao?

I served four more customers before he replied. I asked for shrimp dumplings for Jenny and I, and got a thumbs up and a heart emoji in response.

He was so utterly different to Seb in every way, but that wasn't the only reason why I liked him so much.

Perhaps it might've had something to do with it in the first place, but now Rick gave me a reason to like him every day we saw each other. He was kind, smart, *so* funny, generous. And the sexiest guy I think I'd ever been lucky enough to kiss.

"Maddie?"

I jerked out of my reverie of thoughts of Rick to feel Jenny tugging my shoulder. "Sorry!"

She smiled. "You've got a little drool here." She touched the corner of her own mouth.

"You think you're so funny." I busied myself with the already perfectly-arranged pastries in the refrigerated counter.

"Luckily, we had a quiet moment there, so no one had to see you openly fantasizing about getting into my brother's pants."

"Jenny!"

She rolled her eyes. "Okay, then tell me that wasn't what you were imagining."

I went away to tidy the shelves of pre-packed sandwiches.

Jenny just cackled.

Aunt Laurie arrived around lunch, and I started to tell her she needed to go home and rest, but she held her good hand up, palm out, in the universal *talk to the hand* gesture.

"I'm here to run the register while you two take turns to eat. You've got to have lunch, haven't you?" She scrutinized my face. "You look pretty good for someone so hungover that you sounded like ten elephants leaving my house this morning. I bet your dad still does, too. Annoyingly good genes."

"Um, sorry? And thanks?"

She shooed me away just as I saw Rick's truck pull up through the big front window. I swore that my insides turned immediately to jelly.

Spellbound, I watched as the driver's side door opened and he stepped out. His scarred work boots and ever-present resting stern expression made him look rough and competent. The warm rays of the midday sun kissed the koi carp tattoo on his forearm, highlighting the muscles flexing there.

He was *gorgeous,* and what made him even better was that he'd gone to the trouble of bringing me *xiaolongbao.*

I wanted him to bring me dumplings every day. I wanted to eat lunch with him in the sunshine, ask him about his day, hear his funny little anecdotes in his deep voice. I wanted to be there to celebrate his good days and console him on his bad ones. I wanted to curl up inside his huge heart, make myself cosy there, and never leave.

The wedding – and getting to hold his hand and be with him in front of *everyone* – couldn't come soon enough. A real date!

Everything else fell away as he walked towards the bakery

in long strides. When his gaze met mine a few steps from the door, he broke into a grin.

Aunt Laurie gave me a shove with her one good hand.

"Sweetie, sexual tension doesn't sell cakes. Go get him."

Jenny chuckled. "But make you sure give me my lunch first!"

I untied the apron from around my waist and helped my aunt put it on. "You don't have to stay."

She tutted. "And have you drop even one of these beautiful cookies on the floor because you're too busy looking at Rick? No, thanks. I like this place to turn a profit."

Rick stepped into the bakery behind a mother with two young boys chattering about chocolate cookies, and Laurie started talking to them.

I grinned at Rick as he held up two takeout bags with kawaii-style dumplings emblazoned on them.

"Lunch is served," he announced.

I rounded the counter so fast I almost tripped over my own feet. I honestly couldn't say whether I was more excited to see him or eat the soup dumplings. They would be *the* perfect temperature to eat right now. If you ate them straight away, the skin always popped and all the taste buds were burned off your tongue by gelatinous soup hotter than the sun.

Too late, and they might congeal.

It was a balancing act akin to judging the ripeness of avocados.

"Gimme!" I demanded.

He laughed, handing over the bags. "And here I was, thinkin' you were pleased to see me."

"Of course I am, but we've only got a short window to eat those dumplings! They might get cold! Come through to the back, now!"

"You're really taking these dumplings seriously," he muttered, a smile in his voice, and followed me.

"Oh, my God. I have not had *xiaolongbao* since before I left London."

I set the bags down on a clear area of the counter out back. Shaking his head with amusement, Rick settled on one of the two stools in the prep area.

"These things are that good, huh? It hasn't even been that long since you were home, Maddie. What, ten days?"

"You have *no* idea. Nine days, desolate without my favorite food." I tore open the bags and the scent of spring onions, soy, and ginger hit me immediately.

"*Oh my God,*" I moaned.

Behind me, I heard rather than saw Rick shift in his chair and get up, and then a moment later I felt him at my back, his broad, warm hands on my hips.

"What do I gotta do to hear that noise when I don't bring dumplings?" he murmured, his deep voice curling around me.

I turned into his embrace, *xiaolongbao* momentarily forgotten.

"Keep doing this," I whispered against his mouth, "and you *might* find that you end up ranking higher than little parcels of pure joy."

"That's a high bar." He nipped at my lips, watching me from under those gorgeous lashes.

I grinned. "I'm confident you'll rise to the occasion."

He gently pushed into me, confirming that he already had. I slid my hands around him and slipped them into the back pockets of his jeans. "How are you so hot?" I wondered aloud. "I can't stop thinking about you, Rick."

"The feeling's mutual, darlin'," he rasped, his voice low, the pitch deep and intimate. "Been dreamin' about getting you alone—"

The door behind us was unceremoniously pushed open, and Jenny stood there, framed by the architrave. Her cheeks flushed when she took in our close proximity. "Oh. Sorry. I, ah, came to get dumplings. Sorry."

She backed out.

I laughed, and after a moment, Rick joined in until mirth overcame us and we were weak with it.

I slid my hands out of Rick's pockets, and he took a very deliberate step away.

It was probably for the best, but I ached to pull him back into me and finish what we'd started.

"Can I see you tonight?" he asked, opening one of the containers and passing it to me. The aroma bathed my face, and I sighed deeply.

"I can't. I have to make the fondant decorations for your cousin's cake, over a hundred of them. The wedding's on Saturday, and I plan to make the cake over tomorrow and Thursday, allowing myself time to correct any mistakes."

"You won't mess it up," he reassured me, that irresistible grin sketched on his delicious mouth. "It'll be great. But I don't wanna distract you."

"Good. Because that's exactly what you would be. A distraction that I'd find very much impossible to ignore." I playfully pushed at his arm as he shot me another grin. He fucking *knew* how irresistible he was, the bastard. "We'd better eat so I can get back to work before my aunt breaks her other arm trying to reach something, or Jenny starves to death."

* * *

That evening, true to my word, I focused on decorations for the wedding cake. They had to be perfect. If Jenny was to be believed, this wedding would be the talk of the town, and I wanted the cake to live up to every other part of the event.

It'd taken quite some time to switch gears from daydreaming about that moment with Rick earlier to carefully cutting out icing shapes. I missed him, but as sorely tempted as I'd been to accept his offer of company, my focus on this needed to be absolute.

My dedication paid off, because now, three trays of intricate fondant hearts, each stamped with initials for the bride and groom, sat downstairs in the kitchen, while Jenny laid out over a dozen dresses on my bed. My fingers ached, but the hearts were done, and they looked good.

The cake was the next challenge, but I was taking a much-needed break for the makeover montage that'd had Jenny clapping her hands in excitement.

She had turned up on my doorstep with two enormous black bags of clothes.

"Thank goodness we're similar sizes," she was saying as she smoothed out dresses. "Borrow whatever you like. I won't be wearing anything like this for a little while."

She cast a wistful glance in the direction of her house, where Toby slept while Rick was home. I had immediately imagined going over to snuggle up with him, settling my head into the crook of his shoulder.

I had it so bad.

"Not that I have anything to complain about," Jenny added. "I adore my son."

"That's obvious, but you're allowed to have a life in addition to a child. You have some gorgeous clothes." I stroked my palm down the skirt of a coral and white striped dress with black flowers embroidered up the left-hand side.

"Thanks," she beamed. "Try some on! Music!" She tugged her phone from her back pocket and tapped at it until her playlist started, and then she lined up dresses for me to try on.

Jenny snapped pictures so I could see how I looked in each dress. "After this, we'll rank your favourites from one to ten," she promised, squealing with delight. "I'm so happy we get to hang out again. I had so much fun with you at Molly's."

I stepped into a heavy jacquard fabric dress patterned with tiny violets on a gray background. "Me, too. I didn't come here expecting to find a new bestie-level friend, but here you are, and, time zones be damned, I'm going to blow up your phone with gifs and emojis every chance I get."

She squeezed me back. "I'm so, so glad you came. Let's look at you. Oh, this looks nice with your skin tone!" She snapped a picture and showed it to me. "But I don't think it's *wow* enough. Let me see. Oh. This is the one. I feel it in my soul."

She sifted through a pile of silky dresses and picked out something gorgeous.

The dress was forest green, peppered with tiny stars embroidered in gold thread. The scoop neck was demure, but on one side the dress split up to mid-thigh.

"This is *beautiful*," I breathed.

She grinned so big. "I know. I wore it on Toby's first birthday. Mom and Dad wanted to take us somewhere really fancy on account of me being so sad when I got back here. Rick bought it for me, by which I mean he gave me some money and told me to buy something frivolous that would make me happy."

My heart squeezed. "He's almost too good to be real, Jenny."

"He is, but don't think he has no problems. The Army gave him purpose and widened his world, but it left him with scars. I'll let him tell you about that, if he wants to." As I chewed over that, she added, "Put it on!"

I slipped into the baby-soft jersey fabric, which felt like heaven against my skin, and when I turned to look in the mirror, I knew that this was the one. It made me look and feel like a goddess, like I'd stepped out of an advert for an other-worldly faerie perfume. The dark green complemented the olive-gold tone of my skin to perfection. I looked *fantastic*.

I grinned and gave Jenny a double thumbs up.

She laughed. "Yes. This is *the* dress. My brother's gonna swallow his tongue. I *cannot* wait."

I traced my finger over one of the tiny embroidered stars. The thread shimmered. "How come you're not mad? I mean, I'm so happy you're not, but I've twisted myself in knots thinking about Rick and how, in not too long, I'm going to be an ocean away."

Jenny sighed and plopped down on the end of the bed. "I haven't seen Rick this happy and relaxed for a long, long while, Maddie."

She paused, thoughtfully, worrying a corner of the quilt in her fingers. "When he first got out of the Army, he was twitchy, and a fish outta water. He wanted to help, but was kinda bullish about it, to be honest. Once he settled in, he was fine, but antsy. He's been getting better, *especially* since he started going to that support group, but since you came, it's like he lit up inside."

My heart felt so full. "Oh," I settled for saying, but it came out all dreamy-sigh.

Jenny smiled. "Yeah, that deserved a rom-com kinda answer. He deserves to be happy, and—wait," she added, when I opened my mouth to interrupt. "So what if this only lasts a week? He'll have fun with you. You haven't pretended you're going to move here. You haven't, as far as I know, made him any false promises."

"I swear to you that I haven't," I said solemnly.

"I know. And, the other thing is, what if it lasts longer? Your mom used to live in America before she met your dad, after all."

183

"Jenny..." I hedged.

"I'll stop. But just let me say this. You and Rick need to give each other a chance." She smiled, standing to help me out of the dress. "You can't tell me you don't want to. If this dress is the catalyst for you to stop dancing around each other, then I am *very* happy to facilitate."

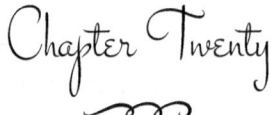

Chapter Twenty

Cathy, the bride whose wedding would take place on Saturday, called on Wednesday and asked if I could go to the ranch to be shown where I should place the cake, so it would be in the best light for photographs. I agreed before considering that I would need a ride.

While Jenny served an older couple out front in the bakery and one of the college girls restocked the muffins, I slipped into the staff area to call Rick.

He answered on the third ring. Classic rock could be heard in the background, and I imagined him working, peppered with sawdust, muscles twisting as he sawed and measured.

"Maddie, is everything okay?" His accent was deep and syrupy and I felt like his syllables stroked me through the phone.

"Everything's fine," I quickly assured him. "I'm sorry to bother you at work."

"No problem. Gimme a minute."

The music was turned down, and I heard him ask someone, "Can you finish those two dovetails?" To me, he said, "I can talk now."

Guilt at relying on him for something like this warred with need. I didn't have time to try to wrangle other transportation. I started telling him about Cathy's request.

"I'll take you," he said before I'd finished. "Happy to. What time?"

I had known this man for eleven days and he was prepared to drop everything for me. My heart bumped at his generosity. "She said after work, but I didn't want to leave it too late to ask you. Thank you so much, it would be a massive help, seeing as I have to bake her cake tonight, too."

"You're welcome, Maddie." His smile came through the phone and I wished I could see him. "I'll pick you up from the bakery."

Relief made my stomach bottom out. We figured out the details about when Rick would get me, and when we would arrive at Cathy's. I couldn't thank him enough.

He chuckled. "It ain't entirely altruistic. I get to spend time in close quarters with you. Not like I won't enjoy this. Plus, Two Rivers is gorgeous. The ride there and back isn't free. You gotta take a country walk with me after."

Anticipation shivered through me. "You've got a deal. I can't be back late, though. As well as the cake, I have to help bake some more stock for the bakery tonight."

"Don't worry. I'll have you back before you turn into a pumpkin," he said, a note of mischief in his voice. "I'll see you later."

He clicked off. I had to really fight the urge to clasp the phone to my chest like a teenage girl getting off the house handset with her crush.

The rest of the day passed slowly. On my lunch break, I messaged briefly with Jess and then my parents. Aunt Laurie arrived to take over from our college helper, and came on screen during my video call with my cousin and reported on her arm.

Jess was predictably hopping mad, but mostly not at me—thankfully. We managed to talk her down from getting on the next flight home, to the obvious relief of Connor, who'd joined her for part of the call. They were both looking pleasingly tanned.

When the sound of the horn of Rick's truck filtered in through the open back door, Jenny practically shoved me out of the shop. "Go, go, your chariot has arrived!"

I glanced between her and Aunt Laurie. "But you still have tidying and closing."

"If your aunt tries to do anything except cash up, I'll give her my best stern mom look until she wilts," Jenny promised.

My aunt rolled her eyes, but nodded in agreement.

As I left, they'd started to chat about who had the best stern mom look, and, satisfied, I left them to it. Jenny wouldn't let my aunt come to any harm.

I practically skipped through the staff area of the bakery and out into the long row of yard behind the avenue of shops. Rick sat in his truck with the engine running and familiar music streaming out of the dash speakers.

His hair was tousled, and his gaze soft as it met mine. He wore another Henley—did he have any other clothes? I hoped not—with the sleeves rolled up, and his face was scruffy with a day's worth of stubble.

I wanted to feel the scratch of it on my skin.

I opened the passenger door and climbed in. "Didn't know you were a fan of sixties Brit tunes."

"Hard not to be. The Beatles are one of my dad's favorite bands. Him and Mom danced to one of their songs at their vow renewal party last year."

I plugged in my seat belt. "They're classic for a reason. Hi, by the way."

"Hi, darlin'." He leaned over and I met him halfway, eagerly accepting his kiss of greeting, both reassuringly familiar but new enough to have nervous butterflies come to life inside me. I wanted to kiss him forever. His hand slid into my hair, cupping the nape of my neck, and I settled my palm on his thigh, firm and warm beneath the denim. Touching him was addictive, *he* was addictive, a sugar rush in madly compelling human form.

Finally he pulled back. "I can't believe I'm sayin' this," he reluctantly pulled away, "but we'd better stop. Gonna be late."

I nodded, although I wanted to tug him back toward me and carry on kissing his mouth—and everywhere else. "Can't stress out a bride on the week of her wedding."

"Yeah, Cathy's always been nice to me, but I don't wanna be on the end of her wrath." He chuckled, putting the truck into drive.

He told me about his day as he drove the handful of miles up to Two Rivers, run by the McLeod family. I told him about Aunt Laurie's determination to come back to work only three days after fracturing her arm.

"It's the way most people here seem to be." He nodded. "We're doers, not waiters. This isn't a big city where someone else might be providing the thing you want or need, so you've gotta be self-sufficient. But generally, we look out for each other."

I was about to tell him that Jenny had shied away from a couple of people who seemed to have had ill intentions at the bakery today, when he turned onto the road that led up to the ranch. The truck passed under a simple metal arch with TWO RIVERS engraved into a wide band at its apex.

"The ranch was floundering a little while back," Rick told me as we got closer to a big house. The clapboard looked a little worse for wear, but there were cheery fresh flowers growing in the window boxes. "I went to school with the Lewis McLeod, the eldest son of the owners. He came back from his job in the city, restored the old barn and turned it into a wedding venue."

"Wow. That must've been a lot of work."

"It was three years ago. My dad did a lot of the woodwork. I think you'll like it. It's real pretty."

We passed the ranch house and drove through an avenue of very young trees, up to a big barn. It was two levels tall, the wood honey-coloured. Mature shrubs of lavender, their flowers a deep purple and beautifully fragrant, ringed the open doorway.

Rick came around and opened the passenger door for me, and I hopped out. I was wondering if I could sneak in a kiss when the woman who must have been Cathy appeared in the barn doorway, followed by a tall, blond man in a gray Stetson and a black and white plaid shirt.

"Maddie, Maddie Liu?" she called. She wore a cute sundress and leather flats. Her make-up was immaculate. I felt very plain in comparison.

I walked towards her, my hand outstretched. "Hi, Cathy."

"Hi!" She shook my hand vigorously. "Oh, hey, Rick."

Rick, who was now leaning against the side of the truck, just nodded. "Hey, cuz."

"Thanks *so* much for making the cake on short notice," Cathy was saying, talking quicker than anyone I had ever met. "How are the fondant hearts coming? Laurie did have the measurements, but do you need them again to check? Do you have a hundred? Come in and see the barn!"

It was tricky to imagine her married to the softly spoken giant whom I'd met at the ballgame on Sunday, but, after all, opposites did attract.

"Excuse me," the man a few paces behind her began, taking off his Stetson and offering me his hand. "I'm Lew McLeod. My family owns Two Rivers." After we shook hands, he slid a business card from his back pocket and offered it to me. "Y'all need anything in the run up to the wedding, don't hesitate to call. Rick," he added, nodding toward the truck.

"Lew. How's it going?"

They started to have a conversation, but Cathy tugged me inside the barn to see everything she'd done, so I didn't catch any of it.

* * *

Cathy was a whirlwind who talked at the speed of light. She was friendly and eager to answer my questions, but even so, I was exhausted by the time we finished, thirty minutes later.

I'd photographed the location the cake was to be placed in, and Cathy had drawn chalk arrows on the floor for where the cake table would be. She hadn't left anything to chance for her wedding, and I had to admire her stellar organizational skills.

After she climbed into Lew's pickup truck and he drove her back down to the ranch house, I walked to Rick's truck on tired feet.

He opened the driver's side door and came to enfold me in his arms. I went willingly, breathing him in; sawdust, clean sweat, minty soap. A combination I knew I would very much miss when I arrived back in London.

I put that out of my mind as I settled my face into the hollow of his chest.

"It go okay?" he asked, his accent rumbling under my ear.

"I think so. She's so organized, Rick!"

"Terrifying, isn't it?" We both laughed. "You want a walk? Let me show you the area Lew landscaped behind the barn. There's an old wooden swing in the style of a loveseat, a little pond, and lots of enclosed grassy areas for clandestine romantic moments."

"Romantic, eh?" He started to walk towards the barn and I fell into step beside him as he walked.

"Yeah, romantic." He reached for my hand and I laced our fingers. "And I've been savin' something for you."

"What is it?"

He reached into his back pocket with his free hand and took out a small cellophane bag. Inside were four white rabbit sweets.

I gasped out loud. "Oh, my God! Where?"

"They gave 'em to me with the *xiaolongbao* order. Honestly, I clean forgot on Monday, and found them in my truck this mornin.'"

I reached for them, but he held them tantalizingly out of reach.

"Rick!" I protested.

His grin was cheeky, and the playfulness on this man was devastating. He let go of my hand and wiggled his eyebrows. "You want it? You're gonna have to come and get it."

And he took off around the back of the tall, golden barn.

Laughing, feeling free, I hot-footed it after him.

Above us, the bright sun hung in the sky, blazing, warming the grass.

It was beautiful here. Lewis had done a great job with the landscaping. A well-kept lawn was ringed by more lavender and other shrubs, each blooming with butter-yellow or pure white flowers. A couple of water fountains bubbled on the left side of the space, the water surrounded by big circles of stone for sitting, or resting glasses.

At the end of the gardens, about six meters away, sat the *pièce de résistance* that I imagined was used plenty for photos, a towering oak tree, with a wooden swing hanging from the biggest branch. The seat of the swing was solid, shiny wood with a heart engraved where the couple would sit. Ivy curled around the swing's hand ropes.

The whole area was stunning. It stole my breath, and I

could *so* easily imagine every kind of wedding here. Big and love-filled and loud, or small and intimate.

"I'm gonna eat 'em if you don't get over here," Rick called from ten feet away, and I refocused my attention. I hadn't eaten since lunch, and even if I had, white rabbit sweets were my absolute favorite. My dad always kept some in his house. It was the treat he'd always carried for me in his pocket when I was a young girl.

"You're going to regret this, Callahan," I warned, but I couldn't keep the encroaching giggle out of my tone. This was too much fun.

I ran towards him. He jogged back a little, but it was clear that he wanted to be caught, and when I tackled him, we fell to the ground in a heap, breathless and laughing together. Rick rolled me on to my back, and I rolled him on to his, and we went like that for several feet, turning over and over in the sun-warmed grass, a tangle of entwined limbs. Finally, I won, maneuvering him on to his back, and pinning his wrists above his head, handcuff style. He was so big that it took both of my hands to restrain him, and I felt the banked power of his broad body underneath him.

He could so easily overpower me, but I knew he was willing prey.

I searched his hands. Empty.

"Give it to me," I demanded, unable to keep the smile from my voice.

"Oh, I'll give it to you."

"You think you're so funny." He was all swagger and arrogance, cocky charm with just an edge of danger, of power, and oh, God, I wanted him more than I wanted my next breath. "You know very well what I'm talking about."

Rick's mood changed, and he freed one of his hands to stroke a stray curl of hair back behind my ear. He did seem to *love* touching my hair, and I did not mind one bit. "Sure don't seem like we're in a position to do anything much like talking. Does it?"

I shifted, constantly aware of the heat of him, all muscle and strength. And the delicious sensation of him, hard and heavy and so needy, between my legs. Layers of clothing separated them, but I swore that I could feel every curve and angle of that gorgeous body beneath me.

"We can talk. Just give me the sweets," I teased.

I ran a hand down his chest, aiming for the front pocket of his jeans.

"Uh-huh. Not so fast." In a heartbeat, he flipped me over onto my back, and pinned my hands above my head.

The ridge of his erection pressed right where I needed it, and without a thought, I bucked up into him, softly breathing his name.

He lowered his mouth down to mine for a kiss, just a brush of lips at first, then more insistent, until I opened for him, and he dipped his tongue inside. His stubble grazed me, marking me, I thought, dazed. Making me his. The thought turned me on even more, revving me up, sharpening my ache for him to an unbearable point, and underneath him, I spread my legs, settling him further into the embrace of my hips.

He groaned. "Jesus, Maddie. You're killin' me."

We gazed at each other for a moment, and I knew that he was asking for permission. This strong, capable man wouldn't do a thing unless I explicitly okayed it, and that was a hell of a turn on.

"Rick," I whispered. "I want you so much."

I didn't know what I was waiting for. Some cosmic sign from the universe that I could have sex with him? I'd given my engagement ring back to Seb, had told him in no uncertain terms that he could essentially take a long walk off a short cliff. So what did I want? Some promise from a higher power that I could dive feet first into something with Rick and walk away with my already-broken heart intact?

"I'm yours for the takin'," he murmured, kissing my forehead.

The gesture was so sweet that my eyes burned.

Why the fuck was I hesitating? My days in Kentucky were dwindling, and I could either spend them dancing around this fire-starter with Rick and then regretting it forever, *or* luxuriating in everything he was offering.

And with a lightning bolt of clarity, I knew what I was going to choose.

I pulled his lips down to meet mine, slid my tongue into his mouth, captured his little groan of pleasure as I slid my hands along his chest and settled my palms on his excellent behind, pressing the length of him into me. He felt *amazing* between my legs. I wanted all of him, without barriers, for as many as hours as possible.

"Please, Rick."

He made some sound of hungry assent and kissed me fiercely, all lips and teeth and tongue, and I lapped up his attentiveness. The world had narrowed to this man and how he made me feel.

The sudden slam of a car door made me start, and I broke the kiss with a sigh of regret, pushing gently at his chest.

"You gotta be fuckin' kidding me," Rick muttered, standing up. He helped me to my feet and brushed off the legs of his jeans, then turned toward the back of the garden, probably to hide his huge and completely obvious erection, and I finished smoothing my hair just as Lew appeared around the corner of the barn, Stetson in place.

"Hey," he said slowly. "Wasn't sure if you'd left. I need to lock up the barn."

"Oh, yeah. Of course, go ahead. It's gorgeous here, by the way. We're just leaving."

Rick turned to face his friend. "I was just showin' Maddie the, ah, swing."

Lew narrowed his eyes and glanced from Rick's face to mine, but he didn't say anything, just nodded.

We thanked him and walked to the truck, not looking at each other. I knew that if I so much as peeked in Rick's direction, I'd burst out laughing.

Rick drove us down the track to the ranch house. Once we were safely on the road back towards Redwing Falls, I started giggling, and Rick's chuckles soon filled the cab of the truck, too.

We ate the white rabbit sweets on the drive back. They were chewy and creamy, the coating of rice paper melting on my tongue.

"Not bad," Rick said thoughtfully of his.

"These are my favorite nostalgia sweets. That's my childhood, that and haw flakes and homemade prawn crackers. I'll cook you some one day. They blow up so big in the hot oil, you can get ones as large as your whole hand!"

As he turned onto Otter Street, I knew home was close, and I set my hand on his thigh. "Do you mind if we get dinner somewhere? I really want to talk to you."

He looked over at me, concern sketched on his handsome face. "Sure. You okay?"

"I think it's time we properly talked. I want to tell you everything that happened with my ex-fiancé."

He made a turn and then pulled the truck into the diner parking lot. "Okay."

I released my seatbelt and leaned towards him, cupping his face with one hand. His day-old stubble rasped against my palm. God, how I wanted to feel that prickly layer of hair *everywhere* on my body.

"I like you so much, Rick. I'm done trying to tell myself

why I shouldn't see you too much, why I shouldn't give into this. But I want to tell you everything."

He leant into my touch, then kissed the soft skin of my palm. His hazel eyes were almost black in the twilight encroaching through the truck cab windows. "Then let's get dinner, and I'll listen."

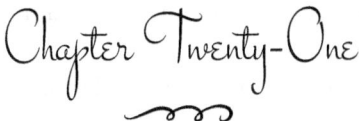

Chapter Twenty-One

Rick

Rick led Maddie into the diner, making himself think about anything except that all too recent prelude to sex they'd been enjoying in the Two Rivers wedding garden.

Boiled cabbage. The exact measurements of the willow tree spindles he'd been painstakingly carving. The tune played by the most irritating of Toby's all too numerous musical toys.

What had he been thinking back there? Making her chase him and then rutting her into the grass like—

He hadn't been thinking. Just *doing*. Wanting.

And for her part, Maddie, had been one hundred percent into it. He would have stopped if she wasn't. Non-consent had never been his thing.

He chose a booth near the back. "Is this okay?"

"Sure." She slid into the seat opposite him, and he watched her scoop her hair back from her face. The diner strip lights bounced off the shiny-black waves.

She was *beautiful.*

And she lived an ocean and several time zones away.

A fact which just didn't seem to matter whenever he got close to her. Ever since he'd carried her into his house after the airport, sleepy and sad, something inside him had been drawn to her, inexorably.

He thought about her constantly. Dreamed about her and woke up with a hard-on like steel.

But it was more than sex. It was the timbre of her laugh, her wicked sense of humour, her softness, her vulnerability.

He picked up a menu and passed it to her, then spread one out in front of himself but didn't look at it. His gaze was on her; the shape of her lashes on her cheeks as she read, the set of her shoulders, the slight smile playing on her lips.

Tori wandered over to them. "Hi, y'all! Second time in a week. That hot brown must've been good," she joked to Maddie.

Maddie grinned. "It was, but I don't have time to digest that tonight. Can I just have a buffalo chicken wrap and a coffee?"

Tori scribbled it down. "Rick?"

"The same. Thanks."

She bustled off, humming along to the pop tune that played on the overhead speakers.

Rick slid his hand into the middle of the table.

Maddie met him halfway, lacing their fingers. "I should have talked to you properly earlier."

He smiled. "Well, yeah. Ain't like you've had anything to do. Not gettin' over jetlag, dealin' with the number your fiancé dealt you, helpin' to run a bakery you ain't ever worked in before while also learnin' the ropes for it, and on top of that, running your online platforms.... You seem kinda lazy, if you ask me."

She laughed a little. "Thanks. I needed that. But still. I've been meaning to tell you about my ex, Seb. Sebastian Yates was his name. Well, is, he isn't dead."

"More's the pity," Rick growled.

Maddie frowned. "I don't wish him dead, you know? I wish that he never gets to have sex with anyone again, or that his dick grows warts, but I don't wish him dead. I'm more cross at myself for not seeing it. What he was obviously really like inside."

Rick turned her hand over in his, smoothed his thumb over the life line that curved down her palm. "Tell me."

Tori brought over their coffee. Rick smiled up his thanks.

Maddie waited for her to leave again, and then cleared her throat, the fingers of her free hand clenched into a loose fist.

As she proceeded to tell him all about how she and Seb had met, their courtship, and her dreams of owning her own shop space, he did his best to listen without interrupting, squeezing her hand when she faltered at several parts in the story, including when Seb had suggested she move in.

When she reached the part about the non-responses from the co-op shops, he had to press his lips together to keep from speaking, because he was almost a hundred percent sure he knew where the story would end.

He stroked his thumb over hers, nodded as she continued, but when he heard about the letter in the bin, Rick couldn't keep his words in. "Fuck. Him."

His temper was held at bay on a short leash, and he wanted to break something. One of Sebastian Yates' limbs, to be precise. He took another steadying breath, so he didn't end up yelling.

"Fuck him, Maddie," he said again, and he made his tone pretty even, considering all the mad he'd built up. "He had *no* right. No fuckin' right."

"I know, believe me, I know." Maddie sighed, and her eyes were brimming with tears. She dashed them away with her free hand. "We fought. He said he was doing what was best for our future. He had railroaded me completely, painted me into a corner, altered my plan so it fit his."

She inhaled deeply, clearly gathering her calm. "He started to explain further, but I didn't want to hear his bullshit.

"I told him to go fuck himself. I stormed out, and I asked my mum to post the engagement ring back through his letter-box. Later, my dad went to get what little stuff I had at his place, too."

Maddie looked at him through sad, hazel eyes. Shiny tears brimmed in them. "And that was just days before I was due to fly here. He called me at least three times, begged me to stay and work through things, but I couldn't renege on the promise I'd made to Aunt Laurie and Jess."

Rick swallowed back his incendiary rage. She didn't need that now.

Tori arrived with their plates, wished them a great meal. Maddie thanked her with a smile that didn't reach her lovely eyes.

"And that's it," she added, easing her hand free of his and picking up her cutlery. "I've got baggage, and I wanted you to know how much. Whatever happens, I'm never going back to him. I think I might finally block his number so he can never call me again."

Rick toyed with his own fork, imagined stabbing Sebastian in the eye with it. Then the dick, then the eye, again.

"Thank you for tellin' me," he managed to say.

She smiled at him, and some of her perkiness was back. "Thank you for being so angry. It's very comforting."

In lieu of Sebastian Yates' eye being available, Rick stabbed a slice of cucumber with his fork. "I was an excellent shot in the Army, Maddie. Hit targets from twelve hundred yards away."

She rewarded him with a watery laugh. "Thanks. I'll let

you know. I like you so much, Rick. You deserve to be more than someone's rebound. So much more."

He let himself drink in the graceful line of her neck, the sweet curve of her lips. "Maddie, you have to know that right now, I'd settle for being your anythin', for as long as you allow."

Setting his fork down, he leaned forward a little. "And for the record, I am *far* from baggage free. The Army was my family for a while, and my ticket to see the world, but it fucked me up in ways I probably will never fully understand. I still have nightmares, wake up from 'em in cold sweats. I hate bein' snuck up on. I attend a support group for veterans every Sunday in Louisville."

Her face didn't change. No pity, no withdrawing from him. "I'm so happy you do that, Rick."

"I wrangled with it for a while. I ain't gonna lie. I went 'round and 'round in my head about how men shouldn't have to talk about feelings an' such. But I have Jenny to think about, and my dad's business, well, it's our business now, I guess."

Maddie leaned toward him, mirroring his pose, and took one of his hands with both of hers, sandwiching his palm between them.

"I couldn't go off the rails, because of them, and because I still want to be able to look myself in the mirror in the mornin'. It helps, talking to people who lived the same experiences I did."

She squeezed his hand. "Do you want to talk to me about it? What you saw, the things you had to do?"

"Not right now. But one day, maybe."

"Well, when that day comes, I'll be here." She rubbed her thumb in small circles over his skin, the little move gently comforting. The fact she didn't add a meaningless platitude or tell him he was *so brave* meant a lot.

Rick studied her expression, grateful she took him as he was, and asked, "Would you like to come over for dinner Sunday? The day after the wedding," he clarified. "I can cook one of the other two things I'm halfway good at."

Her smile was sweet and sunny, and this time it did warm her eyes. "I would love that."

"I'll ask Jenny and Toby to stay over at Mom and Dad's," he added, holding her gaze so she didn't miss his meaning.

Her cheeks flushed. "Maybe you can make me another of your excellent omelets in the morning."

She was so goddamned irresistible that he wanted to cart her out of the diner and into his truck, lay her out on the backseat and use his mouth on her until she forgot her own name.

But she had a wedding cake to make. And more than a few other responsibilities. So, knowing that he'd have her to himself on Sunday, and that he was a grown adult perfectly capable of patience, he settled for keeping the conversation light and enjoying dinner with her.

* * *

Maddie

It was full twilight by the time Rick dropped me home. He walked me up to the porch, kissed me with a fierceness that made everything inside me ache, and then disappeared into his own house.

I wanted to linger in the memory of our talk, of the taste of him, but I couldn't. I had serious work to do, starting with the top tier of Cathy's wedding cake. I made enough mixture for two versions, and I'd pick the best

Aunt Laurie had convinced us to increase our order from

the wholesaler for tomorrow's delivery, seeing as I wouldn't have time to make as much stock, and I was *so* grateful. Some of the staples that got shipped in from the commercial bakery, like cinnamon buns and shortbread, were our bestsellers.

Once the first part of the wedding cake came safely out of the oven, I could relax, at least a little, and I started on a batch of pork sung buns to sell tomorrow. While I was here, I had an ideal opportunity to test out my Asian and Asian fusion baking on a brand-new audience, and I'd let myself get too busy to make the most of it. That ended now.

With baking playlist turned up high, and set out the correct tins, weighing ingredients. I had a cheat sheet for converting American and British measurements, so I could be sure nothing was left to chance.

Everything inside me settled when I started baking. Making food really was my happy place. I didn't have to worry about anything else. Thoughts came and went as I worked; mostly thoughts of Rick, but he was always on my mind these days.

When I was in the zone, my world narrowed to ensuring the measurements were correct and that I mixed and folded and stirred properly. Nothing else needed to enter my frame of mind for this time. I made myself a huge pot of tea, knowing I'd need the caffeine. I ran on tea. That and my favorite brand of imported soya milk that I had first tried on a visit to my dad's family in Hong Kong. It arrived warm, in a tall glass while we rested our aching feet in the cafe area of a busy city market, and it had been love at first sip, but there wasn't an Asian grocery around here, and it felt very frivolous to order it in when I wouldn't be here that much longer.

The little spike of fear that shot through me when I thought about being far, far away from Rick unbalanced me, so I made myself push that aside.

Two hours later, two trays of pork sung buns, the rolled

bread filled with generous helpings of pork floss, spring onions and my own fusion addition, grated apple, sat on the counter, fresh from Jess' second oven. It was *great* to stay in the house of someone who also not only adored cooking but also cooked for a living.

I'd taken pictures of the buns at every stage, including just before baking when the dough was glossy with egg wash and sesame seeds, and now, with everything cooling, I sat down to upload it all to my social feeds, making sure the branded pastry brush and dough slice that a London company had gifted me were clearly in shot. It could be tough, remembering all these little details, but I was never so happy as when I was baking, when I was creating, and if sponsorship allowed me to do it, well, I was all for it.

Thinking of the few companies who'd sponsored me in exchange for featuring their products reminded me of Seb. He'd often insinuated that when we were married, I could give up the sponsorship, as he had more than enough money for us both.

I'd always laughed, thinking he was jokingly trying to assure me he could take care of me, although I didn't need taking care of.

How could I have been so blind?

Rick was totally different. Even only knowing him a little under two weeks, I could never imagine him trying to control the steer of my life, even if the direction I took ended up to his detriment.

I wondered how he had felt after tonight. He'd still invited me over on Sunday. Anticipation of that coming day curled, hot and heavy, in my stomach. The warm pull of attraction was a living thing inside me. Compelling, irresistible. I had to push him from my mind to concentrate hard on anything.

I finished the uploads, and replied to comments on the videos I had shared recently. Nothing more from Seb, thankfully, and only a few borderline-hateful comments about our break-up. It never failed to astonish me that some people felt they could behave however they pleased just because they were saying it with a keyboard and not to my face.

At eleven in the evening, too exhausted to work anymore, I logged off my laptop.

I sank into sleep like a stone.

My last thought was of Rick's soft, warm smile, as he told me not to work too hard. I wished he was here to curl around me.

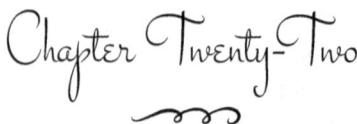

Chapter Twenty-Two

Thursday was a *complete* mess. I slept through the alarm and only woke up to Jenny pounding on the door.

"We're gonna miss the wholesaler delivery! Wake up!"

I scrambled out of bed and we loaded the pork sung buns into her car. I glanced at the two versions of the top tier of Cathy's wedding cake. I was relieved to note that they looked good, although one was a smidge less wonky, so that one would make it to the final cut.

Jenny drove like the wind. As it was only six in the morning, we made it to the bakery in a couple of minutes, just as the wholesaler's delivery truck pulled up. I almost up-ended the tray of buns on to the ground in my haste to get the bakery keys out of my purse.

The rest of the morning didn't go any better. I spilled coffee on myself. Jenny started to come down with what appeared to be a horrific cold, and she said her throat felt like she'd swallowed a pack of razor blades. Aunt Laurie had been planning to come in for an hour or so to give us a lunch break, but I wasn't sure Jenny or I would last that long, and I told her so, hoping she'd get the message.

The saving grace was that my experimental pork sung buns with the additional grated apple had sold out within the hour. Someone from the grocer's had bought one to try it, loved it, and spread the word. The empty display dish made my heart soar, and I texted my parents with the news. My mum replied with three heart emojis. My parents were my biggest fans and my best cheerleaders, even if they were still a little apprehensive about my desire to work in the creative industry. It was a harsh world out there. I lived it every day, putting content into the world to be judged by strangers on the internet. But when it worked, when you connected with others and made them happy with what you did, it was everything, and I knew unequivocally that I didn't want anything else.

By eleven o'clock, I had sent Jenny home. I was about to start packing up, thinking I'd cut my losses even if we missed the lunch crowd, when Molly stepped inside. I took a second to place her, seeing as I'd only met her the one time when I'd played pool with Rick. That seemed so long ago, now.

Her hair curled to her shoulders and she wore a t-shirt printed with the word "sarcasm" made up of elements of the periodic table.

"Hi!" I was overly cheerful, running on fumes and pleased to see a familiar face after a morning of strangers.

"Hi." She offered a sympathetic smile. "Laurie sent me. Said you needed a hand and that Jenny's sick, and your college girls couldn't pull an extra shift."

"I—" I hesitated. I *did* need a hand if I wasn't going to crash and burn in the next half hour. But need warred with my natural British reserve to ever admit that I needed assistance. "Thank you," I settled for saying. "Yes, please. I *so* badly need a hand. Are you sure?"

"Bar doesn't open until six, so you got me until three at least. Use me or lose me." She grinned, with a shrug.

I was planning on shutting by three anyway, assuming I could stay upright that long. I'd burned the candle at both ends for too many days in a row, wanting to do a perfect job covering for Jess. But with Aunt Laurie, the backbone of the operation, out of action, I was pushed for time *and* stressed, and ultimately, something had to give.

Despite the fact she barely knew me, Molly took my direction well and without complaint, restocking cookies, making all the coffees and teas that were ordered, and preparing sandwich fillings. We worked together through the lunch rush, bumping into each other a few times, but on the whole, we made it work.

At one-thirty in the afternoon, I called it a day. I could barely keep my eyes open, and I needed to film some more content for my channel later, assuming I lived long enough to get home and take a nap.

I thanked Molly profusely, stowed all the goods that would keep until tomorrow in the big fridges, and sent the rest away with Molly. She said she'd share them with the bar staff working tonight.

I wrote a sign for the door, telling customers we closed early for the day.

Even though I felt awful for shutting *Cake Away* hours early, my heart was light. This miracle of someone showing up at a moment's notice to help a friend's niece might never have happened in London. Molly hardly knew me, but she'd stepped up to the plate.

The close-knit community of Redwing Falls might be awful for some things, the gossip mill being one, but for others, like calling on a friend when in need, it was invaluable, and I thought that when I flew back, I'd miss it.

As soon as I got home, I texted Jenny to see how she was doing.

Me: How are you feeling?

Jenny: Terrible. Toby must have given me something. He's always touching stuff and then putting his hands in his mouth. I really hope he doesn't give it to my parents.

Jenny: I am so sorry to let you down.

Maddie: Don't even think that. You can't help it.

Maddie: I hope you get well soon. We'll work something out. Do you need anything?

She didn't respond. I succumbed to fatigue and had an hour's nap on the sofa.

When I woke up refreshed, she still hadn't replied.

I got on with making the bottom two tiers of Cathy's wedding cake. The batter smelled divine, and as the stand mixer whirred, I remembered her excited face from our meeting and I felt happy to do this for her.

This was why I baked. To make people smile. To fill them with joy in edible form.

By the time the bottom tiers of the cake were baked, I still hadn't heard from Jenny, and I decided she deserved, and needed, some cheering up, so I'd bake something for her.

I set up my lights, made sure I had all the ingredients measured out, fluffed my hair and washed my face, then started recording as I baked a batch of Chinese almond cookies. They were one of my favorite comfort snacks, buttery and bite-sized, and my dad's all-time favorite kind of cookie to have with coffee. I sometimes added matcha to these when I baked them, but I'd used all my supply on the Mississippi cake and hadn't found any more at Sureway, so plain almond it was.

I texted Jenny to see if I could come over, and I packed up the cookies when she replied.

* * *

Ten minutes later, having used that time to freshen up in case Rick was home (vanity, thy name is Maddie Liu), I knocked on the door.

He answered it, Toby on his hip. Thankfully, the brain fart did not reach my lips.

"Hi," he greeted me, his smile was slow and sweet. I wanted to kiss him, taste that grin.

"Hi. I brought cookies. I know Jenny is under the weather, and I thought she could use a pick-me-up."

"You're an honest to God angel." He bent to kiss me, and our mouths had almost touched when Toby wailed.

Rick jerked back. "Sorry. He's grouchy today. Ain't that rude, little man?"

Toby jabbed a finger in Rick's chest. "Ick!"

"Yeah, he's not happy that I'm in charge, but mama's sick, dude. You've got what you've got." He stepped back from the threshold. "Come on in."

I followed him inside and shut the door behind me, toed off my shoes, and carried the box of cookies through to the kitchen. Unlike Jess' house, where the wall separating the living area and kitchen had been knocked through, Rick's house retained the division. The big concertina door between rooms was open, and I saw Jenny laying on the sofa, a huge blanket covering her from neck to ankle. She waved feebly when I arrived.

"Hey. Don't come too close," she called out.

"I'm sorry you're feeling so awful," I sympathized.

Rick sat down in one of the kitchen chairs, Toby settled on his lap. He shuffled his chair closer to the table and tugged a shape sorter towards him on the tabletop so Toby could play. The toddler clapped his hands and got to work, mumbling nonsense to himself as he turned the shapes over in his cute, tiny fingers.

"It's okay," Jenny groaned. "You brought cookies. You're always welcome."

I opened the tub. "None of you have almond allergies?"

"Nope," the siblings said in unison.

"Great. Oh, do you have—"

Rick pointed to the cupboards above the sink. "Plates are in there."

I fetched one, plated two cookies and took them to Jenny, who gave me the sunniest smile possible, considering she was stuffed up with cold.

"You are worth your weight in gold, Maddie."

Warmth filled me. "I'd hug you, but if one more member of the bakery staff goes down, we'll have to close. I'm not sure if the college girls could manage on their own."

She waved me back. "I don't wanna give you this plague. I made Mom drop Toby off so she and Dad would at least have a chance of not catching before the wedding. Ugh," she added. "The wedding. I might miss it! My *one* opportunity to dress up. And Toby had such a cute outfit prepped! I'm more mad about that than anything else."

"You still have a few days to go," I soothed her, returning to the table in the kitchen and offering Toby a cookie. He took a bite of it and then smashed it into Rick's face, laughing. Rick tried to defend himself, but it was a lost cause, and crumbs cascaded everywhere.

Rick looked very tired.

What would I want in this situation, I wondered, and then, I knew.

"Shall I make dinner?"

Their faces lit up.

Jenny's expression was the first to crumble. "We can't ask that of you. You probably have stuff to bake."

"Jenny's right," Rick added. "You got your own stuff to take care of."

"I can spare an hour," I said, truthfully. I knew I hadn't burned through all the food Jess had frozen, and besides, helping people I cared deeply about ranked top of the list.

Toby threw one of the wooden shapes on the floor. Rick bent to get it, passed it to him, and, delighted with this game, he repeated the experiment.

"Toby, c'mon, honey," Jenny called from across the room.

Toby sent me the most devious look I'd ever seen from a toddler, waited a few seconds, threw the shape again, and cackled.

I decided to stay out of it and opened the fridge to see what I could cook for dinner.

A whole head of cabbage greeted me, along with a carton of eggs, hot dogs, two old- looking carrots, a pack of six fruit yogurts, three ready-made pouches of Bolognese, probably for Toby, and a couple of steaks still in their supermarket shrink wrap.

"I need to go to the store," Rick said ruefully. "But I came right home to wrangle this one." He moved Toby to the side, narrowly avoiding a wooden star in the face. "So I ain't had time yet." To Jenny he said, "I'll drive over tonight while you put this little rascal to bed."

I closed the fridge door and opened the cupboards, looking for what I wanted.

"Soy, sesame, and vegetable pancakes sound okay to you? We can dip them in some extra soy sauce and, if you want, sweet chili sauce, for flavor."

Jenny gave me a thumbs up from the sofa, and Rick mirrored the gesture at my side. They looked so alike in that moment that I laughed.

"Thanks, Maddie," Rick murmured. His gaze was soft and warm, cozy and compelling, and I'd have done pretty much anything he asked right then.

If only I had all day to look at him.

Sadly, time waited for no woman, so I got to work washing and slicing the cabbage, sieving flour, whisking eggs, heating olive oil in a heavy-bottomed pan.

In twenty minutes, I had enough vegetable pancakes for all of us. Rick had been busy too, setting Toby in front of his favorite cartoons for five minutes so he could clear and set the table, pour everyone water, and heat Toby a pouch of the toddler-friendly Bolognese.

"Secret vegetables," Jenny whispered as she settled him into his high chair. "They blend it into the sauce."

I grinned at her as I slid the pancakes on plates and set the soy sauce and the sweet chili sauce into the center of the table.

"Kinda amazing, don't you think, that we've got a famous baker to make dinner for little old us?" Rick asked his sister.

"Yeah!" she enthused, digging in.

I sat down, picking up a fork as my face flamed. *"Semi-*famous. And only in a very niche crowd. I never get spotted in the street or anything like that. Thank God."

"Forty thousand followers aren't that niche!" Jenny protested.

Rick took a forkful of pancake, chewed thoughtfully. "Well darlin', semi-famous or not, these pancakes are *fantastic."*

"This smells absolutely *awesome* and tastes better," Jenny agreed. She cut off a sliver and held it out to Toby. He obligingly took it into his mouth and then spat it out and glared fiercely at his mother.

"Sorry," Jenny said quietly.

I laughed. "Toddlers aren't my target audience. Not to worry."

"We're for sure gonna miss you when you head back to London," Rick murmured, and held my gaze for a long moment.

Hundreds of unsaid words fell into the space between us, and I felt more than a twinge of sadness at the knowledge that my days in Redwing Falls were slipping through my fingers.

Chapter Twenty-Three

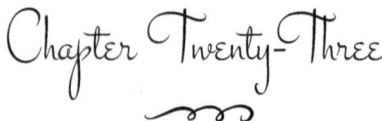

A half-hour after we'd eaten, a very tired Jenny took Toby up to bed. The little one looked exhausted, too, hardly putting up a fight when she lifted him from his high chair.

"Thanks so much for dinner, Maddie," she told me earnestly. "I'm gonna be really sad when you leave, and not just because you bake and cook like a dream."

I smiled after her as she left the room. The door shut behind her, and her footfalls sounded up the stairs.

Rick got up and began loading the dishwasher.

I stood, too. "Can I help?" I asked, standing to join him.

"Nope. You cooked, you don't clean. House rules."

It was nice; I had to admit. "Thanks. I have to go cook some Chinese sponge cake to sell tomorrow. I've been trying to make one thing every day, just for the experience of testing my baking out on a new audience, and I wanted to do rhubarb with this sponge. It's very gratifying when my cakes sell out."

I yawned hugely. In retrospect, the hour's nap I'd had earlier might not have been enough.

"You want some company?" Rick asked as he shut the door to the dishwasher and straightened up. I gave myself a moment to gaze dreamily at how good his backside looked in the dark-wash denim.

"You sure? You won't be bored while I whirlwind around the kitchen?"

He leaned against the sink and folded his arms slowly over his chest, giving me a very deliberate once-over.

"Darlin', even if all I get to do is watch you bake all evenin', I can hand on heart guarantee that I won't be bored."

Lust licked up my veins, and I swallowed back a pang of desire. "Rick—"

"I won't get in your way, I promise." He crossed the very small space and bent to kiss me. "I want to spend time with you, and if you have to spend some of that time baking, well, just know that it'll be no hardship *whatsoever* to watch you do that. And I'm great at doin' the dishes afterwards, too."

I cupped his cheek, and tugged him down for another kiss. "You're a dreamboat." When he huffed out a laugh, I added, "No, really. I can't believe I get to be your date at the wedding on Saturday. Are you going to dance with me?"

He chuckled and rolled his eyes. "I'm a terrible dancer."

"I don't care, so long as you're dancing with me," I countered.

He frowned, but his gaze was warm. "We'll see."

I smiled against his delectable mouth. "You haven't seen my dress yet."

He tickled his hand through my hair, cupping the nape of my neck. "Christ. Probably won't survive it. Don't make me combust with wantin' you too much in front of my damned cousin, Maddie."

I just smiled some more.

Just ten minutes later, I let us into Jess' house next door, preheated the oven and got to work. The sponge cake didn't take long. Whisking the egg whites into stiff peaks was the most arduous part, and luckily Jess had all the best gear. I put Rick to work unearthing the tulip cake cases from the highest shelf in Jess' kitchen while the electric whisk whirred. When the batter was ready, I added a few drops of rhubarb flavouring. These cute little cakes had been a hit for one of my British Chinese friends for her recent thirtieth birthday.

She'd wanted the softness of a typical Chinese sponge cake, but paired with her favourite autumn crumble flavour. I had been skeptical, but they were devoured in record time, and a new fusion bake was born.

"That smells *divine*," Rick commented twenty minutes later as they baked in the oven. He'd been as good as his word, washing dishes and helping me tidy up. "Do I get to try one? You know, as a taste tester?"

"If you behave yourself."

"Oh?" He came up behind me where I stood at the kitchen table, studying the sketches of the wedding cake with the placement of the fondant hearts. I had to assemble it all tomorrow evening, and I wanted to do it *right*. Aunt Laurie would, quite rightly, never forgive me if I messed this up. It was someone's wedding, arguably the event they would remember best for their entire lives, and besides, there'd be no shortage of photographs to catalog my shame if the cake didn't look perfect.

"Yeah," I murmured, turning my head to kiss him. He wrapped his arms around me, nuzzling into my head. His stubble tickled in the best way, set every nerve ending inside me alight, just as I'd fantasized it would.

The oven timer started chirping, interrupting us. I bit back my disappointment. It seemed like we were forever doomed to one interruption or another. Rick stepped back so I could open the oven door and check the little cakes. They'd risen to perfection, and I slid the trays out one at a time.

"Amazing," Rick breathed. "Kitchen magic."

I smiled at him over my shoulder and closed the oven door. "The same could be said of what you do. Wood magic."

"I'd like to give you some wood magic, if you know what I mean." He smirked, and I laughed out loud.

"That was awful. I mean it," I added, holding his gaze. "You make trees into treasure."

He chuckled. "That's one for the next batch of business cards."

I slipped off the oven gloves and yawned hugely, stretching. I felt a pang of guilt as Rick looked at the cakes behind me. I hadn't really had a chance to enjoy him being here, and now I was too dead on my feet to start something. Plus, I didn't know if we'd sort of agreed to wait to... *Do* anything until Sunday.

"I'll let you get to bed, Maddie," he said softly. "I know you've gotta get up early." He came in close for a kiss, and I responded eagerly, melting into his arms.

"Rick?"

"Hmm?" He dropped a kiss on the tip of my nose and my heart warmed.

"Would you stay with me? I mean, I'm so tired, we'd just sleep. I don't want you to go, but also, I'm too tired to do all of the things I want to do with you."

"Yeah," he murmured, before I could make a total fool of myself by over-explaining in my clumsy British way. "It'd be a pleasure to hold you all night, Maddie."

* * *

I was nervous about how to do this, but Rick made it easy.

"You got a spare toothbrush?" he asked, as I finished putting away the clean and dry baking equipment. The rhubarb sponge cakes had filled the room with a sweet, syrupy scent that reminded me of home.

"I'll have a look." I held out my hand, and he took it, flicking off the kitchen light before I led him up the stairs. The layout here was simple; bathroom straight ahead and then two big bedrooms spread out along the hall.

I rummaged in the bathroom cabinet and found a toothbrush still in its packaging.

"Thanks." He leaned against the doorjamb, his beautiful body framed perfectly by the cream architrave. "You wanna use the bathroom first or second? I vote for you to go first. You're about to keel over."

"You know just what to say to make a girl feel good," I groused, but his eyes held such concern that I couldn't truly be mad. Besides, he was right.

He just smiled and stepped back so I could close the door.

By this point I was so sleepy that I didn't even have the energy to get excited about Rick being in my bed. It was a big thing, a *huge* thing, and I wanted it so much, but my body was slowly shutting down. I'd pushed myself too hard, for too many days in a row.

I finished in the bathroom, and then Rick took his turn while I changed into my pajamas and got under the covers. Thank goodness that Jess' spare bed was queen-sized.

The room glowed with diffused light from the bedside lamp and I watched through half-closed eyes as Rick stepped in through the doorway.

"I'll just sleep in my clothes, if you don't mind?" he rumbled.

"Fine with me," I yawned. I made sure to keep my eyes open as he bent to take off his boots and socks, leaving him to pad to the other side of the bed on bare feet.

He slid into bed, his proximity settling everything inside me. There was no table on his side of the bed, so I held out a cupped hand when he took off his dog tags. Rick lowered the chain and metal tags into my palm. The necklace was warm from his skin, and I curled my fingers around it before setting it on the little table by my cup of water.

"Light off?" I whispered.

"Light off. You're sure this is okay?" The gentleness of his tone warmed me from the inside out.

"*Very* okay. Would you please just hold me?" I clicked off the little beside lamp, and the room darkened. It was very quiet, save the sound of me moving to snuggle against him. Rick lifted his arm and I wiggled underneath it, pillowing my head on his chest. His heart beat steadily beneath my ear. He smelled fantastic.

He curled his arm around me, and he ran his thumb up and down my arm. "Thought about holdin' you like this," he said into the darkness.

"Hmmm?" I replied, because I wanted to hear all his thoughts about me, but he was *so* cozy and warm and I was *so* very, very tired.

"Yeah. It's even better than I imagined."

My eyes closed completely. I fell asleep to the rhythm of his heart beating.

* * *

I woke slowly to the sound of chattering birds outside the window. My stomach felt heavy and warm, and I slid my fingers down until they met Rick's arm, draped possessively across my lower belly.

He slept on his stomach, facing me. His face was relaxed in slumber, his lashes long and thick against his cheeks. What was that about? Why did men get better lashes, always?

Fortunately, in this case, I benefitted, as I was the one who got to enjoy just how fantastic he looked.

His hair was tumbled from sleep. I let my greedy gaze

follow the column of his neck and the broad line of his shoulders. He took up over half the bed.

When I gave in to the urge to touch him and threaded my fingers through the silky-soft strands of hair at his nape, he opened his eyes.

"Mornin'," he rumbled, and his sleep-rough voice was *wonderful* and I wanted to hear it every single day.

"Morning, sleepyhead."

He stretched languidly, like a big, beautiful cat, and then curled into me, and I eagerly wrapped my arms around him. He nuzzled into my shoulder.

"We don't gotta get up yet. Right?" He muttered, and he was so adorably grumpy and my heart squeezed.

I checked my watch. "We have about an hour. Reduced bakery hours on account of the double shit storm."

He huffed out a laugh. "Right. Laurie's broken arm and now Jenny has toddler plague. It's the worst kind of all plagues." He smiled against my shoulder. "Within the first week of movin' in with me, Toby gave me some absolutely horrific viral thing. Jesus, Maddie, I've had easier gunshot wounds."

"How many times have you been *shot?*" I demanded.

"I've been shot *at* many more times than I've been shot," he reassured me. "Worst time was when I got shot mannin' a checkpoint in Afghanistan." He took my hand, slid it under his shirt and up so my fingers kissed his bottom rib. I felt the unmistakable pucker of a healed scar. "Took damn near forever to heal."

My eyes burned. "I'm so glad it did heal."

"Me too. Anyway, this *thing*, whatever it was, made my hands and feet burn up. I had ulcers on every inch of my tongue. Least you only get shot in one place at a time."

I gently touched the scar. It seemed so small, but it could have killed him. The enormity of it made me wonder how anyone in relationships with soldiers on active duty coped without worrying every second of their day.

"It's no joke, Rick. I could have lost you before I even found you."

"Sorry. It's gallows humor. Gets you through." He pressed a gentle kiss to my cheek. "Enough about that." He shifted next to me, leaning up on to his side, and pulled me into the warm length of his body. "You said we had an hour. I fully intend to make use of that hour, as long as you want this, too."

Oh, my God, I wanted it.

"Yes, please," I managed to say, which was impressive considering my brain had short-circuited just from feeling the hard press of his cock *right* where I wanted it.

He cupped my cheek and bent his head to kiss me, and when our mouths touched I opened for him, sliding my arms around him and rolling on to my back so I took him with me. His weight on top of me was *delicious,* I spread my legs to feel the heft of his cock, and I bowed up to him on instinct.

"*Fuck,*" he cursed, and I loved hearing the expletive in his scratchy, deeper morning voice. "Maddie. I want you so bad."

"Please, take me."

He smiled against my mouth, then dropped his kisses down over my jaw and along my neck. I arched to give him better access and shivered in anticipation when his fingers worked open the buttons of my pajama top.

He murmured, "Goddamn, who knew flannel could be so sexy?", I laughed, feeling light and free, until the feel of his hot mouth enveloping my nipple rendered me incapable of coherent thought.

He used his tongue and lips to drive me to the brink, and then switched to my other breast and did it all again, using his hand to caress the nipple neglected by his mouth. It was an assault of pleasure and I pressed up into his mouth, both never wanting it to end and also wanting *more, more.*

Rick glanced up at me, and his gaze was dark with wanting. "Okay?"

"Oh, *yeah.*"

He kissed his way down my stomach and then trailed his mouth along the waistband of my pajama bottoms.

"Oh, my God, yes," I encouraged him, and he tugged them down, revealing my plain black underwear. I hadn't worn clothes to seduce, but he seemed seduced all the same, an appreciative groan escaping his lips as he eased them off and was met with naked flesh.

I lifted my legs so he could work off the panties and the sleepwear bottoms, and then he covered me again, his warm, callused hands parting my legs as he settled between them. My inner muscles clenched hard, impatient, and I fisted the sheets in my hands as he pressed kisses to the inside of each of my thighs.

"Please," I begged him.

He lifted his gaze to mine. "You want something?"

His grin was quick and deadly, and I was about to just shove his head where I wanted it when he parted my folds and took a long, considering lick.

I arched off the bed, his name flying from my lips, and he moved one arm to band across my lower body, holding me in place.

Our eyes met when we looked down, and he held my gaze for a moment, making sure I wanted this as much as he did.

When I nodded, burning up too hot to speak, he bent back to the task at hand, murmuring "fuckin' delicious" as he worked his tongue first over my clit and then down to my entrance and back again. I had no choice but to *very happily* take it because he'd pinned me to the bed with one hand and held me open to his ministrations with the other.

I felt the slow coil of an orgasm building in the pit of my belly as Rick circled his tongue over the little swollen bud of my clit. Every time I got close, when the flutters started to build, he changed tactics, writing his name, or the alphabet, or whatever, until he brought me to the precipice of that cliff again.

When I couldn't take it anymore, I speared one hand into his hair. "Please. I'm so close."

"Okay, honey. I got you." He slid one, then two fingers inside me and I readily clenched around him. "Fuck," Rick bit off. "So tight."

And then he applied himself to my pleasure, drawing slow, deliberate circles right where I wanted them, and it seemed like only a heartbeat later, the climax hit me like a freight train, and I was bucking against his face, and he worked me through it with his fingers and lips and tongue, until I gently pushed him away.

"Oh, my *God.*"

He kissed my thigh. "That was one of the hottest things I've ever seen. Fuck, you're beautiful."

"Thank you." I shivered, inner muscles still greedily closing around nothing, around where I wanted *him*. "That was *amazing*. But..." I tugged him up to cover me again. "You aren't going to...?"

"No condoms here, darlin', and besides, we don't have time for me to do it properly, like I want to." Rick pressed a kiss to my forehead.

Christ on a bike. I wasn't sure I would survive *properly*.

I glanced at my watch. "We still have time for *something*." And before he could object, because he was a perfect gentleman and always seemed to put others' needs before his own, I added, "Go sit on the edge of bed."

He dropped a gentle kiss on my lips and drew back, doing as I asked. His gaze went dark and hot when I completely shrugged off my open pajama top and moved to kneel at his feet.

"Maddie. I don't expect this," he said gently, smoothing a hand over my hair.

"Who said I think you do?" I asked cheekily. "Maybe *I* want to do this."

He closed his eyes as if summoning strength. "Thank God."

I grinned and reached for the fly of his jeans, slipping the top button through its stiff eyelet and then drawing down the zip.

He wore plain gray boxers, and he inhaled deeply when I ran the tip of my finger down the very impressive bulge of his erection. "For me?"

He half-groaned, half chuckled. "Are you serious? You fuckin' know it is. Spend all my time around you at half mast, it seems."

Wasn't that extremely gratifying? I smiled at up him, in awe that this gorgeous, kind, funny, capable man was here with *me.*

I tugged at the hem of his shirt. "Off."

He did as I asked, revealing those beautifully shaped shoulders, his Eagle tattoo, and his flat stomach and broad chest. I got to see the little scar I'd touched, and below it, also the tattoo I'd only glimpsed that first Sunday, a serpent whose curving body read *This We'll Defend.*

"U.S. Army motto," Rick added as I traced it with my finger.

"You have some beautiful ink. And something else that I bet is beautiful, too." I parted the opening in his underwear and drew him out, and Rick let out a long breath, like he'd been waiting to feel my touch all this time.

I wrapped my hand around him, giving him an experimental stroke, and his hand slid down to cup my cheek, no pressure in his touch, just affection.

"Hell, don't stop," he murmured.

I hadn't been planning on it.

I shuffled further forward and he widened his legs a little to accommodate me, and I pressed a kiss to the tip of his cock and watched him swallow, his eyes drifting closed. He tasted musky, salty, with just a residual tang of soap, and I licked at him, testing the flavor, gauging his reaction, paying as close attention to his pleasure as he had to mine.

I rested my free hand on his thigh, and Rick moved to hold it. The gesture was unbearably sweet.

After pressing kisses down the length of his shaft, I took him into my mouth, felt the weight of him on my tongue, and his hips bucked.

I released him briefly. "I like knowing what I do to you."

And I proceeded to absolutely rock his world just like he'd rocked mine moments ago.

Chapter Twenty-Four

If everyone in the world could begin their morning with oral sex, I typed to my friend Emma, *there'd never be another war. Everyone would be too happy.*

Since it was later in the U.K., she replied right away.

Emma: OH MY GOD. Tell me EVERYTHING. No detail is too small.

Emma: Don't even think of sifting through the small details deciding what you're going to exclude. I want all of them.

Emma: Is this about who I think it's about??

I laughed and replied.

Me: Yeah. It's about Rick. I'll talk to you properly later, gotta open the bakery.

Aunt Laurie walked toward me as I turned onto Otter Street, a smile on her face and her arm in a sling.

"Morning!" I called.

"Morning." She frowned as we got close enough to speak. "Feels awful strange, being here so late. Still, I enjoyed the lie in. I'm gettin' too old for this. I'm seventy next year."

I pressed my hand to my heart. "Stop. The people I love are not allowed to get old, ever. I forbid it."

Aunt Laurie chuckled as she took the keys from me and opened the door. "It's been an adventure helping Jess and Connor run this baby, I admit it. But I can't see me lasting more'n another year without slowing down. You know? I was leaving it until after this big holiday to tell them, I didn't want to ruin their time away."

She had a heart the size of the state of Kentucky. "You have to do what's right for you."

She nodded, moving to the big fridge. "Did you defrost some of what Jess left in the freezer?"

"Yes, twenty muffins, twenty cookies, and," I lifted the bag I'd carried with me, "rhubarb chiffon cupcakes. Another one of my recipes."

She bent her head so she could smell the bag. "Oh, my. People are gonna miss your baking, Maddie. You should know that."

My heart warmed as I started to unpack the cupcakes. "I'm so touched, honestly. Sometimes..." I rummaged in a drawer until I found a slate cake stand and assembled it to hold the cupcakes.

"Sometimes what, honey?" Aunt Laurie asked from behind me. She'd started to set out the defrosted muffins and cookies on the two big trays that sat in the window.

I fussed with the cupcakes. "Sometimes I wonder if London was the best place to start my baking business. It's so big, there are already a hundred bakeries... It took *so* long to get my name out there. I'm still just another baker."

My aunt *hmmmed* to let me know I had her attention, even as she continued to prep for opening.

"But here, I sell out of everything I make. It's a simple pleasure, but it makes me happy, getting to see people eat what I create immediately. Normally I deliver the cake to the recipient and *they* take it to the party or whatever, and I never see the result. Before coming here, I'd never been able to sell my own stuff."

"I see." I knew Aunt Laurie was thinking something and not saying it. I didn't need sight of her face, I could tell just from the tone of her voice.

Before I could ask what she was mulling over, the whole-sale delivery of rolls and pastries arrived, and then the moment was lost.

I left the bakery at noon, when the college girls arrived for their shifts. I was thankful for the reprieve, considering I still had to ice and assemble the wedding cake on the stand the bride had ordered specially.

Rick had been texting me on and off all day. The most recent message was a picture of a bedframe he and Eddie had made, the headboard carved to resemble a mountain range. Two layers of wood, one dark, one light, flirted with each other to give depth and interest.

Me: It's gorgeous!

Rick: Pick you up at 11 for the wedding tomorrow?

Me: Once again, I live literally next door.

Rick: I have to pick you up. It's practically the law here. Imagine the headline: KENTUCKY MAN EXPIRES FROM FAILURE TO ADHERE TO OL' SOUTH GENTLEMAN RULES.

Me: Okay, we can't have that. See you tomorrow.

Me: xxxxxxxxxxx

He replied with the "blowing a kiss" emoji.

I sighed like a teenage girl when I saw it, allowing myself a moment to relive this morning with him; the sounds he made when I touched him, the way his bare skin felt under my hands.

The wedding cake icing assembly went without a hitch, probably because I moved at a glacial pace with every stage of it. It had to be perfect. I desperately wanted to make a good impression.

Finally stepping back from the cake, I snapped several photos that I would share on my socials if Cathy gave permission, and then I stepped back to admire my work.

Responding to work emails and replying to comments on my feeds, assuming they weren't trolls or spam, ate up the rest of my evening

By the time the clock struck ten, I'd fallen into bed. There was a new message notification on one of my social feeds, but I didn't click on the icon. It could wait, and I did *not* want to look exhausted during the wedding tomorrow. Maybe it was vain, but this was going to be the first time Rick saw me all dressed up, and after all, I was only human.

He was going to be in a fucking *tux*.

I had to bring my A Game.

* * *

On Saturday, I took a ridiculously long time getting ready. Longer than I'd spent for ages.

Of course, when Seb and I had first started dating. I'd made plenty of effort, and every time we'd gone out for dinner subsequently. I was no slouch; I wore heels and a pretty dress, for myself as much as for Sebastian.

But this was my first *proper* date with Rick. I knew now, more than ever, that what was growing between us wasn't throwaway.

I'd wanted to see where it went before our first kiss, and now, somehow only days later, I still wanted that, only *more*. So much more.

I felt such a pull towards him. Did it have to be a rebound? Was every new relationship begun on the heels of a broken one doomed?

No, I couldn't believe that.

Especially not of us.

I felt such a pull to Rick. He was kind, thoughtful, smart, funny. Heart as big as the state he lived in. The exterior package didn't hurt either. He'd helped me without a thought for himself, several times.

I very, very carefully boxed up the wedding cake. Cathy's ideas and my execution had resulted in a beautiful, silver-gray three tier cake. The purple hearts I'd hand-stamped with Cathy and her groom's initials fluttered over the cake like butterflies. The top was bare for the cake topper the bride had commissioned separately.

That done, I checked my creation for even the tiniest imperfections, found none, and got to work doing my make-up.

Once my face was done, no small feat when my hands shook a little from nerves, I stepped into the dress borrowed from Jenny. The silky fabric clung in all the right places and skimmed over others, the color enhancing the darkness of my hair, and also somehow warming my pale-olive skin rather than washing it out.

Rays of sunshine through the bedroom blinds caught on a couple of the gold thread stars, making them twinkle like the rarest of gems.

It was like wearing spun magic.

I texted a picture to Emma, and then Jenny.

Jenny: RIP my brother.

Emma: Man's gonna swallow his tongue. Hot babe alert.

I asked Jenny how she was feeling. She replied that she was well enough to come to the wedding, and that she was waiting until the last minute to wrangle Toby into his little outfit in case he had an accident "from either end" (her words).

I checked my make-up, slipped my feet into the one pair of

dressy-ish shoes I'd packed, and fluffed my hair just as Rick's knock sounded at the door.

He was sin on two legs, devastating in black and white, the lines of the tuxedo perfectly cut to accentuate his frame. He'd left the neck of the shirt open two buttons and a triangle of tanned skin and a curl of chest hair peeked out, the dark blond curls flirting with his dog-tags chain.

The strong sunshine–Cathy was very lucky with the weather, although I supposed rain was less of a risk outside Europe–touched the copper in his golden hair. It was swept off his face, giving me a chance to sigh over his Hollywood-level bone structure.

He'd shaved, showing off that amazing jawline. His gaze held mine for a long, hot second, and I watched his chest rise and fall as he took a deep breath.

A bronze star hanging from a red and blue shield was pinned to his suit jacket.

"Maddie. You look–wow." He shook his head, bit his lip, and he was adorable. "I'm sorry I haven't got any better words. Wow. That dress is Jenny's, isn't it? It looks totally different on you."

"Well, thank God for that."

He chuckled. "I... You look beautiful. Do we have to go to the wedding early? Can the cake just arrive a little late?"

I grinned. "No, and please know that I say this with *immense* reluctance, the cake *cannot* be late. Especially because it's your cousin who's getting married. You look fantastic, Rick."

His smile reached his eyes and warmed them. "Thanks. Been a while since I got dressed up all fancy like this. My razor didn't know what hit it this mornin'."

I stepped out on to the porch, lifted my face for his kiss. When we parted, I said, "While you look *super* handsome like this, I hope you give shaving a rest after today. I like feeling the scrape of your stubble on my lips. And other places."

He closed his eyes, obviously summoning inner reserves. "It's *real* early to try'n kill me off like this."

I pulled him down for a long kiss. "Maybe we can leave the wedding early."

His hands slid down to my hips. "I'd say there's a hundred percent chance of that." He gave me one more kiss, his tongue tangling with mine for a hot second, and then he pulled back, resting his forehead against mine. "This dress looks stunnin' on you, Maddie. The only place I think it'll look better is on my bedroom floor, while I take my sweet time making you forget how to say anythin' but my name."

My pulse spiked. "Rick," I breathed.

He smiled. "Turnabout is fair play. C'mon. Let's get this cake loaded into the truck."

It took both of us to carry it. Rick settled the box in the footwell of the back seats, and packed it with old carpentry sheets, rags and blankets to keep it steady.

"I'll drive two miles an hour."

"Good thing we're leaving early, then."

I couldn't stop looking at him as he drove us up to the ranch. He was a walking advert for sex, basically. I'm not ashamed to say I kept my hand on his leg the entire drive, just to feel connected to him.

I was in full helpless teenage girl crush-lust mode.

We talked about everyday things as he drove.

"Honestly, Maddie, it makes this fuckin' noise at a pitch you can't ignore, and there don't seem to be an off button. He loves it," he described a new toy of Toby's, a gift from Rick. He told me about the bedframe Rick had sent me a picture of, and I shared the fact that all my bakes had sold out each time I'd put them in *Cake Away*.

"That's amazing, Maddie!" he cheered, and the happiness on his face, *for me,* filled me with pure joy.

I was *thrilled* with the results of my little test.

I wondered how I'd feel when I went back to being one baker in a million in London.

The thought of being back sent a little pang through me. I missed my home city, but I thought I might miss Rick more...

The florists had already arrived at the barn when we parked, and they were building a gorgeous flower arch over the big barn doors. I breathed in and smelled lavender and roses. The arrangement looked worthy of any magazine cover.

Rick and I carefully carried the boxed cake in through the open barn doors and set it on the table, which was exactly where Cathy said it would be, draped in a purple cloth.

At the head of the room, more florists were constructing two pillars of lavender, roses and greenery where the couple would say their vows.

With Rick's help, I carefully lifted the three-tiered cake out of the enormous box. It looked fantastic, all shimmery gray and dark purple.

One of the florists approached with a circle of lavender and eucalyptus, and roses. "For the top tier. And here's the cake topper."

"Thanks." I settled it on with the utmost care, then added the delicate clay polymer topper, and snapped some photos.

"It's gorgeous work, Maddie," Rick said softly, his appreciation filling me with warm, happy pride .

When I locked my phone screen, I saw the notification of the message I earlier ignored, deciding not to distract myself from how much I wanted to enjoy today.

My time was running out here, after all.

"Cake looks great."

I turned from the cake table to see Ralph, Rick's cousin, walking towards us, resplendent his robust form all clean lines in immaculate black tie, his hair neatly combed, beard trimmed into a neat goatee, a sprig of lavender and a rose tucked into his buttonhole.

He offered Rick the same flowers on a little pin. "Here you go, cuz."

"You didn't tell me you were in the wedding!" I said to Rick.

He shrugged. "I'm not. I'm just doin' a reading."

"You didn't tell me that, either!"

He ducked his head, looking little-boy-shy. "Public speaking ain't my forte, darlin'. Still not convinced I won't make a fool of myself."

I reached for his hand and squeezed it. "You won't. And hey, if you do, you'll look so handsome doing it, that no one will care."

Rick chuckled and squeezed my hand back. "I guess there's that. Ralph, can we do anythin' for you?"

"Nah. I don't think so. We got at least fifteen minutes before guests arrive, an' that's if they're hella early. Feel free to explore the gardens. They're real pretty."

I agreed that they were, and was about to congratulate Ralph on his choice of venue when one of the florists snagged his attention for something, and he gave us a distracted goodbye.

"Garden?" Rick asked. "Gotta take every chance I get to have that dress alone."

"Oh, sweetie, I don't think it'll fit you."

He laughed. "Smartass."

We walked through the manicured gardens that surrounded the barn and curved around its big back doors at the head of the building, positioned so they would open behind where the bride and groom said their vows. What a gorgeous backdrop.

"Swing?" I asked. "We've got to go on it before everyone arrives. We'll never get a look in afterwards."

"Sure."

I led him towards it and we sat down together. The wood was warm from the sun, and smooth, and Rick curled his arm around me. The bright sunshine kissed the water fountain and the flowers and made everything look so happy.

I reached for my little purse. "Can we take a photo?" The only things I'd taken pictures of so far were cakes, it seemed. I could have been taking pictures of Rick this whole time! I *couldn't* pass up the chance now. Not with how he looked in the tux.

After all, maybe the pictures would be all I'd have left after I flew home.

The thought made me unbearably sad, and I pushed it away.

"'Course we can."

I passed him my phone after opening the camera app and flipping the viewfinder to face us. "You take it. Your arm is longer." I unashamedly snuggled against him as he positioned the phone.

"Done. I took a few. You wanna see if they're okay? Jenny always wants to look."

"Nope. I'll enjoy them later." I clicked the screen off and dropped it back into my bag. "Thank you, so much, for taking me as your date. I love weddings. And I get to be with *you* when you look like *this.*"

"Well, lap it up. I'll be back to normal tomorrow."

"Lucky me, because I love that look, too."

"No accountin' for taste, I guess."

I snorted, and settled next him as he pushed off the ground with one foot, sending the swing into a slow rock. "Stop. You're objectively gorgeous and you know it."

I felt him smile against my hair.

We swung back and forth for a few moments, my head pillowed in the crook of his shoulder.

I lifted my hand to gently stroke the pad of my finger over the little bronze star pinned to his suit jacket. "How did you get this?"

He cleared his throat, and I felt his thumb stroke up and down my arm. "Meritorious service in a combat zone."

"You were very brave?"

He nodded. "Yeah, that's about the size of it, although, when something needs to be done, bravery doesn't come into it. You gotta get it done. My unit was transporting some civilians to Kabul airport. We got ambushed. Not an unusual occurrence, but things had been quiet for a while, so we were hoping this would be an easy run. We defended the civilians, but some of my guys got wounded in the crossfire. Mack, from my unit, covered me while I pulled some of the soldiers into the safety of our Humvee, and then I went back out to shield the others as best I could with my own body until backup arrived."

A shiver ran through me. "That must have been terrifying."

"I was in charge at the time while our CO recovered. It was my job to protect them," he explained.

The sunshine glinted off the medal. "I'm glad they honored you with this."

He kissed my hair again. "Feels weird to wear the dress uniform, but I do if people specify it for stuff like this. Weddings," he clarified. "But, it's nice to pin this on if I wear a suit. Makes me remember the good times as well as the bad times. The camaraderie, all the jokes. The heat, goddamn, the heat over there. And then after, where there was less fighting and more humanitarian stuff. Evacuating people. Helping with medical aid. I'm glad I did it. All of it. Met some amazin' people. A few I still keep in touch with."

I slid my arm under his and entwined our fingers. I didn't say that I was glad he'd *stopped* doing it, because if he was still serving, we'd never have met.

It was a selfish thing to think, but it went through my head anyway.

In a few days, I would have to leave, and everything would change.

"Rick?"

"Hmmm?"

I tilted my head up, and he shifted back so our eyes could meet.

"I feel like our time is running out so fast."

He cupped my cheek, and stroked his thumb along my jaw, his touch gentle as the kiss of a butterfly's wings. "I know."

"I don't know what to do."

His gaze was soft. "Do you have to have all the answers right now?"

I laughed weakly. "It'd be easier if I did."

Rick drew me close again and pressed a kiss to my forehead. "Maddie, I ain't gonna make suggestions as to what you should or shouldn't do. From what you told me in the diner, you've had a gut full of that."

My heart squeezed. "Thank you. I have."

He continued, the timbre of his voice intimate, compelling. "Instead, I'll tell you that I want to spend as much time as possible with you while you're still this side of the Atlantic, and that I wanna see you *after* you go back to England, too."

My breath caught. I'd dreamed of him saying it, but hearing him say it was *top tier fantasy.*

"And," he added, "what you do with that information is up to you."

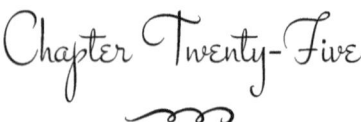

Chapter Twenty-Five

It was a gorgeous wedding.

The string quartet played *Canon in D* as Cathy walked up the aisle on her father's arm. Her fifties style dress hit her mid-calf, the tulle skirt like a confection of spun sugar and lace. A lavender and rose crown haloed her hair.

I grinned from my seat next to Rick as Ralph had to snag his handkerchief to wipe away a tear. Someone behind me, also watching, sighed in a very romantic way.

Rick squeezed my hand and got up when the officiant announced him. His reading was a passage from a novel, about the rush of first love giving way to something deeper, lasting, with roots.

He held my gaze as he spoke about roots growing underground. Despite his earlier shyness, he spoke eloquently, and pride for him made my heart grow two sizes. As I listened, I enjoyed an uninterrupted excuse to drink him in. The broad set of his shoulders, the way an unruly lock of his hair curled over his forehead, and how he made me feel.

He was beautiful, and I could hardly believe that until I flew home, he was *mine.*

I wanted to get him alone so badly.

Ralph and Cathy's vows were handwritten and heartfelt. Ralph's son, the one in the little league, stood halfway through, and Cathy made vows to him, too.

I cried.

Everything inside me warmed as they promised their lives to each other. Ralph made the best heart eyes I had ever seen at his bride.

I wondered briefly what my wedding to Seb would have been like. It was true that he had expensive taste, but, growing up working class, I hadn't expected a big fancy wedding.

In fact, the only part of the wedding I had given much thought at all to was the cake.

Maybe that said more about our relationship than I realized.

After the initial sorrow had subsided, after I'd come down from the adrenaline high of our fight and got over my anger, I'd been left with a feeling of... nothing. I should have been more upset, or, I *expected* to have been more upset.

Maybe what I'd loved most about Seb was that he'd appeared to support my dream and he didn't get in the way. I was so delighted that he'd been willing to work around my baking schedule that maybe I'd ignored the other stuff, like *how he was as a person.*

How he always chose where to eat out, and never asked what I wanted.

How he sometimes picked out clothes for me. *This suits your shape better* or *cutesy sundresses are for younger women.* Had that been genuine advice, or a control thing?

How had I not noticed?

I hadn't had the *time* to notice.

The pace here was slower. Okay, it had been a very busy time after Aunt Laurie had broken her arm, but until then, commuting with my feet had been refreshing.

Seeing people eat my food and love it was amazing instant gratification.

I sighed, and pushed the introspection aside, cradling Rick's hand as he stroked the pad of his thumb along the edge of mine.

Three rows of seats ahead, the officiant pronounced Ralph and Cathy man and wife, and we all stood and applauded. The flash of cameras filled the large barn space as people snapped photos.

The officiant's assistant opened the big barn doors behind the flower pillars and led the happy couple to a small, ornate wooden table to sign the marriage certificate. Rick and a woman who looked like Cathy but with shorter hair witnessed, and then the officiant asked us all to line up outside the big open doors while one of the bridesmaids passed out rose petal confetti in little brown craft paper cones.

After we showered them in confetti and posed for pictures in the beautiful garden, Ralph and Cathy were swept away by their photographer for intimate shots, and a couple of immaculately dressed servers appeared almost out of nowhere and circulated with little bronze trays of beautifully arranged canapes and tall, skinny glasses of fizz.

I took one just as Jenny emerged from the crowd and almost knocked me off balance with a huge hug.

"Maddie!"

I had never heard her voice so scratchy. "How are you feeling?" I embraced her, delighted to see her up and about.

"Like a wet towel that's been wrung out too many times, but, I've stopped sneezing and I'm here. Mom's got Toby. You look gorgeous!"

"So do you!" I stepped back to look at her. She wore a peach wrap dress with a flared skirt and her hair had been curled at the ends.

"Thanks." She blushed, then moved to hug Rick. "Clean up nice, Ricky."

He scowled. "Don't call me that."

"You love it."

I laughed, just as behind me, an older man announced, "You look good, son! Clean u-up well."

When I turned, I was faced with a man with Rick's eyes and a large hook nose. He leaned heavily on a walking stick, but his face was all mischief, taking years off his age.

Rick cleared his throat. "Maddie, this is my father, Bill Callahan. Dad, this is Maddie."

"The f-famous Maddie!" Bill enthused, offering me his free hand. I shook it and glanced at Rick.

A blush had crept up his neck. A *blush!*

"It's so nice to meet you, Mr. Callahan."

"C-call me Bill. Did you make the cake in there?" He nodded towards the barn "It's wonderful."

"I did. And thank you." I *really* wanted to ask him what Rick had said about me, but that wasn't appropriate, was it? *Especially* when Rick looked so embarrassed. That made me want to ask more.

My stomach was full of butterflies. Rick had talked to his parents about me. I mean, I should have guessed that when he invited me to the wedding, but even so, we'd known each other for only a couple of weeks.

That he'd mentioned me to his parents cemented the fact that it wasn't just me who felt this. It wasn't just me who wanted us to be something more than a whirlwind holiday romance.

I want to see where this goes, Maddie. I replayed his words in my head.

Yeah. I wanted to see where it went. For as long as it went. So what if there was an ocean between us? People had surmounted bigger obstacles.

"I'm looking forward to t-trying it later." As a server passed Bill, he asked me to snag a couple of glasses. When I handed him one, he grinned. "Cheers."

"Cheers."

We clinked glasses, and then Bill turned to Jenny and said something about Toby being a fine little man in his tiny suit.

I noticed Rick watch his father with warmth and concern.

"You okay?" I asked, taking his hand.

He nodded. "Yeah. It's just that he looks old, you know? When did he get old?"

I looped my arm through his. "I feel that about my parents sometimes. They're not allowed to be fallible, are they? It's horrible."

"Exactly. They're always there. He's always been there. When I was deployed for months, a year or even more, at a time, he was always *there*. Even if he was a royal pain in the *ass* when I was helpin' out with the business while I was on leave... and then when I thought he might not be...."

His eyes closed briefly. "I was four months from the end of my current tour when my CO gave me the message. My dad had a stroke. He was stable, but very unwell. When I finally got out and went home, Dad couldn't speak that well, and he still has a stutter."

Rick's gaze was far away as he relived what must have been a scary time for them all.

"Jenny was there too, staying in the house we grew up in, with Toby. Her *asshole* boyfriend had made some ridiculous demands, so she'd dumped his ass and came back here. Toby was so young, and she was barely coping." He paused, shaking his head eyes as he recounted the memories. "I decided not to go back. They're my family. They needed me, and I'd done what I joined the Army to do. See new places, experience life outside this little town."

I reached to press a kiss to his cheek. "Not everyone would've done that."

"Maybe, but it was the right thing to do. I got my shit out of the shoebox apartment I kept in Louisville for between tours, bought the house, and Jenny and Toby moved in." He watched as a gray-haired woman wearing a beautiful ankle-length dark blue dress approached with Toby in her arms. "Hey, Mom."

The woman turned, looked up and smiled. "Rick. Come here and kiss your mother."

Rick rolled his eyes but did as he was told, keeping hold of my hand so I went with him. "Maddie, my mother, Edith. Mom, this is Maddie."

Edith shifted Toby to her shoulder, and offered me a delicate hand sparkling with thin silver rings. "It's so nice to meet you. Rick has talked about you. I was *very* excited to hear he had met someone."

"Thanks, Mom," Rick murmured.

"It's nice to meet you, too," I enthused, truthfully. "Rick has your smile."

She grinned, and yeah, they had the same crooked little tilt to the left. "I gave him his good looks, too, don't you know."

Toby chose that moment to say, "No, no, no, Gamma." We all laughed at the timing.

"That's right, little man," Rick said, reaching for his nephew. "I got these looks all by myself. Though the body is courtesy of Uncle Sam."

I couldn't wait to see his body properly. Spend as long as I wanted mapping out every inch with my fingers and mouth. Trail my tongue along the serpent tattoo under his ribs.

Tonight.

The rest of the wedding passed in a happy blur.

As other people started to join the happy couple on the

dance floor once they cut the cake, I felt Rick move behind me, his hand settling on my hip.

"You wanna get out of here?" he whispered next to my ear.

"You just want an excuse not to dance."

He chuckled. "Guilty as charged, but the kind of *dancing* I wanna do isn't something that should be done in public. So, what do ya say?"

I shivered. "Yes, yes, I do very much want to get out of here."

We said our goodbyes. I gave Toby a high five, and it was the cutest thing ever, especially his confused face when I tapped his open palm with mine.

"Go get him, tiger," Jenny snickered in a whisper.

I knew she and Toby were staying at her parents' house tonight. Rick and I would be *alone.*

Cathy gave me permission to use the cake pictures wherever I wanted when we said goodbye to her. "I'll try to make sure you get a piece wrapped up!" she promised.

Rick had stuck with water after his initial glass of champagne, so he drove us back. Through the truck's open window, the oranges and golds of sunset kissed his profile. He was *gorgeous*, and I was head over heels.

"You sure 'bout this?" Rick asked as he pulled up outside the front of the house. "We can go to bed separately. There's no pressure here."

I smoothed my palm over his thigh. "I want to, Rick. Actually, what I really want is to get into bed with you tonight, and stay there until I have to fly home."

His gaze went hot as he looked at me, and then he pulled me into a deep, searing kiss. I tilted my head and opened for him, and he ravished my mouth. I lost myself in the constant wave of desire that never seemed to be quelled. Not when he was near.

"Well, let's see what we can do about that," he murmured when we parted. "We've got all Sunday, don't we?"

I pressed my legs together. God. He'd be lucky if I let him get into the house before I tore the tux off him.

He got out of the driver's side door and came to open the passenger side.

It was only when I got out and turned towards the path to Rick's house, that I saw Sebastian sitting on Jess' porch.

Chapter Twenty-Six

He looked tired. He probably was. Even without the delay, my journey here had been *very* long.

"Is that him?" Rick asked. His hand settled at the small of my back, comforting. The light touch told me he wouldn't do anything without my say so.

"Yes. It's him."

Rick had a little sound in his throat, a half murmur, half growl.

"I can handle it," I reassured him, looking up at him. "You can go inside, if you want."

"Not a chance, darlin'. I'm with you," Rick said softly.

"Okay, then."

No point in pretending I hadn't just come back from a date with Rick, so I took his hand and we walked toward Seb.

My ex-fiancé's glare dropped to our joined hands and then snapped back up to my face.

It was odd, seeing him here. He almost belonged in another life.

I'd been here less than three weeks, but so much had happened that it felt like longer.

I looked at Seb and remembered our fight before I flew here, and the memory made me sad, but no longer in that gut-wrenching way it had at the time.

I'd fallen for him for the wrong reasons. I was so happy that he seemed to support me that I'd overlooked other things, like how his "support" was just a kind of control.

Once he had me where he wanted me, he'd betrayed my trust, and pissed all over my attempt at trying to secure my own shop space.

"Hi," he began uncertainly, standing up.

It was so unlike him. He was normally smooth. Polished. He just looked sad, standing here on my cousin's porch.

"What are you doing here?"

His mouth turned down. "You didn't answer my calls."

"And you didn't think perhaps there was a *reason* for that?" I demanded, keeping my voice low.

His gaze turned belligerent as he regarded Rick again, wariness playing over his features. "Who's this?"

"Seb, this is Rick Callahan. Rick, Seb."

Seb's eyes flicked to the medal pinned to Rick's jacket. "Pleasure," he said, automatically so polite, but the words sounded hollow.

Rick inclined his head slightly but did not speak.

"Is there somewhere we can go to talk?" Seb asked, looking at me.

I considered this for a moment.

And I thought, ire rising inside me: *Nope.* He obviously hadn't stopped to think about my feelings when he'd thrown that letter in the trash, so his meant less than nothing to me.

Even if it was just that one, that was enough for me to know who he was, inside.

I let go of Rick's hand and folded my arms over my chest. "Anything you have to say, you can say in front of Rick," I decided.

Seb went as pale as the white shirt he wore. "You can't be serious."

"I am, though. As serious as you were when you binned that letter. Did you stop and think about it, for *any* amount of time?"

The look on his face turned ice cold. "I did it for *you*. It was the wrong time—"

"The wrong time for *you!*" I thundered, unable to keep quiet any longer. "I didn't know you were planning for me to basically shut down my business and have babies with you! We'd never discussed it properly, and some of that is on me. With time to think on it, we weren't a good fit then, and we aren't now."

"You cannot be serious," he muttered, again.

"You didn't have the *right* to decide what I should do with my life, Sebastian."

"All you did was work," he countered.

He had a point. I nodded stiffly. "But I worked a lot when we met, *and* when you proposed. You knew about my life."

He didn't say anything, so I kept going. "You didn't think to talk it through with me, like a normal person?"

I could feel Rick behind me, and knowing he was there for me, not interrupting, but instead offering silent support, bolstered me.

Seb shifted awkwardly on the porch. "I'd really prefer it if we talked inside. What will people think?"

"I don't care what they think," I shot back, meaning it.

I had friends in this town, and family, who would have my back, and gave me strength. I didn't need to worry about what they thought. They would have my best interests in mind.

Sebastian smiled, but it wasn't a nice smile. "Of course you don't. That's why you've hooked up with the first guy you found when you landed."

Rick shifted to stand next to me, folding his arms over his

chest. He widened his stance in a very military way, and I expected that the stern, *you wanna say that again* look on his face, combined with his height and the very prominent medal on his jacket, might've made a younger man wet his pants.

"Care to repeat that?" Rick grunted.

Sebastian took a breath, and I thought he was going to do the smart thing and back down.

But apparently, he hadn't flown all this way to do the smart thing, because he ignored Rick and continued, to me, "Maddie, think about it. My family has *money*. We can support you. Guide you to the right people to help you. That's what I was trying to tell you."

"Your money didn't matter to me!" I hissed. "I thought you were being generous when you treated me to fancy dinners, took me to those lovely wine bars. I didn't realize you were trying to buy control over me."

The face I had once thought so kind and handsome darkened as he frowned at me. "Think about this, Maddie. My family knows a lot of people. We can help make your life easy." His lips twisted. "Or, we can *suggest* to those people that perhaps your venture wouldn't be a good thing to promote. It's your choice."

My mouth fell open at his *ridiculous* insinuation. Sure, his family were wealthy but was he seriously threatening that he'd block my access to having a little shop or market presence if I didn't hop back on the plane with him?

This was absurd.

"It's embarrassing, Madeline," Seb added. "Me having to come out here. I offered you everything."

"No, you didn't. You took me out to places *you* liked, and I was so happy to have met someone who didn't mind me having my own, admittedly very time-consuming, career, that I didn't look too deeply into it. I should have stopped to think. I was with you because I was flattered, and okay, you deserved more than that. I wish I had paid more attention. That's on me."

But I deserved more, too. I deserved not to betrayed like this.

The feel of Rick beside me, his shoulder pressed warm against mine, gave me the extra little boost to add, "But now I know what I want, and we're done, Sebastian."

His features contorted. He was a man I didn't recognize now.

"Fine. Have it your way. We'll see how you feel when you're back in London, struggling again to be seen, just another cake maker among all the rest. You'll regret it then, you ungrateful little bit—"

He didn't get the rest of the word out, because Rick surged forward and his fist slammed into Seb's jaw.

He toppled like a tree.

The lights went on in several houses across the street.

I lurched towards Sebastian's prone form, and then glanced back at Rick. "Oh my God, you punched him!"

"Yep." He winced, flexing his hand. "Not punched anyone in a real long time, as it turns out."

I spared a glance at the houses with lights on. "This may be talked about for some time."

Rick lifted a shoulder in a half shrug. "I was talked about for defendin' Jenny when she first moved back here, too. I'm happy to be talked about for standin' up for what's right, Maddie."

This man. I would have moved to kiss him, but then Sebastian moaned at our feet.

"We should get him inside. He might have a concussion!"

Rick snorted. "His head seems a little too hard for that."

But he helped me carry Sebastian into Jess' house, anyway.

* * *

Seb wasn't out for long. He protested weakly at being carried into the house and set on the sofa. I dragged his suitcase inside, too.

I fetched a damp cloth from the kitchen, and laid it on his head.

"Unnf," he said. "Head hurts."

"You'll live."

He closed his eyes.

Rick loomed in the doorway to the living room, arms folded, shoulder butted up against the doorjamb. "Should I stay?"

I glanced over at Seb. Over a fortnight's distance now made me wonder what I'd seen in him, besides the fact that he'd pursued me, and I'd been too wrapped up in my business to look for red flags.

"I'll be fine. I'm in no physical danger from him, Rick."

"Yeah. I get that." He glowered at the prone man on the sofa. "Holler if you need me. I'm just next door."

"I will." I squeezed his bicep. "Still on for tomorrow?"

"Hell, yeah," he said, gazing down at me, his eyes soft like I'd hung the moon. "Wild horses couldn't drag me away from you, Maddie."

I lifted my face for his kiss and he obliged. When we parted, I walked him to the front door, kissed him again, reveling in the feel of his long, broad body against mine.

"See you tomorrow," I promised.

He smiled against my mouth, kissed me some more, and I sank into him.

I had thought about asking him to stay, but it didn't feel right with Seb here. And, I couldn't in good conscience go next door and leave my ex-fiancé in my cousin's house. With a potential head injury.

I watched Rick walk over to his house, appreciating the

line of his shoulders in the suit jacket, and I didn't bother to resist the urge to sigh girlishly.

When I closed the door, Seb was sitting up.

"How's the head?"

He shrugged.

"Are you hungry? You flew a long way."

He speared his hands through his hair. "Food would be nice."

He scrolled through something on his phone while I made scrambled eggs and tinned corned beef with a side of bread and butter. I made coffee, too. When I set it all down at the tiny table, he came over, sat, and looked at me through sad eyes.

"Thanks."

I wrapped my hands around the mug. "You're welcome."

He started to eat mechanically, then smiled around his fork. "These are really good. You always could find a way to make eggs sort of magic."

He ate in silence for a little while, while I tried not to think about the fact that I could be naked under Rick right now.

"I'm sorry I called you a bitch," Sebastian said at length.

I smiled wryly. "Well, technically you didn't get the full word out before Rick punched you."

He winced. "I think I probably deserved it. I do love you, Maddie. I genuinely wanted to help you. We could get our family established, and then you could make a proper go of the baking thing."

The way he said *the baking thing* made me see red. "All this time, I thought you not saying anything *against* my business meant you supported it. But actually, you were biding your time until you could maneuver me into what you wanted me to be." I was angry, but my words came out soft and sad. "I meant what I said earlier. I take some responsibility for what happened. But it's over, Seb. I don't want to see you again."

His shoulders slumped. He looked defeated.

"I'd even made appointments at some wedding venues," he said eventually.

"Without even speaking to me? There you go again, just choosing stuff without asking if I want to be involved!" I heard my voice rising and clamped my mouth shut. Why was I engaging? I didn't want to be with him anymore.

Looking at him, sitting there, tired and sad, I felt...

A big fat nothing.

"We're done." I pushed my chair back. "You can stay tonight. But tomorrow, you need to either be flying home, or staying elsewhere."

And I took myself upstairs to the bedroom, shutting the door tight.

Chapter Twenty-Seven

In the morning, I woke wondering if I'd still find Seb downstairs.

Rick and I had texted on and off for a couple of hours after yesterday evening's events, and he'd told me to call him if I needed him, for anything, whatever the hour.

Each one of his messages had filled me with warmth, and I'd reassured him that I really was fine before recording and sending a "good night, I wish I could tuck you in myself" voice note.

He'd sent a husky-voiced one back. "You have no idea how much I want that."

When I got downstairs, I saw that a folded piece of paper with my name on it in front of the coffee maker.

I yawned hugely as I opened it to see a couple of lines of Seb's handwriting.

Maddie,

Flight leaves tomorrow at 2pm. I'm going to see a little of Louisville until then.

If you change your mind, call me.

Seb

I was not going to call him.

The door to that part of my life was firmly shut, never to be re-opened, I thought with relief, texting Rick to let him know Sebastian no longer occupied my house.

He replied with *Good. Let me know if you want to talk. Got my support group this morning, but have a little time before.*

I assured him I was happy. I wouldn't get in the way of his veterans' group. Besides, Lara had texted to see if I wanted to catch up over a coffee. I met her at the window-service coffee part of the grocer's on Otter Street and then we walked to the lake with our bagels and drinks.

We laughed about the quirks of Asian parents and she told me how much she loved my recent videos.

I promised myself I'd keep in more regular contact with her when I got home. Time zones sucked, but they ultimately weren't a barrier to friendship, unless you let them be.

When I got back, I made another batch of *ang pao* cookies. They would usually only be made on Lunar New Year or on the Autumn Festival, but they were one of the most requested orders from my online store, and while I was here, I wanted to show off. I parcelled up two to bring over to Rick's place later, and sealed the rest in containers to keep them fresh for the bakery tomorrow.

My post of Cathy's wedding cake was attracting steady attention. It wasn't my favourite cake I had made, but considering it'd been short notice *and* I had used someone else's oven, I was very proud of the results.

I spent the rest of the time replying to the nicer comments on social channels, having a bath, and painting my nails a red that I'd found in Jess' bathroom cabinet. It seemed appropriate since this evening I was going to seduce and be seduced.

Jenny was staying a second night at Edith and Bill's–thankfully.

I could hardly wait to get Rick alone. No more interruptions. I would personally bar the door.

* * *

Rick

Rick didn't really cook, but he was getting better at one-pot affairs like ham-fried rice, chicken pot pie, and the like.

And, if he did say so himself, he did a mean rare steak complete with hand cut chips. And of course there were omelets. No man could ruin a good omelet.

For Maddie, however, he wanted something a little more.

He cracked open one of the two cookbooks his mother had gifted him when he'd signed up to fight for Uncle Sam. Christ knew when she thought that he'd use them, but the gesture had struck him as sweet, if a little embarrassing. The colorful pages of one stared up at him now, inviting, but also unquestionably a challenge.

He settled for a classic—roast chicken with herby new potato mash and a side of honey-glazed carrots. The pictures made it look easy, but Rick knew better than to believe in the promise of good lighting and glossy photos. He remembered his mother's words. *The best advice I can give you is to read the recipe through at least twice.*

Good advice for any situation.

Grinning, he did so, imagining his mom's face if he told her he was preparing a roasted chicken for a woman. Maddie, no less. He expected his mom and Laurie had already gossiped about it, seeing as his parents loved *Cake Away*. Its rainbow cookies had a special place in his father's heart, and stomach.

As tempting as it was to text his mom and tell her that yes, he was serious about Maddie - the news she'd waited near a decade for - he didn't pick up the phone. No sense in opening a can of worms right now. He had carrots to peel, besides.

And, he didn't want to work his mom up into a lather if Maddie went home and didn't give him another thought.

His gut feeling was that they belonged together. He could tell she felt it too. The pull between them was like nothing he'd ever experienced before.

But, a little part of him still worried he was counting chickens before they'd hatched.

He worked methodically, enjoying himself. Pushed two halves of a lemon into the chicken cavity, shoved bunches of parsley and thyme in after them. Trussed the legs up, smoothed thyme-infused olive oil over the bird, and slid the loaded tray into the oven.

While the chicken cooked and the mouthwatering aroma of roasting meat filled the space, and with Jenny and Toby out at his parents' place, he tidied the small house until it was what he considered "man clean". Probably not magazine worthy, but perfectly fine for guests.

Rick didn't think himself a fussy man, but, thanks to his mom, and in no small part thanks to the Army, he couldn't leave mess lying around.

He smiled to himself, thinking of how she'd pinch his ear as a kid if he left his room cluttered day after day. He soon learned to avoid her iron grip by keeping his toys at least *near* the toy box.

She probably wouldn't let his age keep her from administering a good ear pinch now and again, he thought with a little grin.

When the timer pinged, he opened the oven and popped the carrots and potatoes in. The brief glimpse at the chicken boosted the fantastic aroma of roasting meat and thyme already circulating, and Rick thought he'd done pretty well.

Checking the clock, he dashed up to his bedroom and rifled through his limited wardrobe. He passed over what he typically wore for work. Many of his clothes were looking threadbare in places; fine for a carpenter, but not so much a man looking to impress an important woman.

He pulled out a button-down winter-sky-gray shirt, clean dark-wash jeans, and, after looking at himself in the mirror and running a hand over his hair, he called it good. The heavy stubble some people referred to as a beard was under control today, so he didn't shave. Besides, he had the slight notion that Maddie might dig it.

By the time Maddie's knock— he'd know it was her anywhere, that no-nonsense, somehow very British rap-rap-rap— sounded at the door, he had set out breadsticks with a garlicky dip, laid two places at the table his father had hand carved, and decanted white wine into a glass jug he'd unearthed from the pantry.

After looking at the table for a second, he headed into the garden, plucked some wildflowers and settled them into a mason jar he grabbed from under the sink.

He opened the door and just breathed her in.

Maddie looked refreshed, her eyes crinkling at the corners when she sent him a big, sunny smile, his favorite look on her.

She wore a plain hazelnut-brown dress that should have been utilitarian, but the almost lazy slash cut of the neckline and the clingy, puff-sleeved jersey fabric instead whispered "let's play."

Boy, did he want to.

The smooth fall of her midnight-black hair skimmed over her shoulders, and she wore thong sandals on her feet, toenails painted a deep rebel red.

God, he wanted her more than he wanted to breathe.

"Hey," he settled for saying, rather than, *I've made chicken, but how 'bout we have each other for dinner instead?*

"Hey yourself." Her gaze dipped down his body in an unashamedly appreciative once-over. He didn't mind a bit. Besides, they were beyond games now. She'd come for dinner and then she'd stay so he could explore every inch of her with his hands and then his mouth, and then his hands again.

He had to take a deep breath to will away his hard-on. It was tough.

"Come on in."

He closed the door behind her and heard her short intake of breath.

The overall effect of the set table was pretty and intimate. The wildflowers lent a splash of colour, and the slate table mats were understated, classic. The cutlery gleamed. He'd worked hard to prepare this meal, and its environs, and he was pleased with her reaction, because it mattered. *She* mattered.

"It's beautiful, Rick," she said softly.

"Southern hospitality at its best."

"You didn't have to go to all this trouble." She met his gaze, and hers was warm, her eyes dancing with happiness.

"I wanted to. C'mere." He held out his hand. She took it willingly, and he tugged her close, lifted her chin with one gentle hand so he could kiss her.

She tasted of hope and of promise, and he wanted to lose himself in her mouth. Who needed air? He could live off this compelling, vibrant, generous woman.

She made a small sound of pleasure against his lips and he nearly suggested forgoing dinner altogether.

But he'd worked at this, and he wanted to impress her.

She *deserved* to be treated like a fuckin' Queen.

He gave her one last, longing kiss, and then reluctantly pulled back.

"Sit." He pulled out a chair, and she folded that delectable body into it. "The chicken's about done, just needs to rest."

"It smells *divine*." She leaned back in the chair with a

relaxed sigh, took a breadstick and tapped it against her lips. It was a very particular shape and Rick forced himself not to think about other things of that shape which would look amazing near her lips. Specifically, a part of his body. "I haven't had a roast dinner since my mum cooked one a few months ago."

"Oh yeah?" Rick poured a measure of wine into the glasses. "It's a whole thing, ain't it? A roast dinner. Very British."

"*Very,* except my dad serves his with a pile of roasted garlic cloves, garlic bread *and* chili sauce, always has. He always complained about the lack of them if we went to a carvery, where they basically serve a conveyor belt of roast dinner. It made me feel *so* weird when we had friends over."

"Garlic bread, huh? And how do you feel about it now? Still embarrassed?"

She laughed. "Now, I feel that anyone who hasn't tried garlic bread dipped in my mum's beef gravy can't judge it until they have. I'm still not sold on the chili sauce, but I've always been a bit of a wimp when it comes to spice, much to my dad's disappointment."

Rick opened the oven to check the carrots. They could do with a few extra minutes, so he took the chicken out and lay it to rest on the stone trivet on the kitchen counter.

He watched out of the corner of his eye as Maddie nibbled on the breadstick with those soft, rosy lips.

Goddamn.

"Your mom good with spicy food?" Rick asked, to distract himself from thinking about the myriad of sexy things Maddie could do with her mouth.

"Some. She's got better since she met my dad. No choice," she laughed.

Rick started to carve the chicken into a dish. The scent wafted up, making his mouth water. He'd done well.

Maddie finished the breadstick and didn't take another. Her gaze was focused on him carving the chicken. "What about you? You like heat?"

He liked the heat between *them*.

Clearing his throat, he sliced more chicken. "If there's enough beer to take the sting away, sure." He smiled as a memory surfaced. "I remember when I was a teenager. Thought I was real hot shit, wanted to eat spicy food like my old man. He can probably still eat whole jalapenos. He's hardcore. Anyway, we'd had some kinda fight. I forget what it was about, and I wanted him to know I was all grown and I didn't need his advice."

Maddie chuckled. "What did you do?"

"I upended three tablespoons of habanero sauce on my dinner. *Fuck* me," he added, shaking his head. "Don't think I tasted anythin' for at least three days."

She sent him a warm smile. "You were a little tearaway as a kid, I bet."

"The *worst*. My mom despaired of me. Still does. Jenny's the golden girl in our family." Rick set the chicken he'd carved on to a beautiful slate serving plate, unearthed and cleaned especially for today.

He'd pulled out all the stops, wanting to show Maddie how much she'd come to mean to him.

* * *

Maddie

Chicken carved, Rick opened the oven again and slid out the carrots, parsnips and potatoes. Delicious steam wafted towards me, and I breathed in hungrily. Who knew that a man serving a simple home-cooked meal would be such a turn-on?

No man had ever just made me this simple, warm-hearted home fare. It was refreshing. Just like Rick.

Rather like Rick himself. He had not an ounce of artifice, he was honest, open, and he respected me. I pushed last night out of my mind, closing the door on that chapter of my life. I didn't plan on opening it again.

Today, I was dedicating all my time to Rick, and Rick only.

"It smells *so* good," I moaned.

Rick glanced over his shoulder. "Woman, don't be makin' those noises at me before we eat. I can't take it, and I don't want to waste this food."

I grinned, drawing my bottom lip between my teeth, and I felt *very* gratified when he followed the movement. "Sorry."

"You damn should be." But he was smiling, shaking his head as he removed the vegetables from the oven.

A few minutes later, he set a heavily loaded plate in front of me. Thinly sliced chicken, bathed in caramel-gold gravy, nestled in next to a mound of parsnips, carrots and golden, crisp potatoes.

I'd only eaten a very light lunch, and so my stomach practically sat up and begged.

"Rick. This looks *ridiculously* good."

He sat before his own plate. "Yeah? Well, let's hope it is. Roast chicken ain't one of the three things I do well. I got this recipe from a cookbook."

I lifted my glass. "Well, here's to you mining the rest of that book for ideas on what to cook for me."

He clinked my glass with his own.

I eagerly started on the food.

The wine, an oaked Chilean chardonnay, was a perfect foil for the meltingly tender poultry.

For a few moments, we ate in companionable silence. The flavors exploded on my tongue and I felt a pang for my home country and its frequent roast dinners.

"Rick, this is *delicious.*"

"Thanks."

"I mean it. Thank you. I haven't been cooked for, like this, I mean, by someone who isn't my mum, for a long time."

His brow furrowed as he sliced off a sliver of chicken. "Like this?"

I shrugged, thinking about how any time Seb cooked was a performance for others, and not for me.

"This is proper home food," I replied. "Made with love." I almost added, *not that we're in love of course, or that you love me,* but I decided to just stop there before I dug myself into a bottomless pit of awkwardness.

"That's a real shame, Maddie," he considered. "You deserve to be loved. Spoiled."

I luxuriated in his praise. As ever since the moment I'd met Rick, I was pulled into his orbit, unable and more importantly, unwilling, to break free. Everything about him dragged me closer, made me curious.

Made me *want.*

"So do you," I replied, brushing my hand over his leg under the table.

He rewarded me with a slow smile. The left side of his mouth ticked up before his smile spread, and it was sweet and sexy and unforgettable. *He* was unforgettable. "Well, lucky me, because you *have* spoiled me. I've tried so many new foods and cakes since you got here. It's about time I returned the favor."

I squeezed his leg warmly, and we went back to our food. I wanted to show this glorious dinner the proper attention.

When we were finished, Rick cleared the plates away. "You want dessert?"

I looked up at him, startled. "You made dessert?"

He held both hands up, palms facing me. "*Made* is a very strong word. I went to the Sureway on my drive back from my veteran support group and bought the best-looking tart I could find."

"Er, *second-best* if you please," I joked, and Rick narrowed his eyes at me until he got the joke and then he laughed out loud, and happiness on him was devastating. His laugh was deep and his eyes crinkled at the corners and he was *beautiful*.

"Funny," he said when he'd recovered.

"I try."

"I did have a quick look in the imported food section to see if they had scones, but they didn't, or, I didn't think they did," he said, his head in the fridge.

"Nah, they're normally freshly made. They'd be in the bakery section if they were anywhere. My mum and dad have full on arguments about whether scones and biscuits are the same thing. My dad says you only dip biscuits in tea, and my mum says biscuits are things you eat with gravy."

"Amen to that," Rick agreed, the tart in hand.

"I could never get on board with savoury biscuits."

He lifted a brow. "This from the woman who lives in a country where marmite and baked beans in that funky sauce exist."

"It's *surprisingly* good on toast."

"I'll pass, thanks." He eased the tart from its plastic prison and slid it on to a plate. "I'd rather be eating something like this."

He set it on the table between us and then turned to get forks.

This was so easy. It felt good and right and I wanted to sit here forever and never have to leave him, never have to step outside this warm, perfect bubble of whatever had grown between us. I wanted my life to just carry on from this point, and okay, it wouldn't always be this perfect, but I wanted *him*, and everything that entailed.

When I looked at him next he was watching me, an unreadable expression on his face. The room suddenly felt hot, the tension thick, as if we had both remembered, at the same time, what we'd begun in bed on Friday morning.

And what we were going to finish later.

"You're sure you want this?" he asked, and his voice had dropped half an octave.

I swallowed. I'd have to be an idiot not to realise that his question was loaded with more than an enquiry about the tart.

I wanted it, all right.

I wanted to eat it off him.

Almost without thinking, I stood up. My mouth felt dry, my head pleasantly heavy from the wine, the food, the company.

"I *do* want. I want you, Rick."

Chapter Twenty-Eight

Whip-fast, Rick rounded the table to stand before me, only a breath away from our faces touching.

Anticipation made me tremble a little as he cupped my cheek, stroking the pad of his thumb tenderly over my jaw and upwards. His touch sent tiny rivers of sensations flowing inside me, rivers that all led to the same sensitive, aching spot. When his thumb moved to my lips, caressing gently, my mouth seemed to open of its own accord. I heard myself sigh.

"More?" he whispered.

Helpless to do anything but nod, a low gasp escaped me when his lips replaced his hand, and the sweet flavour of him saturated me. He stroked his tongue over mine in a soft, sensual dance, and the rivers of sensations flooded my every sense.

He nipped my bottom lip playfully, and then his kisses moved down, dotting over my chin, down to my neck, where the gentle scrape of his jaw scruff rendered my skin super sensitive. As I giggled, a sound of excitement and joy, he captured my lips again, the kiss so tender that my heart bumped painfully in my chest.

As he returned to kissing my neck, his hand lifted to cup my breast, his thumb finding the already firm point of my nipple and teasing it to hardness through the soft fabric of my dress.

I strained towards him, only wanting more, more, more. The world and everything else but *us* fell away.

"Maddie," he bit out, and my name came off his lips like a curse and a prayer twined together.

The sound of his lust-rough voice set something loose in me. Maybe it was knowing that he seemed as conflicted by this tug-of-war attraction between us as I was, but it was enough to spur me into action.

I slid my hands into his hair, loving the feel of it, soft and thick, between my fingers. I pressed my mouth to his temple as he continued devouring my neck.

The sensations were divine, and I stopped thinking about what would happen when I got on a plane back to England. I let myself stop thinking at all and started to simply *feel*.

It seemed like Rick was going to take charge, and I-

I would let him.

I *wanted* him to.

And then I wanted to have *my* turn in charge, wanted to ride him until we were both exhausted.

And then rest until we could do it all again.

I arched into his hand as he used the other to pull me closer to him, closer still. With our bodies pressed together there was no mistaking the hard ridge in his jeans pressed to my lower belly. The heat of it, the want of it, made muscles deep inside me clench, over and over.

"Rick, oh, God!"

"Bed?" he murmured against my neck.

I fisted a hand in his hair for a moment. I should choose the bed. Upstairs, where people should have sex. Especially first time together sex.

But this was *Rick,* and I wanted to be memorable for him, in case... In case I didn't see him again after I flew home.

If I had my way, I *would* see him again.

But life had a way of spoiling things. So I would make the most of the now.

"No. Too impatient. Sofa."

He cursed against my neck. "You'll be the death of me, Maddie Liu. But what a way to go."

Almost without warning, he swung me up into his arms as if I weighed hardly a thing and carried me to the sofa. When he put me down gently, I yanked at his lapels until he collapsed on to me, that long, work-roughened, rangy body pressed deliciously atop mine.

I kept hold of his shirt and tugged his face down until our mouths met again, until our tongues tangled. I let Rick drink me in and gave as good as I got, savouring every taste, every new texture.

I wanted to kiss him forever and never, ever come up for air.

He buried his hands in my hair, and I took the opportunity to start on the buttons of his shirt. He'd looked delicious as sin when he'd opened the door to her, the shirt slightly open at the neck, exposing that tempting curve where his neck met his shoulders. His jeans hugged his hips like a lover.

I wanted my legs there tonight.

Almost unbearably impatient now, I tore open the last button and shoved the edges of the shirt aside, feasting on his bare chest with my fingers and palms. When I could endure it no more I broke the kiss and used my eyes, too, allowing myself a visual feast of a body sculpted by Army training and then kept fit by hard labour.

This view would live in my fantasies for some time to come.

I pushed the shirt down his shoulders, and it fell to the floor.

Rick raised a brow, his expression playful. "In a rush, darlin'?"

I grinned back, feeling light. "I'm simply someone who knows what she wants."

"And gets it?"

I slid a hand down his naked back to rest on his belt. "What does it look like to you?"

"It sure looks like you're gonna get it."

We smiled at each other for a second, perfectly in tune, and Rick dipped his head to press a row of kisses along the column of my neck. I reveled in the tingle of his scruffy jaw against my skin, spiky on smooth.

Rick paused at the neck of my jersey dress, his lips skating the line where the soft fabric met my skin. I shivered in anticipation.

"Yes?" he asked, so softly I almost thought I'd imagined it.

"Yes," I whispered back.

Rick eased down the stretchy neck of my dress, inch by hot inch, his lips following the dark material.

"Faster," I whispered.

"I don't think so," he murmured, his breath tickling my skin. "Feels like I've waited forever for this, honey. I want it to last. Want to take my time."

I started to complain, and then he sucked my nipple into his mouth, fabric and all, and my brain simply short-circuited.

The heat of his mouth, the barely-there scrape of his teeth, along with the insistent press of his body on top of mine, made my back arch. I pressed myself against him, wanting more, more, closer, hotter, harder.

I didn't recognise the sultry keen of my own voice as I demanded *more*.

Rick tugged my dress all the way down, flipped open the

front clasp of my bra, and tasted me without barriers. The warm friction of his tongue on my hardened nipple made my cry out.

Later, I would realize that I'd never been this uninhibited with Seb. It just hadn't felt *right* the way this did.

The way *Rick* did.

He gave similar attention to my other breast, and the tickle of his gentle-rough stubble with the soft stroke of his tongue sent my internal muscles into a frenzy of clenching desperately around nothing. I bucked against him, wanting more, *now*.

"You're making it damn hard for me to take my time with you," he groused against the curve of my breast.

"Then don't." I clutched at his hair. The length of him pressed up between my legs, hard where I was soft. "We have all night together, Rick."

He lifted his head and raised a brow, and in his face, I saw that hint of southern swagger that I couldn't help but lust after. "You sure about this?"

* * *

Rick

"Yes. Oh, my *God*, yes. A thousand times yes."

Maddie met his gaze for a hot second, and then she slid her hands between their bodies and grasped the hem of her jersey dress, pulling it up and over her head. Her bra followed, whispering to the floor, instantly forgotten.

She was a goddess on a faded gray couch. Her silky fall of raven hair haloed a beautiful face crowned with a mouth made for sin.

As she looked at him through almond-shaped eyes half-closed with desire, he thought he'd never had a more perfect moment.

Or a more perfect woman.

His heart beat hard in his chest, and he felt uncharacteristically, fearfully, sentimental.

He'd had relationships, of course. But his career hadn't really allowed for permanence and he hadn't minded that. His partners had been aware, happy with brief relationships themselves.

When he'd decided not to re-enlist but instead to stay and help out his family, it'd crossed his mind that maybe he should settle down. Try to find the right woman.

He hadn't expected her to be sleeping at Louisville airport, all silky hair, sad eyes, and gorgeous.

She'd be leaving soon. A plane would take her thousands of miles away.

She wouldn't be here to laugh with, touch, hold.

His eyes burned, and he swallowed as the rush of something that felt a hell of a lot like *love* reared its head in his chest.

"Maddie, I—"

She pressed a gentle hand to his lips. "No talking. No thinking. Just.... This."

He could see her point. They'd have plenty of time for melancholy when she was on the other side of the ocean.

"Yes, ma'am."

He captured her mouth again, delighting in the sweet taste of her, and how easily she gave to him, how easily those walls dropped down. He wanted to sink into her and never, ever come up for air.

They had tonight, and he would make it enough, even if he only had his memories and his right hand forever after.

Maddie locked her arms around his neck and shifted to wrap her legs around his hips. Fuck, he wished he could think away the layers of denim and cotton between him and paradise right now. But he'd said he wanted to take his time, and so he would. He was a man of his word, after all.

He moved down her body, as much as the couch would allow, taking time to worship her amazing breasts. She pressed into his mouth, letting out that breathy moan he'd never get enough of, even if he lived be to a hundred.

No—On second thought, *that* was the sound he'd never tire of hearing. His name falling from her lips like a prayer.

He lifted his head, and she met his eyes. "As sure as I'd like to have you on this couch, and anywhere-the-fuck-else you'll have me, this time, the first time... I want you to be comfortable. I'm gonna take *a long time* over this. We're gonna need a bed."

She nodded.

Needing no more encouragement, he stood and scooped her into her arms, delighting in her little gasp.

She curled up into him, and he swore he felt a crack across his heart.

This woman, who baked like a dream, who had a heart as big as her country, who made him laugh until his sides hurt, would be the end of him.

I don't want her to go.

I want her, even if that means long-distance calls and long flights.

Even if it means months apart.

The realization should have rocked him, but it didn't.

He'd known from the beginning that she was special.

"Mind your head," he warned, and she ducked her head under his chin as he took the stairs as fast as he dared, saying a silent prayer of thanks that he'd thought to make the bed before preparing dinner.

The door was ajar and Rick shouldered it open, placing Maddie gently on the bed. He wasted no time in divesting himself of jeans, boxers and socks. When he glanced up,

Maddie had propped herself up on some pillows, naked except for black lace panties, and was watching him, like Queen Cleopatra waiting for Anthony, knowing he was hers in all things.

Normally in this situation, in any other brief relationship or on a one-night stand, he'd have let loose with some quip or another, such as *like what you see?* Or, *look all you want, babe.*

But to do so with Maddie felt trite. Unworthy of her perfectness.

So he just smiled, drinking her in with his gaze, wondering if it was possible to take a permanent picture with his brain.

He'd have done any number of illegal things right then for a polaroid camera in that moment, so he could snap the warm welcome on her face, the confident sexuality.

He'd slip it into a little leather wallet so light would never fade the image, carry it everywhere with him. Be buried with it.

She crooked a finger in invitation.

In that moment, he would have done literally anything she wanted.

* * *

Maddie

Holy shit.

I'd had a handful of lovers in my lifetime, but Rick.... Rick's body knocked every single one of the other guys out of the park. His charm, the stubborn good-person streak, his looks, *everything about him*.... He knocked every other guy out of the *universe*.

I let my gaze trail down his magnificent torso, and over his hips. I wanted my legs around them, and finally, his mouth-watering erection.

I knew firsthand that it absolutely tasted as good as it looked.

I'd felt it on my tongue and now I wanted to feel it *much* further down.

Why had I waited so long for this?

Rick joined me on the bed and when he got close enough, I pulled him over me, sliding on to my back and wrapping my legs around his hips, slotting the solid length of him right against that sweet spot between my legs. *Wow.*

He rasped my name against my neck as we moved together for moments that stretched.

I stroked my palms down Rick's back, enjoying the play of smooth skin and strong muscles under my greedy hands, and then I settled my heels on his calves, arching my neck so he could press kisses to it as he moved against me. Settled in the cradle of my hips, the head of his cock pressed against my sensitive folds through the skimpy lace of my underwear.

With each stroke, shivers of pleasure flooded my entire being. I could die happy like this.

My muscles clenched in anticipation. I wanted to feel him there, in my most intimate place, wanted to be joined to him in every way possible.

Rick leaned on his forearms. His face was contorted with concentration. "If I keep this up, it won't last long."

"I don't mind."

He groaned. "I *do.* And I said I was going to take my time."

He was going to kill me through too many orgasms. It was okay. I'd had a good life. I'd achieved a lot.

"*Please.*"

"While you're here with me, I want to take care of you, honey. Please let me."

He said it so softly that I lost the will to respond. I wanted to be taken care of, and I wanted it to be *him*.

He was a dream that I never wanted to wake from.

Rick moved down my body and hooked his fingers in the edges of my little lace knickers. He eased them down my legs and dropping them silently to the floor.

I closed my eyes and let my head tip back on the pillow when he gently parted my legs. I waited for him to settle between my thighs again, but at the first touch of his tongue where I was soaked and begging for attention, my eyes flew open.

He licked me in sure, smooth strokes. By the third one, I thought my every fiber of my being was going to explode from the pleasure streaming from my clit to every cell in my body. I trembled in delight as he kept the pressure up, knowing just how to stroke that bud of nerves to set me alight. He'd only done this to me once. It had been amazing then, but now it was *incendiary*.

I sobbed his name as he curled one, then two fingers inside me, hearing his curse when I helplessly clenched my internal muscles around him, wanting, no, *needing*, more, more. Let it be now...

He flicked just the right spot with the tip of that talented tongue and I came in a burst of light and heat, pressing into his mouth, his name falling from my lips again and again, like a desperate prayer.

When I came to, he lay next to me, head propped up on his hand, gazing down at my face, a smug little smile playing on his lips.

I didn't have the energy to do anything but lazily grin. I'd come like a freight train, and we both knew it.

And I wanted *more*.

There was a rapidly expiring time limit on the time I could

spend with Rick, and I wanted to make the absolute most of every second.

Rick reached into a bedside drawer for a condom, and after watching him roll it onto the delicious column of his cock, I picked my moment, and lunged for him.

We rolled over the bed—thank goodness his bed was king-size, not unlike the man himself—and I wrestled my way on top, settling my legs either side of his hips.

I looked down at him, impossibly handsome, with just that hint of cocky southern charm, that glint in his eye. I'd never get enough of looking at his face, taut with desire for *me* - maybe as long as I lived.

And maybe it was all very soon for these kinds of thoughts, but I'd fallen hard for this man.

Perhaps this was the meaning of *whirlwind romance.* It was a whirlwind, but I was safe in the eye of the storm, happy to just be close to him in whatever way he wanted. Whatever way *we* wanted.

But I knew, solidly, that I didn't want to let him go. Even though an ocean separated us, I wanted to see where this fire between us took things.

I held his gaze as I slowly slid down on to him. I saw the moment he felt my muscles close around him.

His eyes widened slightly, and he uttered, *"Fuck, Maddie. Oh, Christ."*

My heart raced as I took him all in, to the hilt, then held still, allowing us both the time to enjoy the feel of each other.

Rick stroked his hands down my sides, then settled them on my hips, squeezing gently. He wanted me to move.

I obliged him for us both, going slowly at first, the feel of him against my tight walls sending pleasure spiralling through me. When I set a faster pace, wanting to bring him to orgasm, knowing it was *me* who got him off, he positioned his hips up to meet mine. The feel of every ridge of him dragging quickly against my inner walls was *heaven.*

I watched something like pain flash over his face.

"Goddamn it, Maddie, I can't..."

One of his hands left my hips to strum that sweet spot at my apex. I was already so wet from his earlier loving and his powerful thrusts had stoked the fire, and I flew apart, the orgasm slamming into me.

A few seconds after, I heard Rick's hoarse cry as he emptied himself into me.

Limp, I slid down to meet him, chest to chest. His arms curled lazily around me, and I felt my eyes drift closed. The little aftershocks of *fantastic* sex rocked my insides pleasantly, like late, but very welcome, fireworks.

"Darlin'." He pressed a kiss to my temple. "Condom."

Reluctantly, I let him shift me off of him, and felt cold for a few moments as he went to take care of business.

But he came back and pulled me to him, settling my head under his chin. I snuggled into him, quietly delighting in the lazy pound of his heart under my ear.

He threaded his fingers through my hair, a soothing caress.

"Maddie." His voice was soft. "That was...."

He trailed off, maybe because he couldn't find words. Neither could I.

"It was," I agreed, spreading my palm over his chest. He was solid and warm and made a wonderful pillow.

I dropped into a dreamless sleep.

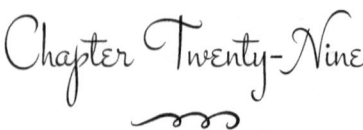

Chapter Twenty-Nine

We stayed in bed until the wee hours on Monday morning, only venturing out from between the covers for food—buttery scrambled eggs on toast, which Rick made.

Expecting to have to get up and prep food for the bakery opening, I was surprised when I blearily checked my phone at three a.m. only to find a text from Jenny.

Jenny: Take the day off. Laurie and I have it covered. Enjoy what, or whoever, you're doing.

I swear I had a whole-body blush reading that, especially as *who* I was doing was Jenny's brother. She seemed remarkably not grossed out about the whole thing.

Rick arranged to start work late and meet his apprentice, Eddie, at the job site at eleven, confident that Eddie would handle the wood that needed to be cut prior to Rick finishing off the parts that needed finer manipulation.

Taking the time as intended, Rick and I spent ninety percent of it curled around each other, learning each other's bodies with lips, hands, tongue, and teeth. He made love to me on the bed, in the shower, against the wall.

We talked and talked. I told him about how my Asian

fusion baking had started as a way to express myself and celebrate my mixed-race heritage. I felt lucky to have grown up in London, a melting pot of race and culture. I went to school with kids from diverse backgrounds, and we'd all had something different to share with each other at lunch.

Rick told me about how his desire to see something outside this little town had led him to join the Army when a recruiter had come to his high school. He'd all but bitten their hand off, even though he'd shown an aptitude for carpentry when his dad had tried to train him.

"I was young an' full of piss an' vinegar. I wouldn't be told. The Army gave me friends, an extra family, but also made me learn how to be an adult."

He'd started helping out his dad when he was on leave, and ended up liking it. He enjoyed seeing old friends, reconnecting with the town he was born in, and making something with his hands. After that, when Bill had a stroke, it seemed only natural to take over.

He took me into the garage to show me the wooden toddler-size car he was making for Toby's Christmas present. It was *gorgeous,* all sleek but cute with it. He planned to paint it a sunny yellow with blue race car style stripes and emblazon Toby's name on it. My heart melted. Then I realised that I wouldn't be here to see him receive it, and I felt a pang in my chest.

After Rick left for work, I let myself back into Jess' house and started work on the seventieth birthday cake, triple-checking I used all the correct flour and such for the allergies of those who'd consume it.

Three hours later, it was iced, and I snapped some photos, pleased with the result. The "70" was constructed of gingerbread and iced in a snazzy turquoise, the birthday boy's favorite color, so I'd been told. The glittery gel icing sparkled under Jess' overhead kitchen lights.

I texted Rick to see if he'd finished work yet. He replied with a photo of himself on my doorstep and the caption: WAS JUST ABOUT TO KNOCK.

I rushed to the door, opened it, and, grinning, dragged him inside by his dog tags.

He took his time tasting the smile on my face.

We went straight to bed.

* * *

Rick stayed over, but he got ousted at five on Tuesday morning when I got out of bed for my final shift at *Cake Away*. He was adorably grumpy when woken up, pulling the pillow over his head and begging for five more minutes.

When I walked up to the bakery, I saw Aunt Laurie through the window, but I went around the back anyway. The door was open, and she waved when she saw me.

Two stand mixers whirred in symphony with each other and the smell of the ingredients was divine.

"What're you doing here alone?" I demanded.

"One of the college girls is on her way," she replied, shrugging, incorrigible as always. "Wanted extra money, and Jenny's tired. Toby's got a tooth coming through."

I winced in sympathy. "What can I do?"

She nodded to the door. "Wholesalers are due any second. I ordered some extra stuff, iced buns and such, so I'm just mixing a batch of rainbow cookies. Can you unpack the order when it arrives?"

We worked seamlessly together now. By the time today's college girl arrived, the wholesale order was unpacked into the window displays, leaving space for the rainbow cookies and Madeleines that Aunt Laurie had mixed. I carefully spooned them into the correct trays and slid them into the oven.

The day passed happily. Jenny and Toby, who was very

grumpy due to the teeth thing, popped by for a rainbow cookie and a coffee. At two, I headed back to Jess' place to make sure everything was tickety-boo for her imminent arrival. I also spent a happy hour making a WELCOME HOME banner to string across her doorway, decorating it with whatever craft items I could scrounge from around her house, like mini pom-poms and scraps of ribbon. The result was... Eccentric, but lovable. Or so I hoped.

Rick called just as I was wondering what to do for dinner.

"Wanna drive out to the highest point in town later and go stargazing?"

I all but sighed girlishly into the phone. "I really do. And make out?"

He chuckled. "Most *definitely* make out."

He invited me over, made a *divine* chicken pot pie for all for us, and then he drove me to a place known for people taking photos there.

We spent some time looking at the view, but longer making out in the truck bed.

Rick had connected a string of fairy lights to a little electric battery and strung them across the back of the cab, filling the truck bed with blankets and pillows. After the sun bled out below the horizon, we were cocooned in the golden glow from the tiny bulbs. The effervescent light warded off the dark, and my increasingly frequent thoughts about what would happen when I left.

He made love to me slowly and tenderly, our bodies cushioned by the layers of blankets. I wrapped myself around him, keeping my legs tight around his hips. We moved languidly. I didn't want us to be separated by even an inch, relished the feel of his skin on mine, the rasp of his scruffy stubble against my neck, the sound of his groans.

I wanted to record our moments together to store in my heart forever, keep them crystal clear so I could get them out and sigh over them whenever I wanted, like a teenager with one of those instant photo booth strips, or a regency heroine with a miniature portrait in a locket.

He held me close as the stars winked at us overheard, and I knew that I might be going home in a few days, but a large piece of my heart had already broken off and settled down with Rick Callahan.

I wouldn't be able to take it back; and I didn't want to.

* * *

I'd like to say that I woke up naturally on Wednesday morning, delighted to find Jess and Connor home, but instead they crashed through the front door at two a.m., startling me out of sleep, and I rushed down the stairs in a panic thinking the house was being burgled. Instead, I saw them in the hallway, a jumble of tired eyes and bulging suitcases, and I leapt down the last two steps to greet them.

Jess and I shared a long, tight hug before she pulled back to say, "I'm aware that some *things* have happened, but I am in no state to talk about it now. I'm practically asleep standing up."

After helping them get everything inside and bidding them goodnight, I lay awake in the darkness for a long while, staring at the ceiling, my gaze trailing the little crack of light across it spread by the glow of the moon through the curtains.

My cousin's return twisted up joy and sadness inside me; delight at being close to her again and anticipation of seeing her holiday snaps, twinned with a wrenching dread at leaving the happy alternate life I'd settled into here.

Sleep evaded me for some hours.

On Wednesday night, after rounds of catching up with people, haranguing Aunt Laurie for hiding her fractured arm, sleeping off jetlag, and assuring herself that *Cake Away* had not, in fact, burnt down or been otherwise harmed, Jess threw a going-away party for me.

Upstairs in the guest room, I smoothed down the skirt of my cheongsam, eyeing myself critically in the mirror. The rational part of my brain said, *"Stop focusing on how you look! Just be in the moment!"* The vain emotional part of my brain argued, *"You want him to remember you like this, not with unwashed hair and in jogging pants."*

Stupid brain.

I applied the finishing touches of my make-up and grabbed my purse to go next door. When I opened the door, the scent of barbecuing hot meat reached me, and my stomach sat up and begged. I crossed the short distance to Rick's house, heard the clink of glasses and snatches of laughter, kids running about in the big yard. I rounded the house and let myself in through the gate. Rick was manning the barbecue with Eddie, and as if he'd heard me, he looked up as I shut the gate behind me, and his gaze went soft. Something inside me yearned to stay longer. Maybe forever.

He said something to Eddie, passed over the barbecue tongs, and crossed the yard to greet me.

I tipped my face up towards his, and he obliged me with a kiss. I tried to keep it light, but all I could think was that by midday Saturday, he'd be an ocean away from me, and my lip wobbled as I pressed into him.

"Baby, what's this?" he asked, cupping my cheek, thumbing at a stray tear.

"Nothing." I hiccupped a sob at the endearment and then laughed sadly at myself. "I don't want to leave you."

He curled his arms around me, and I pressed my face into his chest and breathed him in. "It's just for a little while, sweet thing."

"Really?"

"Soon as I can get things under control with work, I'll

come out and see you."

My heart clenched. Over the last few weeks, I'd got the distinct impression that Rick only ever said things he meant, but sometimes, holiday romances didn't work out. What if I crossed back over the ocean and he didn't miss me?

"I wanna see where this goes," he added, repeating the words he'd given to me that day at the lake.

"Me, too," I whispered.

He kissed me again, and I sank into it, into the moment.

I swallowed back my anxiety as he cuddled me close and then added, "Come and join the party."

"Will you dance with me?"

I felt the movement of his chin on the top of my head and grinned because I knew he was scowling.

"Maybe."

"That's a no if ever I heard one." I looked up at him and pouted a little.

"C'mon, Maddie, that's not playin' fair."

I didn't change my expression, but against my will, my mouth twitched a little.

Rick skated a hand down my ribs, exploiting a ticklish spot.

"Hey!"

"Man's gotta protect himself from public dancin'."

We were interrupted by Rick's dad, leaning heavily on his cane. I turned in Rick's arms as his father approached. "Evening, Mr. Callahan."

A smile broke out on his face. "I've told ya, girl, call me Bill. And come on. Our wedding song is playing, and damned if Edith and I will be the only ones out there!"

Rick rolled his eyes, but he was smiling.

"Did you put him up to this?" He wanted to know.

"No. Girl guides' honour."

"That's not a thing," he groused.

"It is in the UK."

He scoffed, but let me lead him into the party. Bill and Edith were already swaying to their song, Edith supporting her husband's weight as he smiled down at her like she'd hung the sun and stars with her own two hands.

Jenny was dancing with Toby in her arms, his little face pillowed sleepily on her shoulder.

I tugged at the apron Rick wore. "This has to come off. No grease on this dress."

"Which is *sensational,* by the way," he murmured, just for me. He pulled the strings and draped the apron over a garden chair. "You look like a million bucks, darlin'. You had this in your suitcase the whole time?"

I laughed. "I wasn't thinking straight when I packed, really, but I'm glad it found its way in."

"Me, too," he all but purred.

"You don't look so bad yourself."

Rick wore a pale grey button-down, no tie, and the edges of the open neck flirted with the triangle of tan skin the open garment revealed. His jeans were dark-wash, and either new or kept for best—no torn work clothes here.

He settled one big, warm hand on my waist and tangled his other hand with mine. I slid my palm up his chest, felt the drum of his heart as he started to sway me.

"You okay?" I asked.

He dipped his head to press a kiss to my hairline. "Feel a little like I'm back at high school, and the prettiest girl agreed to go to prom with me."

My face heated, and I grinned up at him. "Oh yeah, and who was that?"

He started to speak and then laughed. "Oh, hell no. I know a trap when I'm about to walk into one. 'Sides, I don't wanna talk about the past tonight. I just wanna spend it with you."

My heart melted.

I scooted closer to Rick, winding my arms around his neck, feeling the comforting heat of his big body against mine, and he sighed and rested his chin on my shoulder, and for a moment it was us against the world, and I wanted to take this moment and clutch it selfishly, never let it go, tuck it away from the light so it never, ever faded.

I love you, I nearly said, but I kept the words back.

What if he didn't say it back?

Could I be sure that this wasn't just a fling for him?

After all, hadn't I told myself a million times that I couldn't start anything, being an ocean away from him?

Yet here I was, with less than two days left in the U.S., dancing in his arms in his yard, as his parents' wedding dance song played.

I was sunk.

Completely and irretrievably.

I had gone back and forth about a little no-strings fun with Rick, but really, once I fell for him, resistance became pointless.

I'd never tried a long-distance relationship before. How would it work? *Would* it work? Was I an idiot to even try? Would video chat and texting... And maybe *sexting* be enough? Could we realistically keep up with each other's lives?

Rick sung softly along with the music, his lips moving in my hair. His voice was scratchy and out of tune, but that somehow made it all the more perfect.

I considered him a man of many facets. A soldier, a loving son, a man of patience who made treasure out of wood, who threw his nephew in the air and made him laugh with tickles, a man who'd passed the time on deployments with Tolkien novels. A man who could make me scream his name while I was spread out underneath him.

"Didn't know you knew this song. Aren't you just a vault of secrets?"

"Nah." He lifted my hand, and I followed the movement as he spun me lazily out of his arms and then back into them.

For a man who avoided dancing so much, he did pretty well. I hoped I'd have the chance to test out his skills at future parties.

Jess and Connor whooped from somewhere in the yard as Rick tugged me back into place, and I felt a shiver that I'd be leaving my newfound second home soon. "I'm a simple man. Easy to read. Easy for people to know what I want."

I loved being in his arms. "Is that so? And what do you want now?"

His gaze dropped to my mouth. "You can't figure it out?" Rick teased. "Somethin' I can't do here, for sure."

Excitement stirred in my belly. "Do you think I'll be able to skip out of my own leaving party early?"

"I feel sure that can be arranged, darlin'." He sighed and kissed my forehead. "But not yet. Lotta people've come here to see you. You should talk to 'em."

I leaned up on tiptoes. "It's a shame that all I want is to be under you, right up until I have to leave for the airport," I whispered into his ear.

He went still for a second, and then murmured, "Damn, woman." He very deliberately dropped my hand and squeezed the one he held at my waist. "Go, before I can't let you go."

"I'm coming back for you later," I promised.

He sent me a wink, and it made heat fill every fiber of my being. I let my gaze linger on his *fabulous* ass as he went back to the barbecue station, and then I made a beeline for Molly, Jess and Connor, who whistled at me as I neared them.

"Holy shit, I ain't never seen Rick dance," Molly laughed. "Should've filmed it."

Jess hooted. "He'd never let that footage see the light of

day." She offered me a cold bottle of beer. "Saved this for you."

"Thanks." I took it from her and we clinked the glass together, and I also tapped bottles with Molly and Connor. "Can't believe I'm going soon."

My gaze flitted to Rick, and I saw him plating up some food for his parents, leading them to some seats, a softness sketched on his face as he said something to his mother.

No doubt about it, he'd taken up residence in my heart, with his kindness, wicked sense of humour, the love of crafting we shared, and his loyalty to his family.

I'd waited a lifetime to meet him, and I refused to let geography stand in the way. Plenty of people made long distance work.

So could we, I hoped, with every fiber of my being.

To make the most of my time with the other people here that I loved, I shelved those thoughts to chat with my aunt, and then Lara and her parents. Danced with Jess to three songs, convinced Jenny to join us for two, before she pleaded an early night because of Toby. The toddler was already dozing as she hugged me and carried him up to bed.

We turned the music down after that, but it continued at a pleasant low buzz as we ate a second round of burgers and then Aunt Laurie served a batch of perfect cookies shaped and iced to look like airplanes.

Rick disappeared for a second and when he came back, he handed me a cookie with a piece of paper wrapped around it.

I took it with a raised eyebrow, leaned into him as I unwrapped it. It was the booking confirmation for a night's stay in a *very* fancy hotel in Louisville, on Friday night.

"So I get you all to myself for the maximum amount of time," he murmured into my hair.

I love you, I thought. *I love you, I love you.*

It was only a matter of time until the words came out of their own accord.

Chapter Thirty

On Thursday, Jess jokingly granted me a lie-in to thank me for everything I'd done, but I wasn't working anyway.

I spent it saying my goodbyes. I stopped by the Han's delivery place to have congee for breakfast, and promised Lara I'd try to stay in touch more regularly. We agreed that time zones sucked.

I enjoyed a long coffee break with Aunt Laurie. The doctor had seen her arm, and it was healing as expected. "Jess will never let me go near another step ladder ever again," she teased.

We talked and hugged and talked and hugged. I wished her luck, telling Jess she wanted to step back a little from working so much in *Cake Away*.

She didn't ask what my plans with Rick were, and I don't know if I could have told her. I just held so, so much hope for us close to my heart.

I promised to nag my mother and father to visit more regularly, and then, on my mum's behalf, I nagged my aunt about visiting England.

I spent an equally long time with Jenny and Toby.

"You'd better stay in touch," Jenny threatened, looking as intimidating as possible, while wearing a floral skater dress and flip-flops, with her hair in a top knot. "I'll hunt you down if you don't."

I hugged her very, very tightly and promised to stay in touch. We swapped every sort of contact detail it was possible to swap.

I hugged Toby, and he pulled my hair. It hurt, but it was also the most attention he had ever given me, so the smile didn't leave my face.

"Rick is totally gone for you," Jenny added when I hugged her for the last time. "Completely and utterly. I haven't seen him so dreamy for years. I mean, there have been other girls, but not like this. I hope you feel the same way about him."

Everything went still inside me, hearing those beautiful words. "I really do. My life had been turned on its side when I came here, Jen. I didn't expect to have it righted so thoroughly by someone so amazing." I squeezed her arm. "Several some-ones. *You* are a big part of why I loved this visit so much."

"Stop!" she groaned. "I'm so hormonal. I can't cry!"

She cried anyway.

I cried a little, too.

That evening, Jess and I hustled Connor out of the house. He muttered something about going to Molly's with Levi and Eddie as Jess shut the door on him. We took a trip down memory lane, painting our toenails, watching absolutely abysmal reality TV, and eating pizza. Jess took out the old photo albums, and we looked at ourselves, so confident in our teenage style choices, me covered in blue snakeskin print, Jess' hair in huge curls, streaks of it dyed a garish emerald green. We laughed ourselves silly over several bottles of wine and fell asleep curled up together on her sofa.

I couldn't have asked for a better final night in Redwing Falls.

* * *

On Friday, I packed the last dribs and drabs of my possessions, and hugged Jess and Connor. I walked to *Cake Away,* waved to Aunt Laurie through the window, and grabbed a brownie.

And then Rick came to take me to Louisville.

I watched him as he drove. I tried to catalog every detail of his profile, the way he sang along to classic rock off-key, and the way that one unruly lock of hair curled over his forehead. The play of rays of sunshine through the truck window over the koi carp tattoo on his forearm. The softness in his smile when he glanced over at me after stopping at a red light.

We checked into a fabulous hotel.

As Rick gave our details in the lobby, I admired the leather chesterfield sofas, exposed brick walls, and hanging pendant lamps styled like naked bulbs with glowing, bright orange filaments.

"I wish I'd had time to get something a little lacy for tonight," I murmured to Rick once the elevator doors closed on us.

He pulled me close. "Your naked skin is just *fine* with me. Can't think of anythin' fancier."

I snuggled into him, breathed in that perfect scent in the spot where his neck met his shoulder. He settled his chin on top of my hair and we stayed like that until the doors opened on our floor. Rick let us into the room, and I gasped.

The clerk might have said *junior suite,* but this was *huge.* The bed was enormous, big enough for four people. I found a bathroom with a luxurious claw-footed tub *and* a walk-in shower, and a little seating area with a faux fireplace.

The suite boasted a stunning view of the city. It was early, the sun still bathing the buildings and streets.

Below, the snaking body of the Ohio River sparkled.

"This is beautiful, Rick."

He came to stand behind me, enfolding me in his arms and bending to kiss my neck. "Wanted you to have a night to remember."

"You already gave me nearly three weeks to remember."

He smiled against my cheek. "Never hurts to be sure you don't forget me."

I turned in his arms, looked up into his dear, dear face, and smoothed my hand over his prickly jaw. "How could I? Besides, you're coming to see me in London." *Or you said you would,* I didn't add.

He might change his mind after I was gone, and that thought opened up a dark pit of dread in my stomach.

But he nodded, and his gaze was firm on mine as he said, "And I intend to, Maddie."

A man who used his words.

How could I not love him?

Despite the fact the restaurant downstairs looked great, we skipped dinner and ordered room service.

While we waited for it, Rick ran a bath using the rose-scented bubbles provided by the hotel. The air filled with the aromas of cassis and patchouli.

We undressed each other slowly. I kissed every inch of his chest with my greedy fingers, wondering if it was possible to commit the feel of him to my muscle memory. I tried to save specific details to my memory like I had on the drive here; the dark crescents of his lashes against his cheeks. The curve of his biceps. His intricate, fascinating tattoos. The arrow of dark blond hair that led from his navel down to his beautiful, heavy, erect cock.

We bathed each other languidly, like we had all the time in the world. I lay back in his arms, content as the water lapped at the tops of my breasts and Rick stroked lazy patterns on my inner thighs.

I never wanted the night to end.

We made love as the sun set, the nightly spectacle flooding the sixth-floor room with tongues of red and pink and gold, and then we fed each other steak, chips and beautifully tender broccoli, lying in bed.

After I was lax and boneless from food and sex, Rick padded naked to his duffel bag, gave me an *excellent* view of his ass as he crouched down to look for something, then came back to bed with a small parcel.

"Made you something."

Charmed and surprised, I took the prettily wrapped little gift. "I didn't make you anything."

"Darlin', I beg to differ. You have spent your *entire* time here making me things. The brownies. The pancakes. The almond cookies."

"Well, when you put it that way."

He sat on the edge of the bed. "Open it."

I carefully unwrapped the pretty red paper. A little cardinal bird fell into my hands, perfectly carved, smooth as butter under my fingers. It was so perfect it could have spread its wings and flown off my hand. A little hole had been carved in the bottom, the edges perfectly curved and smooth.

"Rick! This is stunning!"

"So you remember our little part of the world. And one more thing-" He went back to the bag, took out a long, thin parcel. I unwrapped it to find a wooden spoon. After I exclaimed over its craftsmanship, he showed me how the bird slotted on top of the spoon. "Thought it'd be better if you could take 'em apart. For cleaning."

It was almost too beautiful to use, but I didn't say that.

Instead, I crawled over to him and climbed into his lap.

He held me for the longest time as I listened to the soothing rhythm of his heartbeat under my ear.

And I tried to only enjoy him, and not think about how

distance, time zones and work schedules and the emotional detritus of life might erode our closeness.

When I woke in the wee hours, Rick's side of the bed was empty. I swung my feet to the floor. Moonlight bathed the little seating area of the suite, and I found him sitting on the couch, looking out over the city, naked save for his gray boxers.

"Hey."

He looked up as I approached. "Hey." He reached for my hand and pulled me onto his lap.

"Couldn't sleep?" I asked, nuzzling into him. I'd put on his t-shirt before going to sleep and the material was pliable and warm between his body and mine. His heart was beating a fast tattoo.

"Bad dream."

"You want to talk about it?"

He was quiet for a long moment, and then he settled his cheek on the top of my head. "It's not really one narrative. More, I just get to relive snatches of things I wish I'd done differently. Moments when men from my unit were lost, or when they received life-changing injuries."

"I'm sorry."

He kissed my hair. "I'm working through it in the group. Guy who runs it's an Operation Desert Storm/Shield vet, so he gets it. I'm gonna keep going."

"Good."

His heartbeat had slowed. I kept my hand there, feeling the drumbeat of it, wondering how it would feel to be an ocean away from him.

It was ridiculous, really. I hadn't even known he existed until around four weeks ago. I'd been in his company only twenty days.

Even so, when I left, I'd be carving off a piece of my heart and leaving it Stateside.

"We should go back to bed," he rumbled. "You've got a

long enough journey ahead as it is, without bein' exhausted durin' it."

I shifted out of his hold so I could lift my head and kiss him. "It's late enough that I would rather stay awake and be with you than sleep more. Make love to me, Rick."

He scooped me up and carried me to the bed. "You know, it was the first time I carried you that I knew I was toast."

I frowned as he lowered me. "Really? After the airport?"

He chuckled, moving to brace himself over me, caging me in, leaning on his forearms. The moonlight from the big window picked out the pale copper in his dark blond hair. "Yeah. I tried to wake you up, figured I shouldn't start raisin' my voice in the middle of the night, carried you upstairs. It'd been a long time since I'd held anyone like that."

I slid my hands over his back, gently pushed until his lower body rested flush against mine. He was hot and heavy right where I needed him, and I luxuriated in the sensation.

"I don't remember much about it, but you made me feel safe. The days before I flew here were erratic, so I *loved* that." I cupped his face, stroked my thumb over his bottom lip. He pressed a kiss there.

"Maddie, I love you."

Everything in me went still, hearing those words.

"I didn't mean to just blurt it out," he continued softly, his gaze holding mine. "But it's been there at least a few days. Maybe longer."

I should have given him those words in return. But I was scared, scared that once I went back to London, he'd forget about me, and so I just cupped his dear face in his hands and kissed him, and tried to give him the words that way.

And he made love to me, slowly and tenderly, until the sun came up.

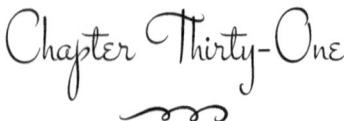

Chapter Thirty-One

He took me to the airport the next day. We spent the longest time just sitting in the truck, holding hands, kissing, watching people walk past towards the two-level terminal.

"I don't want to go," I said in a very small voice, cuddling into him, fitting my cheek into the slight hollow of his chest.

He smiled against my hair. "If you miss me enough, you'll come back. It's a strategy."

I hiccupped a laugh through eyes brimming with tears. "I'll miss you. You don't have to worry about that."

"Never had a long-distance relationship before," he said at length, playing with the ends of my hair idly.

"Oh? I thought a lot of soldiers did."

He *hmmm*ed. "Yeah. A lot of guys in my unit had sweethearts, and families. Twice I started seein' someone while on leave, but both times they never wrote once I went back out."

"I can't say I'm sorry. Their loss is my gain." I leaned up and pressed a kiss to his jaw. "You're special, Rick. I don't know what's going to happen, but I don't want to lose you."

He squeezed me tightly. "Maddie, I've waited half my life to find you. I'm not lettin' you go now. Not for anythin'."

After he finally walked me into the terminal, I held him as tightly as I could, as if I could press the memory of his body into mine. We snapped a photo so I could have one more picture of Rick.

He waited while I checked my enormous suitcase. Then, I took the escalator up towards security, and at the top I leaned over the railing and waved at him, blowing him a kiss.

Rick caught it, tucked it into the front pocket of his shirt. And then I watched as he walked back through the automatic terminal doors. He turned as they opened, gave me one last searing look, and then he was gone.

The flights back were uneventful.

The next day, Mum and Dad collected me from Heathrow, took me back to my childhood home, a beloved, drafty terrace in Holborn, and made me tea as I told them everything.

That night I settled down in my childhood bed, called Rick to tell him I'd arrived safely. His handsome face filled the screen, and behind him was bright sunshine. I missed him and Redwing Falls so much that I had to resist buying a ticket back.

Instead, I threw myself into work.

I had over twenty orders for cakes and bakes.

I didn't get in touch with the co-op shops and markets I'd written to months ago, because I wasn't sure what I wanted to do long-term. Was I staying? Or would I try to make a go of things across the pond with Rick?

I couldn't ask him to move here. His dad was still recovering from the stroke, and Jenny and Toby needed him.

Emma and I had a couple of movie and ice cream nights. Meanwhile, I continued to make my social media baking tutorials, teaming up with a few other local bakers, including one who'd become a friend, Lacy, an Anglo-Korean baker who made cake pops decorated to look like K-Pop band members.

However, after being in *Cake Away,* my heart wasn't in vlogging anymore. I didn't get the same kind of rush as selling my bakes to actual people.

Jenny and I texted regularly, and she sent lots of pictures of Toby.

I posted a care package of British chocolate to their house, to Aunt Laurie, and to Jess and Connor.

Rick and I texted every day and video-called twice a week. Usually, one of those sessions involved us getting naked for each other on screen. During those moments, I drank the broad lines of him in, caressing the screen with my fingers, wishing I could touch his warm skin.

We'd set up a streaming playlist to swap favorite songs, and a shared a list of our favorite books.

I was learning more about him every day, and loving each new fact.

Six weeks after I'd come home, I missed him more than ever.

I missed him when I woke up and when I went to bed.

I love you, I almost texted him, every day. But he deserved to hear it in person the first time.

When I wasn't baking, or on the phone to Rick, I tried to plan out what my business would look like in Redwing Falls. I dithered about discussing it with Jess. Would she think I wanted to muscle in on her turf? Could I somehow make cakes to order and support *Cake Away?*

I also reached out to all the American vloggers I knew, telling them I'd fallen for an American and was looking for tips on moving my cake business across the ocean. They had some interesting ideas, and I had a lot to chew over.

It was so much; it was overwhelming.

But if it meant being with Rick, then I'd do it.

He booked a plane ticket for September, so he'd be here during the Autumn Festival. I was eager for him to try a mooncake and to see the annual lion dance in London's Chinatown.

The day before he arrived, I received an email that meant I needed to do some serious thinking about my—*our*—future.

* * *

An Autumn breeze crisped the air the day I met Rick at Heathrow, my gaze eating up his long, lean form as he tugged along his suitcase and held his coat. When our eyes met, I started running, dodging people, and launched myself at his tall, broad frame when I got close enough.

Rick dropped his coat and caught me in mid-air, burying his face in my hair, and I just breathed him in.

He smelled of sawdust and clean soap and fresh air, somehow, even after hours on a plane.

I love you, I thought.

We hugged for long heartbeats.

He felt so good.

"Flights okay?" I eventually asked.

"They were just fine, darlin'. Half-watched a film. Ate some plastic food," he replied, without letting me go.

We held each other for a little longer, and I wished we could just portal into my flat without breaking our embrace. He was *here,* and I didn't want to let him go for even a second.

We took the tube home to my shoebox flat, holding hands all the way. Every fiber of me felt awake and alive, urgent with the need to dissolve all the barriers of space and clothing between us.

He was on me the moment I closed the door. He set aside his suitcase and covered my body with his, pressing me up against the back of the front door, and I reached for him.

His mouth was hot and eager on mine as he settled his hands under me and boosted me up, so my legs wrapped around his waist, his erection hot and hard against me even through our clothes. He bit off my name as he rutted into me like that, and I held on as tight as I could, pressing our mouths together and drinking the taste of him in.

Eventually, dry humping wasn't enough, and he scooped me up in his arms, carrying me to the futon which served as my bed and sofa.

We made love and napped and cuddled for the next four hours. For every moment, I savored his nearness.

That evening, I took him into Chinatown. I had set my website to holiday mode for the duration of his stay, wanting to make the most of our time together.

The Chinese Association of London always arranged a lion dance for the Autumn Festival and Lunar New Year. I tried to see it when I could.

Huddled together in a busy, crowded street, squished between revelers, some of whom carried paper lanterns or dragons on wooden sticks, Rick and I let them ferry us along. Overhead, fireworks had already started. Fairy lights were strung up between telegraph poles, casting a glow on the rows and rows of red and gold paper lanterns on display overhead.

I reached for Rick's hand and he squeezed mine, grinning down at me.

"Excited, huh?"

"Very. I've lived in London for years, but each time I go out, it surprises me with something new. There's something different around every corner. Especially at festival time. I'm so glad you came."

Two huge gates, decorated with gold, red, and Chinese lanterns flanked the main street. A huge crowd had already gathered. Nearby, a popular Chinese bakery sold round, flaky red bean pastries as well as tiny, perfectly intricate mooncakes.

Outside a Chinese general store, a young woman sold glow sticks and sparklers to a long line of chattering children, some clapping their hands and wiggling their bottoms with excitement.

The crowd talked among themselves, but fell quiet when, from around the corner of one of the gates, a huge dragon head appeared, bright red and brilliant white, with saucer-round golden eyes.

Moving sensuously like a snake, the dragon and its long red body, made up of four people and decorated with hundreds of gold and white tassels, traveled down the street. It paused, waiting, undulating, like a lion sizing up its prey.

Then the music began. From behind the dragon a procession of men in traditional Chinese dress appeared, drums around their necks, beating out a rhythm that the dragon swayed, bucked and danced to, its motions enthralling.

Around them, children held sparklers and lanterns, but the only other light came from restaurant and shop windows.

In the evening darkness, the white of the dragon's fur stood out like virgin snow. The drums beat out an increasingly mesmerizing tattoo of sound.

I glanced up at Rick. He looked spellbound as the dragon reached the end of the gate-to-gate pavement stretch, and came back towards us, the drums still beating.

"You watch this every year?" He wanted to know.

"If I can." I grinned up at him. "Look at all the smiling faces, filled with hope and joy. Listen to the music. Later, when the lantern procession goes through the streets, it just seems so magical and exotic, right here, in ordinary London."

"London is *not* ordinary."

"I have to agree," I smiled. "I love it." I looked up at his profile, lit by the glow from sparklers and overhead fairy lights, and cuddled into him.

"Wonder if we have anythin' like this near Redwing Falls."

"There's a Lunar New Year dragon dance in Louisville.

The Han family told me. Their daughter, Lara, goes sometimes."

The dance ended, and a woman I recognised as owning a couple of the bigger restaurants in Chinatown ascended the little stage to talk about the evening's proceedings. There would be crafts for the kids, a visiting *xiaolongbao* stall, and other activities.

We queued up for the soup dumplings. The carton they gave us was almost too hot to hold, so in other words, perfect. I taught Rick the perfect way to eat them by cupping one in a big spoon, biting a tiny hole in the skin to let the soup inside cool down and then eating them whole.

I tugged Rick down a street with a tiny cafe that sold only chicken skin in various forms.

"The triple fried is the best."

He made a face. "Ain't chicken skin already basically fried by the oven when you roast it?"

"Psh. This from the man who encouraged me to eat a pile of meat, carbs and gravy within days of making his acquaintance. When in Rome, Richard Callahan."

He shuddered. "I'll do anything you want, as long as you never, ever call me Richard *ever* again. It was my grandpa's name, apparently."

We got a big bag of the triple fried chicken skin and, despite his earlier misgivings, Rick ate most of it. We washed it down with some mango Boba tea before stopping at a small bakery, where I bought a big, fat wedge of bright green pandan cake that we ate, back home, in bed.

Night slanted in through the curtains, the walls illuminated by the soft glow of my bedside lamp.

I settled in next to Rick, beyond pleased to have him here with me. I had missed him so much. I already knew I'd never get enough of him. These months apart had increased my love for him, not dampened or lessened it.

I'd nearly blurted out the words three times just *today*. I'd daydreamed about making one of those big welcome-style signs with the words on.

I was officially a lost cause.

I needed to tell him.

We fed each other bites of the cake, and then I put the plate aside and tugged him down onto the mattress. He smelled like home, like happiness, and if there had been any doubt before, there wasn't now.

I belonged with him.

"Perfect," he whispered against my neck, and kissed me there, his stubble tickling. I arched into him. I wanted the beard burn, the tiny hurt, the fact I'd be marked, even temporarily, as his.

Touch me, I wanted to beg as we undressed each other, but couldn't seem to form words. Fire ignited inside me everywhere he touched, and spread along my limbs until they felt dreamy and heavy, but hot, so hot.

Don't stop touching me.

"I've been thinking almost non-stop about this ever since the last time," he admitted as he gently eased down the straps of my lacy red bra.

I watched him out of half-open, heavy-lidded eyes. "Really?"

He rolled his eyes. "Are you fuckin' kiddin' me? Yeah. Really. Can't think about much else, it seems."

"Since the *first* first time, or the video call last week?"

"Both," Rick answered softly. "These days, I seem to live for being with you, in whatever way I can get. Had to get fuckin' *Eddie* to check my work the other day, because I was daydreamin' about *finally* being here with you."

His face was perfect in the play of moonlight and shadows.

How was it possible, I thought, looking up at him, that nature had endowed one man with so much?

He's incredible. Kind, sweet, smart, insanely handsome.
And he wants me. For as long as this lasts, I'll be happy.
I hope it lasts forever.
I have to follow this, him, and my heart.

I knew I wanted to go to Redwing Falls to be with him, I just didn't quite know what I was going to do once I got there. Maybe once I figured it out, I'd finally tell Rick that I was absolutely in love with him.

But apparently my heart, and my brain, thought they'd waited long enough, because when Rick settled me into his lap and lined himself up to enter me, I took one look at the stark desire and *love* on his face, and I heard myself say, "I love you, Rick."

He went very still as our gazes met and then held. And then he let out a long breath, cupped the back of my neck, and drew me in for a long, tender kiss.

A knot I didn't know I'd been harboring in my stomach unfurled, and when he slid inside me to the hilt, it was like being home.

Rick was my home.

Once we showered together, and we were sitting in bed, I turned to face him. "Rick, I need to tell you something. Remember those co-op shops I'd written to before? One of the letters Seb binned was from them."

He nodded, his gaze holding mine.

"They emailed me because they hadn't received a response to their letter. One of their founders found my social media posts and *loved* them, and they want to offer me a space there for half the usual price."

Rick's brows winged up, but I caught the sadness in his expression before he said, "Wow. That's somethin'. You deserve it."

I settled my hand over his heart. "I've decided to say thank you, but no. As much as I was so stoked for that, everything has changed. I've been doing research into how I can take my business across the Atlantic."

Joy lit up his face, and he leaned in to kiss me, cupping my cheek. "Baby, as delighted as I am to hear that, hold that thought."

"Why?"

"Laurie said you'd start talkin' about what you were gonna do, and she said when you did, to give you this." He went to rummage in his duffel bag, then returned and handed me an envelope with my name on in Aunt Laurie's writing.

I looked at him, puzzled.

"She made me promise not to read it. Not that I would. It's between you and her," he said as he slid back into bed.

"I know. You'd never do that sort of thing." I dropped a kiss on Rick's bare shoulder, then opened the letter, settled down next to him, and read.

Maddie,

I needed time to get my thoughts together, which is why I didn't tell you about this while you were here.

Also, I didn't think you'd have a problem with my choice of courier! Handsome, isn't he? I'd like to say that I called this thing between you two very early on after you arrived. And I was right. You don't have to say it. I know I was.

A few days after you left, I told Jess and Connor about my decision to retire. My arm still aches, and I don't want to get up at the crack of dawn anymore. They weren't surprised, and they're looking for someone else to share the bakery with them.

Which leads me to this: would you be interested in part ownership of Cake Away? *Running it with them, you'd get to bake your Asian-fusion cakes and cookies as often as you wanted. Lord knows based on the response while you were here, they'll sell well.*

And, you'd have time to make your videos and such, if you're still doing that.

You could maybe even put our little town on the map.

I've floated the idea with Connor and Jess. They're fully on board.

People were asking about your baking for weeks after you left. You really started something here, Maddie, and I wonder if you'd want to continue it.

I realize my sister would miss you terribly, but it isn't as if she never visits here.

As for the other reason you'd want to shift your life Stateside, well, I imagine he's been stuck to you like glue since stepping off the plane.

All my love,

L x

Tears streamed down my face as I finished reading, and I looked up to see Rick watching me with concern.

"Darlin'," he began, very gently. "What's wrong?"

I swallowed back a lump of emotion, unable to stop myself from grinning so big that my face hurt, but crying at the same time. "Nothing's wrong. I'm coming home with you, Rick."

And after I'd finished smothering his face in kisses, I told him all about it.

Epilogue

Six months later

It was officially Aunt Laurie's last shift at *Cake Away*.

Jess, Connor and I posed outside of the bakery window in our branded aprons as Jenny snapped some pictures. Toby stood next to her, Rick holding his hand. Everyone we knew had come out to ring in the change of staff, and I'd made some taro bao and angpao cookies to mark the occasion. We'd sold out of half the plate of cookies already.

Moving had been stressful. There was so much paperwork, but as soon as Rick met me (and my four giant suitcases) at the airport, I knew I'd made the right choice. My heart belonged wherever he was, and here, I got my other heart's desire, too.

I *loved* having a space here. Loved having a real, tangible home for my creations.

I posted on Instagram less these days. I had retained a lot of my following, but interaction had dropped. I didn't mind at all.

I still planned to do the odd video with local vloggers, some of whom had started to become friends since I'd moved.

I had everything I needed.

My parents were, of course, sad to see me go, but happy for me. I video called them regularly and last week a parcel of British chocolate from them had arrived.

Rick smiled at me as the camera clicked, and my heart turned over as it always did, although I'd been living with him for three months now.

Waking up next to him in the morning and sliding into sleep with him at night made my heart light with joy. We were making our home together, and I was looking forward to every single day of the journey.

When he'd suggested I move in, I didn't hesitate like I had with Seb. Some part of me must have known that we weren't right.

But with Rick, everything had been easy. It just felt... *Perfect.*

By mutual agreement, Jenny and Toby had moved in with Aunt Laurie. It meant they both got company. My aunt doted on Toby and babysat for Jenny sometimes. Toby had started to attend a daycare, and Jenny had a job at the retirement home a couple of miles outside town, coordinating a programme of events for the residents. She'd already asked if I would teach a baking class there once a fortnight, and I was going to say yes.

I felt exceptionally lucky.

When the photos were done, I crossed over to Rick and lifted my face for his kiss. Before our lips met, several people around us groaned good-naturedly, but I ignored them.

"You miss me?"

I chuckled. It had been only three hours since I'd left the house. "I have, actually."

Toby wiggled in between our bodies and I scooped him up. "You want some attention too, huh?"

"Aaaadie!" He exclaimed. It was the first time he'd said my name and I was delighted.

Jenny came to hug me and Toby immediately lurched for her. She *oofed* when she shouldered him. "Dude. You have to start walking more. You're getting heavy."

As the crowd dispersed, Connor and Jess settled back behind the counter to serve the remaining queue. Rick snagged my hand before I could go inside. "Not so fast. Gimme some somethin' sweet."

I grinned and kissed him, allowing a second to linger over it. "That's all you get until tonight. I'll bring a couple of left-over bakes home, if there are any, shall I?"

He smiled against my lips, as the sun shone down on us. "You're all the sugar I need."

Acknowledgments

The Parcel & Page team: Thank you so much for your hard work shaping and honing this book.

Claire A. Jones: Thank you for basically everything. Letting me scream at you about the characters, the plot, and all my ideas. Thank you for advice on U.S. stuff. I love you.

Katie Beard: Thank you for hanging out in the doc and advice on U.S. stuff.

C. Carter, Chrissy D., Emma J., Laura M., Shevi E., and (fellow Parcel & Page author!) Kate Chambers: Thank you for your support, looking over pitches, beta reading, and buoying me up.

A.G.: Thank you for your U.S. military advice.

Ricardo Garcia (Operation Desert Shield/Storm): Thank you for answering my very specific U.S. military questions. You were invaluable.

The Hive Gang: Thanks for keeping me sane while I wrote this.

My husband: Thank you as ever for your love and patience.

About the Author

An Anglo-Asian romance writer living in Wales, Jasmine has been penning romantic fiction since she was a daydreaming teenager. Her work has featured in three short story anthologies, and her romance novels are available online. She lives with her very patient husband, one son, and one pampered tortoise.

www.ingramcontent.com/pod-product-compliance
Lightning Source LLC
Chambersburg PA
CBHW070650180626
46817CB00006B/2310